4|17

DAKOTA TRAILS

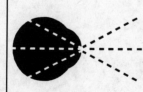

This Large Print Book carries the
Seal of Approval of N.A.V.H.

DAKOTA TRAILS

ROBERT D. MCKEE

THORNDIKE PRESS

A part of Gale, Cengage Learning

GALE
CENGAGE Learning

Farmington Hills, Mich • San Francisco • New York • Waterville, Maine
᠈nn • Mason, Ohio • Chicago

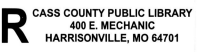

LIBRARY OF CONGRESS CATALOGING-IN-PUBLICATION DATA

Names: McKee, Robert, 1948– author.
Title: Dakota trails / Robert D. McKee.
Description: Large print edition. | Waterville, Maine : Thorndike Press Large Print, 2017. | A reissue of the Fayetteville, Arkansas, Pen-L Publishing edition, 2015. | Series: Thorndike press large print western
Identifiers: LCCN 2016055519| ISBN 9781410498397 (hardback) | ISBN 1410498395 (hardcover)
Subjects: LCSH: Frontier and pioneer life—Fiction. | Wyoming—Fiction. | Dakota Territory—Fiction. | Large type books. | BISAC: FICTION / Historical. | GSAFD: Westerm stories. | Adventure fiction. | Love stories.
Classification: LCC PS3613.C55255 D35 2017 | DDC 813/.6—dc23
LC record available at https://lccn.loc.gov/2016055519

Published in 2017 by arrangement with Pen-L Publishing

Printed in Mexico
1 2 3 4 5 6 7 21 20 19 18 17

*For my wife, Kathy, and my children,
Kent and Jess*

ACKNOWLEDGMENTS

I wish to thank my friends John D. Nesbitt, PhD, and Jim Morgan, MD, for their invaluable assistance over many years and many thousands of words.

ONE

Neil Bancroft glanced at the young woman who stood in the shade of the stable. She had watched him work for the last half hour, and she still stared as he collected his pay from Sergeant Dooker.

"All right," the sergeant said, "it looks like you done us a fine job."

The old cavalryman conducted business at a rough pine desk next to one of the corrals where Neil had spent the last seven days, much of it flat on his back in the dust.

With his thumbs hooked into the top of his jeans, Neil waited as Dooker fiddled with a six-inch stack of paper. It never paid to rush the sergeant.

"Let's see now," Dooker finally said, "you busted us thirteen broncs at a dollar fifty apiece. That comes to . . ." He licked the tip of his pencil.

"Nineteen dollars and fifty cents," Neil said. He was impatient to get his money and be on his way.

Dooker ignored Neil and multiplied it out anyway. Judging by the place's scragginess, Neil figured the troops stationed at Fort Fetterman here in the middle of Nowhere, Wyoming must be on a tight budget and could not take the chance of making a mistake in arithmetic.

"Nineteen dollars and fifty cents," Dooker said, as though he hadn't heard the same amount quoted not a minute before. He opened a small cashbox and counted out the money. As he did, he squinted up at Neil. "We're expecting another bunch of these crockheads next month. Come back then, and you can bust us a few more."

"We'll see, Sarge." Neil knew even as he said it that he'd only be returning if nothing better came along. It was his practice to travel from ranch to ranch saddle-breaking horses, but sometimes when he needed the work, he'd hire out with the Army. He tried to avoid that, though. Since his discharge from the cavalry three years before, he had little use for Army posts. Besides, judging by the ache in his back from hitting the ground so often, he wondered if it might be wise to consider a new line of work.

He tucked the wages into his pocket and looked again toward the stable. The woman who had been watching him was still there. "Who is that over yonder?" he asked, jerking his chin in the woman's direction.

Dooker turned in the rickety chair he sat in most all of every day and had a look. It was clear that the two men were talking about her, but her cool expression didn't change. Lifting the blue kepi perched on his skull, Dooker scratched his bald head. His scalp was as white as paper, but beneath the line of his cap, his corrugated face was berry-brown. "Never seen 'er before," he said. He made a noise like he was sucking something out of a tooth — not a difficult task since he only had one — and added, "Damn, but she's a purty thing, ain't she?"

The sergeant was right about that. She was a pretty thing — about a hand over five feet tall with raven hair, and even from this distance, Neil could see that her eyes were as blue as a cornflower. She wore a light summer dress that clung to the lines of her body in a way that could not be ignored.

"She's been watching me work for the last half hour."

"Maybe she finds you appealin', Neil." The old man cackled. "Maybe she wants to see if you can ride everythin' the way you do them buckin' broncos."

Neil looked down at the old, leering

soldier. The man's one tooth — an eyetooth — hung obscenely from his pink gum.

"Be seeing you, Sarge," he said.

He gave the woman another glance and turned toward his roan gelding.

Before mounting up, Neil offered a few soothing words. It paid to go slow with the spooky horse. The animal could be nasty. He was quick to bite and kick, and he had the kind of kick that got a man's attention. Neil stroked the horse's neck, said, "Easy, now, roan," and climbed aboard.

He started to leave, but the sergeant hadn't yet finished with his joke, and he tried again to make the younger man laugh. "Yes, sirree, Neil," he called out, jerking his thumb back toward the woman, "I'd say she's a bucker. Why, I expect that she could throw ya fer sure."

It didn't work. Neil didn't laugh. He figured he had as much of a sense of humor as the next fella, and he might've laughed if anyone else had said it, but over the course of his hitch as a private in the United States Army, Neil had acquired a poor attitude regarding army life in general and a particular dislike for noncommissioned officers. It was a prejudice that had not diminished since his return to civilian life.

Ignoring the man, Neil nudged the roan

with his right spur and put the horse into a trot.

Earlier that afternoon, supplies had arrived at the sutler's just outside the fort, and Neil expected there must be a few kegs of lager mixed in with the other goods. He'd have a drink and then visit Archie Faulkner's Café for his supper. For the last few days, he'd been eating nothing but beans and biscuits at his camp down by the North Platte River. A beefsteak sounded like just the thing.

Neil was halfway into his first beer when the woman from the corrals stepped through the saloon's open doorway. As she crossed to the bar, Neil noticed she eyed him at the table where he sat.

"Excuse me, sir," she said to Dick, the bartender. "Could I trouble you for a glass of water?"

"Why — why, sure, ma'am." Dick's awkward behavior made it obvious that except for the local whores, he was unaccustomed to a woman coming into his saloon. He reached beneath the counter, came up with a pitcher of water, and filled a tumbler. She thanked him with a pretty smile and took a sip.

It was still early, and the place was not yet

crowded. No more than a dozen men sat around the dimly lit barroom, all of them with their mouths agape, watching the young woman drink her water.

She blotted her lips with an index finger when she was finished, and then she turned her back to the bar and looked out over the room. "Afternoon, gentlemen," she said. Everyone stiffened, but no one said a word. "My name is Kathleen Burke. Katie Burke." She patted a small pocketbook she carried. "In my purse here, I have a Liberty Double Eagle that I will give to any man who is willing to knock that cowboy over there unconscious." She lifted her hand and aimed a finger at Neil Bancroft.

For a long moment, no one responded. It was Neil himself who finally spoke up. "What in the devil are you talking about, woman?"

He couldn't believe what he was hearing.

She shrugged. "I'm saying that if any one of these fine men here is willing to make a reasonable effort at beating you senseless — whether he is capable of getting the job done or not — I shall pay him the sum of twenty dollars, hard gold money."

After another silence — a shorter one this time — everyone in the place, except for Neil, burst out laughing.

"Excuse me, ma'am," said Dick through his chuckles, "but you can't be serious."

"Oh, sir, but I am," the woman said, and to prove it, she opened her purse, took out the coin, and gave it two solid raps on the surface of the bar.

A corporal from the fort pushed himself away from the table where he was drinking whiskey with two other soldiers and said, "Mind if I take a look at that?"

Neil didn't know the man's name, but he'd seen him around Fetterman City. He was maybe twenty years old, big, and unfriendly. He stood better than six foot two — at least three inches taller than Neil — and had shoulders that threatened the seams of his shirt.

The corporal crossed to the bar and took the coin from the woman. He scrutinized it and then put it in his mouth. He gave it a bite and checked it again. Holding it out so the light could hit it better, he rubbed his thumb along its surface.

"Well, boys," he said to his two drinking partners, "it's the real thing, all right." He turned his attention to Neil. "Better'n a month's pay just to whip some tramp cowpoke. Hell, most weeks I do that for free."

His two pals thought that was funny.

Neil stood and offered the soldier a good-natured smile. "Now, hold on a minute, Corporal," he said. "Aren't you just a little bit curious as to why she'd want you to do something like that?"

"Nah, I sure ain't."

"Well, I am. I've never met this woman in my life."

Katie Burke reached around the soldier and took the double eagle out of his meaty paw. She dropped the coin back into her pocketbook and said, "I'll keep this for now." She patted the big man on the arm, gave his biceps an extra little squeeze, and said, "Oh, my." She then turned her bright smile on Neil.

"Who *are* you?" Neil asked, but before she could answer, the big corporal took a step in Neil's direction. Neil held up his hands, palms forward, and said, "Come on, soldier, let's talk about this." Neil despised fistfights, especially the ones he figured he would lose, and he made his best effort to avoid them.

Dick smacked his hand on the bar to get the corporal's attention. "If you're gonna knock him out, Corporal, do it outside."

Neil, who until that moment had counted Dick a friend, said, "Thanks a lot there, Dick."

"Well, I'm sorry, Neil, but I can't afford

to have the place all busted up. And I hate mopping up blood." He rubbed his stomach. "It makes me kind of queasy. Always has."

The corporal, who clearly had heard enough chitchat, said in a reasonable voice, "We can sure do 'er outside, Dick. It's all the same to me." He spat into his palm. "That ain't no problem at all."

And with that, he cocked his arm and plowed his heavy fist into Neil Bancroft's jaw. Neil was knocked back through the open barroom door, across the narrow boardwalk, and into the dusty street. He landed facedown, not three inches from a fresh pile of horse apples.

Only moments earlier, Neil had been enjoying a beer in the quiet and comfort of Dick's barroom, and now he was in a predicament that was turning darker by the second.

He rolled onto his back just in time to see the big corporal bend toward him. With his right hand, Neil made a fist, but before he could swing it, the corporal took him by the front of his shirt, lifted him to his feet, and punched him in the gut. Air exploded from Neil with the sound of an ox falling on a bellows. He went down to one knee, and again the corporal hit him in the face hard enough to send him reeling back toward the boardwalk.

Neil landed with a thud and looked up to see a flash of fireworks. Through the bangs and sparkles, he could see the fine-boned face of Katie Burke. She stared down at him, her arms folded beneath her breasts. Shaking her head, she gave him a disgusted look.

Neil spat a mouthful of blood into the dirt and asked, "Are you having a good time yet, Miss Burke?"

"No, sir, Mister Bancroft, I'm not. In fact, I am finding you to be a great disappointment."

Neil was surprised she knew his name but assumed she'd gotten it, for whatever reason, from Sergeant Dooker before she came to the saloon.

"Well, I would hate to see you fail to get your money's worth. I'll try to be more entertaining if I —" But before he could finish, the corporal once again pulled him to his feet and was swinging at his head. This time Neil ducked before the soldier's fist could connect, and as he came back up, Neil threw a right cross that caught the big man in the mouth, cutting his lip and knocking him back a step. It wasn't much, but it made Neil feel better to know that he had gotten in at least one decent lick.

The corporal brought a hand to his lips and rubbed at the blood that leaked out and puddled in his beard.

That seemed to make him mad, and he took a wild swing that Neil saw coming and was fast enough to dodge. He shifted his weight to counter, but before he could, the corporal caught him with a right above the left eye. It was a glancing blow, but it still hurt like the devil.

Neil hated the thought of letting this moron knock him out, but it was clear that there was no way he could win a fair fight, and since he was not above fighting dirty, he looked around for something heavy and hard to hit the man with. But out here along the edge of the street, the pickings were slim.

He glanced behind him toward his roan tied to the hitching rail. His saddlebags were thrown over the back of the horse, and they held everything Neil owned in the world. His short-barreled Colt was tucked into one of those bags. If he could get to it, he could use it to crack the corporal over the head. Getting to it, though, did not appear likely.

Neil turned back to face the soldier just in time to see him swing an uppercut that started at his knees. The punch lifted Neil a foot off the ground, and when he came crashing down, he smacked his head on the street hard enough to turn the fireworks he'd seen earlier into exploding rockets. They burst in his skull like the Fourth of July, and once their fire dimmed, things started turning black.

He was going out. Somewhere back in the corner of his mind, Neil knew that to be a fact.

No, by God, he told himself, *you're not letting it happen. You'll not give that damned woman the satisfaction.*

He knew if he closed his eyes, he was a goner, and he fought to keep them open. It seemed a losing battle, but in his effort to maintain his senses, he forced himself to stare up into the afternoon sky.

It was a soothing place, that distant sky, but after a bit, it was blocked by the corporal's huge, round head.

"Are . . . you . . . knocked . . . out . . . yet?" the big man asked, looking down at him. It was as though Neil were hearing the corporal's question from somewhere deep underwater.

He gazed up into the ugly face. It had been pleasant watching the clouds scud across that blue sky, and Neil resented the man's obstructing his view. He tried to look around him, but it was impossible. Neil could see only two things: directly above was an enormous head, and to his right was the ass-end of a horse.

He blinked a couple of times and took another look. The horse was the roan. Neil was lying on the ground behind his own skittish roan.

Slowly the world slid back into place, and as it did, he shook his head and smiled at the corporal.

The big man seemed confused. "What the hell're you grinnin' at, saddle-trash?" He sounded disappointed — as though he'd thought Neil was knocked out for sure.

Neil didn't answer. Instead, he allowed his smile to widen as he reached up and took a handful of the roan's long tail. With all his strength, he gave the tail a jerk. He pulled on that tail like he was ringing a bell.

When he did, the snorter gave a loud squeal, lashed out its right hind hoof, and caught the corporal square in his face. The big man was lifted up and spun around, and when he came down, he hit the ground like a steel kite.

He landed next to where Neil lay, and with some effort, Neil reached over, took hold of the man's shoulder, and gave it a vigorous shake.

When there was no response, Neil looked

toward Katie Burke, who still watched from the boardwalk.

"I hate to disappoint you, Miss Burke, but it seems your hireling here is sleeping on the job."

TWO

"Sleeping, huh?" the young woman said as she stepped off the boardwalk. "It looks to me like he's dead."

Neil pushed himself up and started the long climb to his feet. It wasn't easy. His head felt like a basket of dead fish.

"I don't reckon the world would be any worse off with one less surly corporal," he pointed out. It was hard to muster any sympathy for the man.

After making it to his feet, he laid a hand on the horse's rump, trying to calm the animal. When the roan got to kicking, he rarely kicked just once. "It's all right, fella," he said. "You did just fine." Neil kept a small sack of oats and a feed bag tied to the back of his saddle. He poured some of the oats into the bag, and, rubbing the roan's neck, he whispered, "I apologize for all those times I called you nasty names. If I ever do 'er again, you're welcome to one free bite." He strapped the feed bag on and added, "There you go, roan. I figure you've earned a treat." The animal blew a puff of oat dust through the airholes and went to munching.

Neil expected the horse would gladly kick corporals in the head all day if it meant extra portions.

Now that he had that tended to, he dug in his pocket for a kerchief and applied it to the blood flowing down his face in a half dozen tributaries and dripping off the end of his chin. As he patted at his cuts, he watched Katie Burke bend over the still-unconscious corporal.

Neil was pleased to see the man's poor condition. He was far bloodier than Neil. The best part was the way the corporal's nose was folded over flat against his face.

"Well, he's not dead," Katie said.

That was easy to see. Little bubbles of blood and snot sputtered from his nostrils.

"You boys better get him to the infirmary at the fort," Katie said to the corporal's drinking partners. "I expect he could use some doctoring."

One man lifted the corporal's shoulders, and the other lifted his legs. When they hefted him up, Katie took the double eagle out of her purse and tucked it into the man's pants pocket.

"That was sure money well spent," Neil observed.

Dick, the bartender, who now seemed a bit sheepish, bent and picked up Neil's hat. He handed it over, and Neil took it without saying thanks — a rebuke the bartender noticed.

"Ah, hell, Neil," Dick said, "come on back inside. I'll give you a wet towel and a whiskey on the house."

Neil waggled the bloody kerchief at the man's face. "You sure you can handle the sight of me bleeding, Richard?" he asked.

The bartender winced and lifted his hand to ward off the gory rag, but he squeaked out an apology. "I'm sorry about that, Neil. I truly am."

Neil gave the man a frown but stepped onto the boardwalk just the same and headed back into the saloon. "All right, Dick," he said. "I guess we can forgive and forget if you're willing to make it two whiskeys instead of just the one. I fear a toothache's coming on." He used his tongue to probe a wobbly molar. He hoped the tooth tightened back up in the next day or so. He'd hate to lose one of the big ones.

They all made their way back into the saloon, and Neil headed for the table where he'd been sitting earlier. There was a moment as he crossed the room when things started spinning, and he wasn't sure he was going to make it. But he did, and once he dropped into the chair, he closed his eyes and let out a sigh of relief.

"Mind if I join you?"

He looked up to see Katie Burke, her white smile beaming as bright as the lamp on a locomotive.

"I can't think of anything in all this world I would dislike nearly as much," Neil said. Katie pulled out a chair and sat down anyway. When she did, Neil grumbled. "Why did you bother to ask?" It was clear this was a woman who did pretty much as she pleased.

The beer he'd been drinking earlier was still on the table. He took a sip and swished it around. Mixing with all the blood, it tasted as coppery as a mouthful of pennies. He turned his head and fired a shot in the general direction of the nearest spittoon. He then took another sip, and this time he swallowed.

"What do you have in mind now, Miss Burke?" he asked. "You gonna make a deal with one of these fellas to shoot me?"

By anyone's standards, this woman was a beauty, but that was even truer when looked at through the sore eyes of a man who'd spent the last eight years in the West where fine-looking women were a rarity. But a beauty or not, Neil sensed that she was poison.

"Shoot you?" she answered. "Why, I wouldn't dream of such a thing." She reached across the table and gave his hand a reassuring pat. "And I apologize for that unpleasant business with the corporal. It's just that I had to be sure, and I couldn't think of any other way."

Dick stepped up carrying a tray. "Here you go, Neil," he said. He placed two shots of fine Kentucky whiskey on the table. Next to the drinks, he laid a clean, white bar towel. The towel was wet and hot enough that steam floated from it.

"Thanks, Dick." Neil tossed back one of the shots, then held the hot towel to his face. Dick left, and Neil was tempted to tell the woman to do the same, but his curiosity wouldn't allow it. From behind the towel, he asked, "You had to be sure about what?"

"Your competence."

"What's that supposed to mean?"

"I'm looking for a man who can help me to . . ." she seemed to search for the way she wanted to put it, "perform a certain task. I need this man to be both honest and competent. I figure you're honest by the way you make your living. No dishonest man would still be busting broncs all by himself at your age."

Neil pulled the towel from his face. "What do you mean, at *my* age?" He was liking this woman less by the second.

She shrugged. "Most men willing to climb on a string of rough horses are men in their early twenties or even younger. Fellas your age usually do the finishing and the gentling, not the actual busting."

"Just how old do you think I am?"

She hesitated. "I don't know, late thirties, maybe." Neil sensed she was offering a guess she believed to be low, which made him even angrier.

"I'll have you know I am only thirty-five."

This woman was a real irritation, but although he'd never admit it out loud, she did have a point. Sitting atop a raw, wild-eyed jumper was a chore for someone with fewer years under his belt than Neil had. He knew that. It was just that he hated giving up any of what little he made to some cocky young cowboy just because Neil might be brushing the corral dust off a little slower than he used to.

He put the towel back to his face, and with a wince he adjusted how he sat in the chair.

28

The corporal's beating the hell out of him had caused him to forget the more or less constant ache he felt in the lower part of his back. Now, though, Katie Burke had brought that to mind as well.

This woman had a knack for souring a man's day.

"Here," she said, standing, "let me do that." Placing her hand on the back of his neck, she took the towel and daubed his cuts and bruises. For some reason, it felt much better when she did it than when he did it himself.

"It really isn't too bad," she said, inspecting his wounds. "I don't think you need any stitches."

"That's comforting."

She paused and stared down at him. "You're kind of a smart aleck, aren't you?"

Neil pulled the towel out of her hand. "Well, that might be, but don't take it personal. I get a little testy every time some strange woman hires a dim-witted trooper to knock me out. I'm funny that way."

"I told you I was sorry."

"Sorry? This wasn't some mishap, lady. It's not like you bumped into me on the street and accidentally knocked off my hat."

Without responding, she took the towel back and reapplied it to his face. It seemed

29

to Neil that her touch was a little less gentle than before.

"I need a man, Mister Bancroft — an honest, capable man who can take care of himself. I was convinced of your honesty, but I had no way of knowing whether you were capable of taking care of yourself. This seemed to be a good, quick way to find out. I felt that you were probably competent. I mean, you look fit enough —"

"Considering my age."

"You look fit enough," she repeated, "but I needed to be sure."

"So you thought this was the way to do it?"

"A person can't very well ask for references for that sort of thing. This way seemed logical. As it turned out, it was ideal. What better test than to pit you against a man who is bigger, stronger, and . . ." she gave him a hesitant smile, "younger. It would take a very competent man, indeed, to prevail in a situation like that. Yet you did."

"Lucky for me," Neil said, "that he happened to knock me down next to my own spooky horse. It was also lucky that the horse happened to kick the corporal in the head and not me."

He had stopped bleeding, and Katie wiped the last of the blood from his face.

Dropping the towel onto the table, she said, "I believe we make our own luck in this world. A man who's able to think fast and take advantage of anything and everything that he might have at his disposal is just the type of man I'm looking for. And I'm happy to tell you, Mister Bancroft, I was very impressed with your ability to do just that. You passed my little test just fine."

"Well, now," Neil said as he lifted his second whiskey, "I'm sure a prize."

Although his steak was tender enough, Neil found that the hinges of his jaw weren't working too well, and after a couple of bites, he gave up on the meat and settled for slurping potato soup.

"Just what is it that you need this honest, competent man to do, Miss Burke?"

As compensation for Neil's battered face, Katie had suggested they go to Archie's Café, where she would buy their supper. It went against Neil's better judgment to spend another minute with this woman, but after one more Kentucky whiskey — also purchased by the young Miss Burke — Neil had agreed.

"It's not *Miss* Burke," Katie said after a bit. "It's Missus."

The spoonful of soup Neil was lifting

when she made that statement stopped halfway to his mouth. "Missus?"

She cut her entire steak into neat little cubes as she added, "I guess it'd be more accurate now to say *Widow* Burke. My husband was killed in October. Murdered over in the Black Hills when he was returning to our home in Amarillo."

"Murdered by who?"

"Bandits," she answered. "Robbers." She laid down her fork without having taken a bite and settled back in her chair. "We were married when I was twenty-two. That was five years ago. We had a little dry-land farm there in the Panhandle, but Edward was never much of a farmer."

"How'd he end up in the Black Hills?"

"Dissatisfaction, I suppose. After two years of trying to scrape out a living, he came in from the fields one afternoon and said, 'Katie, it's time we did something different.' He'd been talking for months about the strikes in Dakota, and he decided he wanted to try his hand at locating some of that Black Hills gold."

"I've given that idea some thought myself." And he had, but he'd never done it. Even though he was tired of his hard life of riding lonesome and violent western trails and busting horses to the saddle, prospecting was an even more difficult way to make a living, especially now that a few thousand other folks had the same idea. "A man looking for gold, though, needs to know what he's doing," Neil added. That was another problem with Neil's becoming a prospector. He didn't know the first thing about it.

"Edward did know," Katie said. "He talked to everyone he saw who'd hunted gold in California, and he sent off for everything that had ever been written about the various ways to find it." She pushed her plate away and pulled her coffee cup and saucer closer. "I didn't want him to go, and I told him so, but there was no stopping him."

"Why didn't you go along?"

"He said it was too dangerous. He insisted I move into town with my mother — a proposal that I did not find appealing. If you ever met my mother, you'd understand why." She rolled her cornflower eyes. "She can be a pushy, headstrong woman."

Neil bit his tongue.

"But Edward had made up his mind, and there was no changing it. He left three years ago, in the spring of '78, and that was the last time I saw him." She lifted her napkin and touched it to her mouth. "The only contact I had with him was through letters

— letters and the bank drafts he sent back home."

"Bank drafts?"

"Turned out Edward was much better suited for prospecting than farming. He did find gold Dakota. Not so much at first, but more than enough to support himself and me. Even so, I urged him to come home. I told him we didn't have to go back to farming. I'd saved most of what he'd sent. With that and what he had put aside, we'd have enough to start some sort of business. But he'd have none of it. The prospecting had taken hold of him. He was always hoping — and expecting — that he would strike it rich."

"Did he?" Neil asked.

Katie lifted her eyes to his and nodded. "About a year ago, I received a letter from him, and it held a bank draft three times larger than usual. In the letter, he said he'd hit a vein of ore as thick as an elephant's leg. He said I wouldn't hear from him for a while because he was going to stay at the site and work it until it played out. Then he'd come home, and we would be set for life. In November, though, I got another letter. He'd written it the month before from some doctor's clinic in Custer City, Dakota Territory."

"What was he doing in a doctor's clinic?"

"He'd been wounded — shot. He was dying, and he knew it, and he wanted to write me one last time. He said he'd have the doctor mail it for him."

"What'd happened?"

"He'd dug out the vein, and when he was finished, he figured he had close to sixty thousand dollars' worth of ore as pure as any ever seen."

"Sixty thousand? Lord, that's a tidy sum."

"He said instead of selling the gold in Deadwood, as he'd done in the past, and taking his money in cash or bank drafts, he had decided to bring it home."

Neil wasn't sure he'd heard right. "You mean he planned to haul sixty thousand dollars' worth of gold from Dakota down to Texas?"

"That was his plan."

He let out a soft whistle. Up to then, Neil had figured this Edward Burke for a pretty smart fella. His opinion of the man had just dropped.

Katie went on with her story. "He knew it was foolish, but he suspected that as time went by, the price would go up, and hanging onto the gold itself would be like an investment." She took a sip of coffee. "Mostly, though, he said he just wanted me to hold it in my hands and see how beautiful it was."

Neil nodded. "I reckon I can understand how he might feel that way, but still, carrying gold in any amount is a risky business."

"Too risky," she said. "Turns out he didn't even make it out of the Black Hills."

"Did he say in his letter what had happened?"

"Some," she said. "Are you familiar with the Hills at all?"

"I've made their acquaintance." He had entered the Black Hills back in '74 with the Army's Black Hills Expedition and had been in and around the Hills during most of the five years he'd served in the army.

"Well, he had made it from the Deadwood Gulch area, which is in the north, all the way over to near where he eventually died. It was there that he ran into three men. He saw them on a ridge following him for a while before anything happened, but after a bit, one of them drew his rifle and shot him. The bullet hit Edward in the side, but he was able to stay on his horse."

She took another sip from her cup and made a face. Motioning to get Archie's attention, she called out, "Could we get our coffees freshened up over here, please?"

Neil was surprised by her behavior. He'd

never seen a woman call out like that in a public place. But he suspected that Katie Burke was a woman full of surprises, and something about her made him believe she was willing to do whatever it took to get other people to do what she wanted.

When their cups were refilled, Katie continued. "Edward said after the shot was fired, he lit out as fast as he could. He had two pack horses. One carried his gear, and the other carried three bags containing the gold. While the robbers made their way down from the ridge, he put some distance between them and himself, and once he'd gotten out of sight and deep into some trees, he dismounted, pulled off his jacket, and checked to see how badly he was hurt. He said it was clear the wound was bad — probably even mortal." She lifted her cup but didn't drink, just held it in both hands. "He said he knew his only chance of getting away was if the men got what they wanted. There was no way they could know how much gold he was carrying, but just by the quality of his outfit, they'd figure he had something of value. He took one of the bags of gold and tied it to the pack horse that carried his gear. He then sent that horse in one direction, and he and the horse still carrying the two other bags headed off in the opposite direction. He got away from the men for at least a little while, so he figured they must've found the one pack horse and assumed they'd gotten everything of any value he had."

"Smart," Neil allowed, "although expensive."

"There was the possibility they still trailed him, and he wasn't even sure he could make it to town before he bled to death, so he buried the two remaining sacks. As it happened, he did get into town. Custer City was right at five miles to the south, but there was no hope. The doctor told him all he could do was offer something to ease the pain." She replaced the cup in its saucer, then added, "That's when he wrote me the letter."

Neil's next question was so obvious that she answered it before he could even get it asked.

"Yes, sir, Mister Bancroft," she said, "I do know where the gold is buried. More or less, anyhow." She reached into her pocketbook and brought out a crude, hand-drawn map. "My husband enclosed this with the letter." She pushed the map across the table. "But it's rough, wild country out there, and the map's not very good. I doubt I could find it on my own."

THREE

Neil felt his anger bubble as he gazed into the age-darkened mirror at his swollen, beat-up face. This woman was crazy, and he figured he must be crazy too or he wouldn't have a thing to do with her. She did, though, make a tempting offer — a thousand dollars if they found the gold. And if they were unable to find it, she would pay him five hundred dollars for his trouble. There were a lot of things he would rather do for the next couple of weeks than roam the Wyoming and Dakota Territories dodging bandits, killers, and renegade Sioux, but a thousand dollars was an amount worth some risk. He'd taken risks this big and bigger for a whole lot less.

He pondered their route into the Black Hills and the camping spots they could hit along the way. It had been his plan, after the last bronc was busted here at Fetterman, to ride fifty miles east of the fort to visit an old army buddy of his who'd set up a homestead along Lance Creek. Neil figured he could still do that, even with the crazy woman. It was on the way, and it would mean one less night of sleeping under the stars — a prospect he expected would appeal to her.

"You look like you was dragged by a horse." That observation came from a seedy-looking man who appeared to be in his mid-forties. He sat on a cot in the corner of the sleeping room where both he and Neil had spent the night. The man pulled an eight-inch knife from a leather sheath sewn right into the outside thigh of his left pants leg. He then picked up one of his boots and began to slice mud off the sole, letting the scrapings pile up on the floor. After a bit, he stopped and took a sip from a pint bottle he held tucked into his crotch.

"Is it common for you, Mister, to substitute whiskey for your morning coffee?" Neil asked.

"I do when I'm lucky enough to have some whiskey for the substitution." He offered Neil a toothy grin and returned to his scraping. "I can't guess where all this mud come from," he said. "It only rains in this country a couple-a times a damned year, and here I wake up with mud on my boots.

How do you figure a thing like that to come about?"

"Could be you were wading in the river," Neil suggested. The North Platte was the only place around where that much mud could be found.

The man looked up, blinked, and snapped his fingers. "By God, you're right. I remember getting the hankerin' for frog legs last night, and I decided to try to locate me some."

"Did you have any luck?"

"Nah, hell, I was too drunk. I splashed around a bit but gave 'er up. I went back into Dick's Place for a while, and then I got me a bottle and come over here to this bed bug plantation." He waved the knife in the air, indicating the room he and Neil shared.

Next door to the stage depot, there was a small hotel with three or four rooms. Attached to the hotel was this larger room filled with cots. Once Neil had agreed to work for Missus Burke, she gave him an advance and provided him enough money for lodging, but instead of spending two dollars for a private room, Neil, being frugal, paid four bits for a bunk. He was accustomed to a bedroll on hard ground, so these accommodations suited him fine.

The man with the knife laughed. He had

41

a high-pitched cackle that sounded as though it should have come from someone older. "I watched that Army fella beat the stuffin' outta you yesterday afternoon," he said. "That was quite a show. Hell, if someone had wanted to charge, I woulda paid good money to see that exhibition. It was a real bonus to have it takin' place for free right there in the street for all to enjoy."

"Glad you had a good time," Neil said. The man at the general store had said the same thing when Neil and Missus Burke had gone over after supper to purchase supplies for their trip. Later, he'd heard it again from the liveryman when they bought three horses. At the time, Neil had joined in with their joking, but his willingness to be a good sport was wearing thin.

He dipped his shaving brush into his mug and painted his sore face with lather. He would need to be gentle with his razor. Otherwise, the cuts would start to bleed again. As he stared at himself, he felt his usual affable nature begin to fade.

"So you ended up havin' to bunk in here after all, eh?" the man said. There were a half dozen cots along the wall, but he and Neil had been the hotel's only two bunkhouse customers. Even so, now that he was getting to know this fella a little better, Neil wished he had spent the extra dollar and a half and taken a private room. "I figured that's the way it'd be," he added. "You sleepin' alone."

Neil could see the man in the corner of his mirror. "What's that supposed to mean?" he asked.

"Oh, nothin', 'cept seein' that girl tendin' to your injuries the way she was, and the two of you leavin' together, and all, a few of the boys at Dick's suspected that you'd be havin' a cozier spot than this to lay your weary head last night, that's all." He carved a hefty hunk of mud away from his boot heel. "I knew better, though. Ain't nobody never has no luck with that female."

Neil dropped his brush into his shaving mug and turned to face the man. "What the hell're you talking about, Mister?"

"That Katie Burke, she's a hard one. Why, I seen a dude-lookin' fella down in Cheyenne a few days back offer her a fifty-dollar national bank note to go upstairs with him, but she would have none of it." He grinned. "The funny thing was, I got the feelin' she didn't have nothin' in particular against goin' upstairs. It's just that the price he was offerin' weren't nearly high enough." His grin widened.

Neil crossed the rough wood floor to

where the man sat whittling on his boots. Smiling, he asked, "If you don't mind, could you put that toad sticker down over yonder for just a second?" He nodded to a small table near the head of the cot.

The man's face screwed up, and he asked, "What for?"

"Because I want to visit with you for a bit, and long knives make me nervous. They tend to put a damper on the art of conversation."

The man gave Neil a curious look, but he did as he was asked. "What do you want to visit about?"

Neil reached down, took a couple of handfuls of shirt, and lifted the man from the bunk. When he did, the bottle in the man's lap dropped, spun a half turn, and came to rest against Neil's right foot. Neil pulled the little man so close that their noses almost touched. "I don't have a lot of patience this morning, Mister. What is it you're saying?"

The man, whose tiptoes danced along the floor, squirmed and struggled to get away. "You got a damned funny way of visiting, cowboy," he said, gritting his teeth and pulling at Neil's wrists.

"So I do, and it'll get a lot funnier unless you make a quick effort to get to what you're driving at. Now spit it out. Are you saying this Burke woman's a Cheyenne whore?"

Still squirming, the man said, "No, I ain't sayin' she's a whore exactly, but she is fond of a dollar — I know that — and even if she ain't willin' to sell what she's got, for the right price, I expect she'd be willin' to rent the thing out."

Neil stared into the man's rheumy eyes. The whites looked like nests for a couple hundred tiny red snakes. After a bit, Neil let him go, and the man dropped to the bunk. Neil must have grabbed some hair when he lifted him up because the man winced and rubbed his chest.

"What's your problem, anyhow?" the man whined. "I was pleased when you won that fight yesterday. Now I ain't so damned sure."

"Who are you?"

The man must have thought that by Neil's asking him that question, the situation was again turning friendly. His scowl softened. "Name's Waldo Brickman," he said, sticking out his hand. When Neil didn't return the gesture, the scowl returned, and the man went back to rubbing his chest. "I'm a silhouette cutter by trainin' 'n' trade."

"A silhouette cutter? I haven't seen one of them fellas around in years."

"Well, sir," Waldo Brickman allowed, "I have to admit that the demand has declined since photography's become so popular, but the rustic folks on the frontier still appreciate my skills. Ain't many photographers make it out this far."

"No, I guess not. How do you know Katie Burke?"

"I can't say as I do know her. The first time I seen her she was buckin' faro in the Golden Spur down on Seventeenth Street in Cheyenne."

"She was dealing faro?"

"Yes, sir. She's quite a hand, too. John Foster, the man who owns the place, gives his dealers a percentage of their tables, and the way I hear it, Katie Burke was making more money than any three other dealers combined. Dick told me that fellas'd stand in line for hours to have that little minx relieve 'em of their spondulicks."

"Are you sure about that?" Neil asked.

"Course I'm sure. I seen 'er there myself. I've been known to while away an evenin' or two in the Golden Spur."

Neil expected that to be the truth.

Brickman bent and retrieved his bottle. The line of whiskey had been low enough that when it fell on its side, none had spilled. He examined what was left and polished it off.

"What else do you know about this woman?" Neil asked.

"Not much. I reckon it's a good thing she was making good money at the Golden Spur, though, seein' how she likes to throw it around on frivolities."

"What do you mean?"

"What do I mean? Do you have to ask? You're the fella that she paid some corporal twenty dollars to beat into unconsciousness."

Neil didn't respond.

"Also, I heard a rumor down in Cheyenne that she give the fella behind the counter at the stage depot a half eagle extra to tell anyone who come by askin' for her that he had never seen her."

"Why would she do something like that?"

"Not being a mind reader, I reckon I couldn't know for sure, but if I was gonna guess, I'd say she was tryin' to avoid the three fellas who come into the Spur a couple of nights ago. She weren't there at the time, but these three mean-looking boys come in wantin' to know where they could find her."

"Who were they?"

Waldo Brickman shrugged. "With two of 'em, there ain't no way of tellin', but the third one, the one doin' all the talkin', well, sir, he said he was her husband."

Despite how it looked, Neil's jaw felt some better than it had the night before, and he decided to eat a healthy breakfast before he met Katie Burke at the stables where they had boarded the horses and stored their gear. He had a lot of questions he wanted to ask the young Missus Burke, and he wanted to do it on a full stomach. He put away four eggs, a rasher of bacon, and a half pot of coffee before he finally pushed himself away from the table.

One question he intended to ask was how her husband could be looking for her two days ago at the Golden Spur in Cheyenne if he had died in a doctor's clinic in Custer City back in October.

Neil was beginning to suspect that there was only a nodding acquaintance between the truth and Kathleen Burke.

It didn't matter, though. As it stood now, he didn't plan to quit. She was paying his expenses and had given him a fifty-dollar advance against his future earnings. With the kind of wages she provided, he would be happy to stay in her employ, at least for a while.

He complimented Archie on the breakfast

and headed off for the stables. Katie had said that she was not fond of rising early and had wanted to meet him at ten o'clock. Neil had insisted it be no later than eight, and after a considerable fuss, she had agreed. Despite the job's handsome pay, Neil feared that going off into the prairie with this woman would prove an ordeal.

He arrived at the stable at seven thirty, greeted the liveryman, and then saddled his roan. From the three horses they had purchased the night before, Neil chose a handsome sorrel with four white stockings for Katie to ride. He saddled that animal, too, and then he and the liveryman loaded the gear atop the two remaining horses.

After that was done, he checked his watch. Twenty past the hour. This was making for a poor start. If they were to cover any distance at all on their first day, they needed to get going. He'd have to round the woman up.

Just as he left the stable and stepped into the street, he heard a crash and turned in time to see a straight-backed wooden chair bouncing into an alley beneath a broken window in one of the hotel rooms. Following close behind the chair came a leather satchel. Neil watched as Katie Burke kicked out what glass remained and climbed over the sill. Picking up the satchel as she went by, she ran into the alley. When she spotted Neil coming toward her, she stopped.

He almost didn't recognize her. She wore boots, jeans, and a red shirt that was at least a size too large. On her head was a stiff canvas cap, and beneath its short bill, her blue eyes stood out, large and frightened.

"What's going on here?" he asked.

Her only answer was to turn back toward the window. Neil followed her gaze and saw a man step through.

He was mid-sized, maybe two or three inches shorter than Neil, but his shoulders were thick and wide. The sleeves of his shirt were rolled up above his elbows, and Neil could see the corded muscles of the man's forearms flex as he stepped into the alley. Along his cheek were four long streaks where his face had been clawed. The marks were fresh and glistened red. He blotted them with the heel of his left hand, fixed his eyes on Katie, and said in a soft, husky voice, "You'll pay for this, girl."

Neil came up beside Katie, jerked a thumb in the man's direction, and asked in an amiable tone, "Who is this gent?"

As he spoke, Waldo Brickman, the silhouette cutter, who had been watching from an open window of the adjacent sleeping room, said, "This here's one of them fellas who I told you come into the Golden Spur t'other night." Brickman climbed through the window into the alley.

When she saw Brickman, Katie's wide eyes grew even wider.

The burly man turned the heat of his gaze onto Brickman, held him riveted for a second, and then looked back to Neil. "What's it to you who I am, shitkicker?" he asked. His voice was even and carried a note of self-assurance. It was the voice of a man who had been in tense situations before and didn't mind them a bit.

"Shitkicker?" Neil's eyebrows lifted. "That's not very nice. Hell, I've usually gotta know a fella for ten or fifteen minutes before he starts calling me insulting names." He gave the man a wink and a big smile. "You're way ahead of schedule, pard."

Katie said, "He broke into my room, Neil. I had to fight him off. I just barely got away."

Neil looked past the man at the glass scattered over the ground. "It does seem that she was in a hurry to get away from you, Mister, which makes me think that you might mean her harm."

Again the man ran his hand along the claw marks on his face. "You're damned right I mean her harm, you son of a bitch. Now stand aside. The first thing I'm going to do is knock out a few of her teeth. Maybe, just for the hell of it," he added, "I'll break an arm."

Without looking away from the man, Neil asked, "Missus Burke, is it your desire to have this gentleman knock out any of your teeth?"

"No, sir, it surely is not."

"How 'bout bustin' an arm? What're your feelings about that?"

"If it's *my* arm we're talking about, I'm against it."

Neil offered the man a what-can-you-do shrug and gave him his most ingratiating smile. "Seems like, at least for now, she likes her teeth and arms the way they are. I guess you'll just have to save that for another time." Under his breath, he said to Katie, "Head to the stable."

Katie left the alley, and the man started after her.

"Now, just hold on there a second," Neil said, his smile still wide and friendly. "What's your interest in this woman anyhow? What is it you have in mind?"

The man stopped and turned his dark eyes toward Neil. His jawline was large, rock-solid, and thatched with a three-day growth of beard. His wide mustache was trimmed close but grew down past the sides of his mouth.

He paused for a moment, seeming to take Neil's measure. It was clear that Neil was something he was going to have to deal with before he could do what he was there to do.

His gun belt crossed from the left at a slant, causing the holster to hang low against the outside of his right leg. It was tied to his thigh with a thong. Using both hands, he adjusted it on his hip.

He and Neil locked gazes for a moment, and finally, the man let out a little frustrated sigh, the kind a man might give a troublesome kid. He made a slow pivot on the sole of his left boot and faced Neil dead on.

"What I have in mind, cowboy, is to go into that stable over yonder and get that woman, beat her 'til she can't walk, then toss her over my horse. There's business to be tended to with her." He seemed to stand just a bit straighter, and his steely gaze took on a harder look. "Another thing I have in mind," he added, "is killing anyone who tries to stop me, and that starts with you. If you don't step aside, I'll drop you where you stand." Until then, he'd had both thumbs hooked in the front of his gun belt. Now he lowered his hands to his sides.

"Damn," Neil said, shaking his head, "I

was afraid you were going to say something like that. I don't mind telling you, I just hate these awkward moments. What d'ya say we head over to Archie's and have us a cup of coffee and talk this over. I'm sure we can come to some kind of understanding. Hell, if you haven't had your breakfast yet, we can have Archie fry you up some bacon and eggs. I'll buy. I just had some, and they really hit the spot."

For a brief second, the man seemed confused by Neil's manner, but after a bit he smiled. It wasn't much of a smile — nothing more than a crinkling at the edges of his eyes and a quick flicker at the ends of his mustache. "Why, you're nothing but a damned fool." He said this as though he had just realized that he was dealing with something less than he had expected — something not worth his trouble.

"Well, sir," said Neil, still keeping his smile roomy, "I've been called a fool before. So what d'ya say? How 'bout that breakfast? If you're not interested in eggs, Archie makes some fine flapjacks. Covers 'em in the best apple butter you ever tasted."

The man gave his head a disbelieving shake, made a sound that was a cross between a laugh and a snort, and dismissed Neil by waving his left hand in Neil's direction as though he were shoving away the nose of a horse. He then spit into the alley's dirt and started toward the stable.

"Now just hold it," Neil said, not trying to hide his exasperation. "Does you walking off like that mean you're not even willing to talk it over?"

The persistence of this fool must have been more than the man could stand because he jerked his head in Neil's direction, and in one quick, fluid move his right hand went to his holster. The movement was so fast it was a blur, but before he got his shooter pulled, Neil drew and sent a bullet into the top of the man's right foot.

When the slug hit, the man's boot exploded, sending blood and leather flying and leaving a black, gaping hole that showed raw meat and white, jagged bone. The man screamed and fell to his back in the dirt.

Neil realized that the standard rule of gunfighting was to put the first shot in an opponent's chest to slow him down and the second shot in his head to stop him. He also knew that when a man was drawing, it was risky to shoot him in a less than lethal location, but they were standing close, and Neil was sure of his skills.

With his gun still out, Neil crossed to where the man lay. Neil had dropped his genial smile. "I'll ask you again, Mister, what is it you want with Katie Burke?"

But the man didn't answer — he only screamed and rolled and clutched at his foot, which now spewed blood like water from a spigot.

Waldo Brickman came over, and looking down at the screaming man, he said, "I doubt he'll be answering any questions since it don't appear like he can concentrate on much more 'n that big ol' hole you just put in his boot." He glanced at the short-barreled Colt which still smoked in Neil's right hand. "You're fast with that thing." There was a wonder in his voice that could not be missed. "Damned fast," he added.

Neil holstered the weapon and dug into his pocket. He pulled out a half eagle and handed it to Brickman. "See that he gets a doc or someone to look after that shot-up foot, would you?"

The worst of the man's screaming had stopped. Now he merely whimpered and watched Neil and Brickman with vacant, glassy eyes.

Brickman took the five dollars and said, "You bet, but that's pretty generous of you, ain't it? I mean, hell, it appeared to me like the son of a bitch aimed to kill you. Maybe you oughta let 'im get patched up with his own damned money."

Neil shrugged. "Nah," he said, "it'll be my treat. After all, the way it worked out, I didn't have to buy his breakfast."

They both shared a smile, and Neil said, "Be seeing you, Mister Brickman," and he turned and left the alley.

He had not gone ten feet toward the stable when he heard the man on the ground let out another scream, and this scream was more piercing than any sound he had made before. Neil spun around, expecting the worst, and saw Waldo Brickman's long toad sticker protruding from the center of the man's chest. It was buried in him up to the hilt. In the man's hand was the gun he had been too slow to pull on Neil a couple of minutes earlier.

Brickman looked at Neil. His eyes bulged, and he stammered when he said, "Th-th-the b-b-bastard was gonna shoot you in the back."

Neil ran to the body and searched the man's neck for a pulse, but even as he did it, he knew he wouldn't find one. He was as lifeless as granite.

Brickman staggered across the alley and leaned against the outside wall of the sleeping room. "I had to d-d-do it," he explained. "He just pulled his gun and was gonna plug you as you walked away. I *had* to do it. I didn't have no choice."

Neil came over and put his hand on the older man's shoulder. "Thank you," he said. "You saved my life."

"I ain't never seen nothin' like it," continued Brickman, his eyes still wide. "The cold-blooded bastard was just gonna *murder* you. Shoot you down."

Brickman looked as though he might be sick. It seemed this was not the sort of thing that a drunken silhouette cutter was accustomed to.

Neil looked back at the body. The handle of the knife rose from the dead man's chest like a fence post. "I reckon I should've just killed the son of a bitch in the first place," he said. "It would've saved us both some trouble." His gaze returned to Waldo Brickman. "But I thought that maybe this time I could get by without anybody dying."

FOUR

Once they had ridden a few miles out of Fort Fetterman, Neil reined in and dismounted. He wanted to check how the gear was riding on the pack horses, and once the animals had relieved themselves of their morning hay, he tightened their cinches.

"Stand over yonder while I do this," he said to Katie, motioning to a spot out of the way. It was the first time he had spoken to her since they had mounted up and left the stable.

"I can tighten my own cinch," she said as she swung her leg over the sorrel's rump and dropped to the ground.

Neil didn't respond but just went about his business.

After a while, Katie said, "Thanks for your help back there."

She didn't look at him when she said it, and Neil didn't act as if he had even heard. He finished with the pack animals and roan while Katie dealt with the sorrel. He then checked all the horses' legs for prickly pear spines. The low-growing cactus was everywhere and could be a nuisance. When he was satisfied the horses were fine, he mounted up and gave the roan some spur. Katie fell in behind him.

He hoped to reach the confluence of Box and Lightning Creeks before dark. It was a distance of maybe thirty miles from the fort and was a good place to camp. The cottonwood trees provided cover, and there was plenty of grass for the horses. Even though it was a low spot, the grassland sloped up gently in all directions, making it impossible for anyone to come in without being spotted.

Because of their late start, they wouldn't make it unless they pushed hard, but since the horses were fresh, Neil kept them at a steady trot. They should hit the western end of Lightning Creek in three or four hours. Once they did, they could take a short break, water the horses, and maybe share a can of peaches.

Neil had a weakness for the canned fruit packed in thick, sweet syrup. Canned goods were convenient, but he rarely carried them when he traveled alone — they were heavy and took up a lot of space. But since he and

Katie had a couple of sturdy pack horses, a few luxuries were allowed.

Waldo Brickman had been right about Katie's throwing her money around. Besides the horses and supplies, she had also purchased two brand-new Marlin 81s — one for Neil and the other for herself. She claimed to be an excellent shot.

Going with the Marlins was Neil's idea. He knew most folks favored Winchester, and over the years, Winchester's refinements to the original '66 made for an outstanding weapon. But to Neil's mind, the new Marlin was the finest long gun around.

Neil had allowed Katie to trade in the Whitney-Burgess he'd bought used a couple of years before, but it was unclear whether he'd get to keep the Marlin once the job was finished. He hoped so. It was a beautiful piece, but he hadn't asked yesterday, and he didn't plan to mention it now. He'd just wait and see how things turned out.

The events back in town had made him feel low, but he was better now. A breeze coming in from the mountains had rubbed the edge off the morning heat, and he looked up into the cloudless sky and took a breath. The air was full of the tart scent of sagebrush — a fine aroma. It was a prairie smell, a Wyoming smell. There was sure nothing like it back in Oswego, New York, where he'd been born and raised. And there was nothing like it in that damned Fort Fetterman, either. It was good to leave that dingy place behind and return to the open prairie.

What had happened in Fetterman was bad, but that sort of thing wasn't rare. The West was a place with few laws and fewer lawmen, and because of that, men like the one back there who had attacked Katie Burke were common. Most were men who'd had no success in the East and had brought their failings with them to the frontier, and many, like this one, met a premature end. For some, it was getting shot in the street. For others, it was dangling from a rope. For this one, it just happened to be a long-bladed knife to the heart in a back alley of some two-bit army town.

It was a thing Neil had seen before.

Through his teeth, he gave the roan a little "click-click," and the animal picked up the pace. Neil enjoyed the saddle, especially when he had a good horse beneath him, and, despite a nasty temperament, the roan was a good one — strong and fast. He found the animal's rhythm and aimed his muzzle at the horizon.

■ ■ ■ ■

They had been riding a couple of hours — still in a stony silence — when Neil saw the vultures. A few circled a quarter of a mile up ahead, but beneath the ones still flying, there were eight or ten hopping about on the ground. He applied the spur and loped toward the large black birds. By the time they were close enough to make out the ugly buzzards' red, featherless heads, most had taken flight, but a couple of the braver ones lingered, refusing to abandon their booty.

"What is it they're going at?" Katie asked.

Neil didn't have to dismount. He could tell from fifty feet away what it was the vultures were making a meal of.

"A gut pile," he answered. "Judging by its size, it's probably from an elk." Like the buffalo, the elk were a plains animal. Unlike the buffalo, the elk were adaptable. When the white man came along and started depleting their numbers, the majority of elk herds migrated into the high country. A few, though, still roamed the prairie. It wasn't unusual to run across one.

But it was not the elk innards that had caught Neil's interest.

He moved in closer, and one of the two

buzzards that remained spread its broad black wings and lifted off. The other stood motionless, a shiny string of intestine dangling from its hooked beak, and fixed Neil with a beady eye.

Neil lifted his hand and stopped Katie before she could come any closer. He checked the tracks around the gut pile — unshod horses, half a dozen, and the heelless footprints of moccasins.

Slowly, Neil moved around the pile of entrails, and when he found the area from which the riders had departed, he breathed a little easier. The tracks moved off toward the southwest — the opposite direction he and Katie were headed.

"It looks like a few bucks have left the reservation," he said, staring out to where the sky met the grass.

"Shoshone?" Katie asked, looking down at the tracks and following Neil's gaze. "Arapaho, maybe?"

Neil could hear the hope in her voice. Both tribes from the Wind River were docile and rarely caused a fuss.

"I doubt it," he said. "We're too far east." He took off his hat and pushed back the shock of hair that always flopped across his forehead. "Nope, I figure these boys're from the big reservation in Dakota."

"Sioux?"

"That's my guess."

Katie swallowed. "Do you think it could be a war party?" The hope in her voice had been swapped with dread.

"Oh, I doubt it. They're probably just out hunting where they shouldn't be and having themselves a little fun. I expect they're young. It's the young ones that've been roaming off the Res the last year or so. The thing is, you never know what some crazy nineteen-year-old full of piss and vinegar is apt to do. I'd like to avoid 'em if we can."

He glanced again toward the southwest, hoping the unshod ponies continued that way. Then he turned and faced the opposite direction. "Whenever possible," he added, "I like a hot meal at the end of the day, so we best make some distance before it gets dark. Once the sun goes down, we'll not want to risk a fire."

He looked at Katie and could see her concern. He knew she was hoping for something reassuring from him — at least a smile — but he didn't give her one. He still had a bone or two to pick with her. And besides, he didn't feel much like smiling. They still had miles to go, and it had already been a long day. First there was the man at Fetterman drawing down on him, and now there were signs of Indians. A hell of a way to start a journey. He hoped it didn't augur bad things to come.

"Let's hit the trail," he said, kicking the roan. "Daylight's a-burning."

Just past seven o'clock that evening, they got to the spot where Lightning Creek and Box Creek came together, and it was a welcome sight. The lower part of Neil's back throbbed. It had been his experience that the first day of any trip was always the hardest, and this first day bolstered that belief.

He led the way into the cottonwoods along the creek, pulled up, and dismounted. There had been enough of a breeze earlier to fill the dusty air with the tangy scent of sagebrush, but down here among the trees, the smells were sweet with grass and water. He let the horses drink a bit and then unsaddled the roan and sorrel and took the gear off the pack horses.

He nodded to one of the packs and said, "Dig out the hobbles, there, would you, Missus Burke?"

While Katie did as he asked, Neil let the horses drink a little more, and then he brushed them down and hobbled them.

The fetters were necessary. He hadn't yet learned the nature of the three horses they had purchased the night before, but he had been around the roan long enough to know that the scamp could be a hard one to catch. If some belligerent young Sioux showed up, Neil did not want to have to ask if they were willing to postpone their scalping long enough for him to chase his horse.

Once the animals were tended to, he gathered some wood and built a fire. When he had the fire going, he crossed to one of the packs and dug down for a frying pan. "You told me last night you were a farmer's wife. That might've led me to thinking that you have some cooking skills, but since then, there's been a thing or two happen that make me question your story." He turned to check her reaction, but she provided none. "Since I can't be sure what's what, I guess I gotta ask. Do you know how to cook, Missus Burke?"

She let the question hang there for a bit before she answered. "I suppose I'm handy enough with a skillet."

He placed a bag of flour and a tin of lard into the frying pan and handed it all to her. "Then, if you don't mind, whip us up some gravy. Milk gravy would be nice, but since I don't see a milk cow standing around, I guess creek-water gravy'll have to do." He returned to digging in the pack. "While you do that, I'll put on some coffee and slice some meat. Does a chipped beef supper sound okay to you?"

"It sounds fine."

More silence set in as Neil sliced and diced the salted meat and Katie made the gravy.

After the meat was cut, Neil dropped it into the skillet and sat back to watch as Katie stirred it all together.

She wore a pin on her dress. It was an unusual piece of jewelry, made up of two swooping lines of gold that connected in the middle. The first thing Neil thought when he saw it was that it was a bird in flight, but he didn't know why he should think so because there was nothing about it that looked much like a bird.

"That's an interesting pin you're wearing. I noticed it yesterday, too."

"I always wear it," she said.

"It almost looks like a bird flying."

Her eyes came up, and she looked surprised. "Funny you should say that. The man who designed it called it the Flying Swan."

"Is that so?"

"His name was Henri Chenal, and he was from Paris. I met him when I was just a girl."

"Where was that?"

"St. Louis. We were living there for a while, and he was touring America. He was an artist. He did sculpture, designed jewelry, painted. He had studied painting back in France with a man named Manet."

Neil leaned forward and looked closer at the pin. "It's strange, isn't it, how it can make you think of a bird without really looking like one?"

"Henri Chenal had a gift for making folks see things the way he wanted them to." She took the skillet from the fire. "I expect this is ready now," she said as she filled both of their plates.

"Tomorrow will be a shorter day," Neil said when they had begun to eat. "A friend of mine I was in the Army with has a place on Lance Creek about twenty or so miles from here. We'll have to leave the trail, but it's not far off. I hope you don't mind."

Katie looked back the way they had come and squinted into the distance as though watching for something. "Leave the trail?" she said after a bit. "No, I don't mind leaving the trail. Not at all."

"We'll stop there and have a roof over our heads for the night. That is, we will if he hasn't been run out of the country by now."

"What do you mean?"

"He's a Basque from . . . well, the truth

is, I guess I never could figure out just where Basqueland, or whatever it's called, is located exactly."

"The Pyrenees. It's a range of mountains at the top of the Iberian peninsula between Spain and France."

Neil's eyebrows popped up, and Katie shrugged. "I read a lot," she said.

It was becoming clear this woman was a long shot smarter than he was. He hated it when he ran across a female like that, even though it seemed to happen a lot.

"Anyhow," he continued, "ol' Raf grew up a shepherd, and after he had a look at this country around here, he said it'd be a perfect place for sheep. Since there weren't many around, he figured it was high time to bring some in."

Katie took a sip of coffee and then pointed out, "I doubt the locals would agree."

"I tried to explain that to him, but after knowing Raf for about eight years now, I've come to the opinion that the Basques are a stubborn race."

"How did a Basque end up in the US Army in the first place?"

"Oh, I figure thirty or forty percent of my outfit was foreigners. Mostly Irish, but some Germans and a few Frenchies and Italians. So far as I know, Raf was the only Basque.

He and I joined up at the same time in Chicago back in '73, served our whole hitch together, and were discharged in '78."

"What did you do in the Army, Mister Bancroft?"

"A lot of the time, I did what I was doing as a civilian — chopping down trees to use for firewood, lumber, what have you. I was lumberjacking there in Illinois when I saw a parade one day with a band and marching soldiers all in handsome blue. They looked like something grand, something I wanted to be a part of, so I enlisted. That's when I discovered that things are often not what they seem. That was not the first time events had tried to teach me that lesson, but it seems it was a lesson hard for me to learn. I sometimes wonder if I've learned it yet. Being a fool has proven to be a burden over the years. Anyhow, as it turned out, the one real difference between army life and life as a civilian was that the Army had me chopping down trees for a whole lot less pay than I was making before, plus they also provided several real good opportunities for me to get killed. If a fella ever sets a goal for himself of dying young, why then, the Army is the place for him."

Neil took the last bite of his supper and then crossed to the creek and washed his tin plate, spoon, and frying pan. Katie was finished as well, and he did the same with her plate and spoon. He then wrapped the utensils in a large cloth and laid them on the trunk of a fallen cottonwood where they would be handy for breakfast in the morning.

Katie poured them both another cup of coffee while Neil again rummaged inside one of the packs. He came out with a bottle of brandy and a partially smoked cigar. He had tossed three bottles of brandy and a couple of handfuls of smokes in with the other supplies at the sutler's the evening before. He figured only a fool would start a journey without a stock of tobacco and strong drink.

"I've only smoked maybe a third of this long nine," he said, "and now seems like a fine time to polish off the other six inches."

He sloshed brandy into his coffee, and without bothering to ask if she cared for any, he poured some into Katie's coffee as well. He then jammed the cork back in the bottle and set it within easy reaching distance if the need should arise for more.

Katie took a sip, made a face, and then sipped again. "Did you see battle, Mister Bancroft, during your years in the Army?"

She was leaned against a large rock, and

Neil sat down across from her. He reached into the fire, pulled out a burning twig, and lit his cigar. He blew out an acrid puff of blue smoke and said, "I think we've talked about me enough. Let's talk about you awhile."

She stiffened and set her cup on the ground. "I wondered when you were going to get to it."

"Now's the time." He blew across the top of his coffee, slurped some in, and added, "I reckon you can begin by telling me who that fella was who was chasing you around your hotel room."

"I didn't know him," she said.

"Uh-huh." Neil was skeptical. "He seemed to know you well enough. And Mister Brickman, that fella who was in the alley with us this morning, said the man was one of a group who'd been asking about you in Cheyenne."

She nodded. "I heard him say that."

"Well?"

"Well, what? I don't know what you want me to say. This morning, while I was getting ready to meet you at the stables, this man came pounding on my door. As soon as I opened it, he pushed his way in and grabbed me. I kicked and scratched and bit. I fought him for all I was worth and was able to get

73

away. That's when I saw you."

The sun was getting low, and Neil would soon have to douse the fire. Now, though, he stared into it, watching it dance, and without looking up, he asked, "Why would anyone be looking for you in Cheyenne anyway, Missus Burke, since you're from Amarillo?"

"All right," she said. "I admit I wasn't entirely honest with you last night."

Neil put a false note of shock into his voice. "My goodness," he said, "could that be so?"

"Are you going to start being a smart aleck again?"

"All right, tell your story."

"Not long after I got my husband's last letter, I traveled up to Denver. I wanted to get to the Dakotas as soon as possible. It was my hope to go by rail the rest of the way, but I learned that there was no rail service all the way to the Black Hills. The farthest north I could go by train was either Sidney, Nebraska, or Cheyenne, Wyoming. I chose Cheyenne. From there, the only means of travel was the stage to Deadwood, but it was early December, and a day after I arrived in town, the entire region was hit by the worst blizzard in years."

"So you wintered in Cheyenne?"

"I did."

"It was lucky for you that your husband had been sending you those handsome sums of money. Otherwise, you might not've had the means to survive."

Her lashes lifted, and she raised her eyes toward the purpling sky. "I guess I exaggerated some about that, too. I wanted you to be convinced that what I was saying about the gold was the truth, and . . ." she paused, "I didn't want to have to explain how I came by the money I had."

"Why's that?" Neil asked. "Did you rob a stage?"

The blue of her eyes was flecked with gold, and when he asked that question, she turned her head toward him in such a manner that the fire caught those golden flecks and caused her eyes to flash. "Why, no," she said, "of course not. What a thing to say." She gave him a hard look, then lifted her cup and sipped. After a bit, she said with a shrug, "I didn't want to have to explain how I came by the money because I was dealing faro in a saloon, an occupation that my strong-willed Baptist mother would not approve of."

Well, well, Neil told himself, *she admitted the truth about dealing faro.* He had withheld his knowledge of that in order to see if she would come out with it on her own.

"Why did you ride the stage up to Fetterman," he asked, "instead of taking the one to the Black Hills like you'd planned?"

Her lips tightened. It was clear that she resented his quizzing her. He could see she was a woman who enjoyed being in control, and his questions threatened that.

"I fear that the men who were asking about me are the men who killed my husband," she finally said.

"Whatever'd make you think that?"

"I'm sorry, Neil, but I wasn't entirely truthful with you about that, either. I guess I was afraid if you knew there were others after the gold, you wouldn't agree to help me."

"Go on."

"The men who attacked Edward on the road weren't strangers. He knew them. One of them, the leader of the group, is named Randall Frost. Edward told me in his letter that he'd had trouble with Frost in the past. Frost and his men were aware that Edward had found a large vein of ore."

"Which made Edward's traveling with it even stupider."

"Yes," she agreed, "but he would've had to haul it down the mountain at some time anyway. In the letter, he said that he feared

76

for my safety because they knew who I was as well."

"How would they know that?"

"In the confusion after he was wounded, Edward left our letters and a photograph of me among the gear on the pack horse he allowed them to take. In the letters, we had discussed the size of the vein he'd found, so they would realize that he'd been carrying more gold than he'd allowed them to find. If they discovered that he made it to Custer before he died, which I'm sure they eventually did, they would have to suspect that he'd gotten word to me where he hid the rest of the gold."

"And they would come looking for you to find that out."

She nodded.

"But they'd go to Amarillo, not Cheyenne."

"They went to Amarillo. When I was in Denver, I had wired a friend of mine back home telling her I was going to Dakota through Cheyenne. Three days ago, I received a letter from her telling me that a couple of weeks earlier, some friends of Edward's from the Black Hills mining camps had stopped in to say hello."

"And she told them you were headed back to Dakota and had stopped in Cheyenne?"

She stared into the fire. "I suppose she must have."

"One of them," Neil said, "told the owner of the saloon where you were working that he was your husband. How do you explain that?"

She shrugged. "I guess he figured his hunting me would raise less suspicion if he said I was his wife. A husband has the right to do whatever's necessary regarding a wayward wife."

The woman was a quick thinker and had a skill with words, Neil thought.

After a bit, she said, "I'm sorry about being less than forthright with you. I needed your help, but I know it wasn't fair to let you take the job when you didn't know the whole story. The truth is, though, I didn't think there was any danger. I really didn't. I left just as soon as I heard they were there looking for me. I didn't think there was any reason to say anything about them."

She finished off the last sip of what remained in her cup.

"Care for a little more?" Neil asked, reaching for the bottle of brandy.

She gave a quick laugh. "No," she said, "but thanks. One's more than enough for me. I already feel a flush." She rolled her eyes and waved the long fingers of her right hand in front of her face as if to cool herself down.

Neil poured a bit more into his own cup. It was making his back feel better. "Suit yourself," he said.

"I wouldn't blame you if you just left me at the first town on the trail," said Katie. Then, after a pause, she added, "Is that your plan?"

"No, no," he said. "I told you I'd see it out, and I will. Besides, there aren't any towns on the trail."

There was no doubt that she'd been dishonest. Now, though, she was admitting that there were thieves and murderers after her. The thing that surprised Neil was that even knowing all that, he was still willing to stick around.

He asked himself why in the hell he would ever agree to such a crazy thing.

Of course, there was the promise of a thousand dollars — that was a real temptation — and he had to admit that the opportunity to share the company of a beautiful woman was also appealing. Those things counted, all right. But he knew the reason he would stay was the same reason he had done most everything else since his schoolboy days back in Oswego — simple curiosity.

Katie was smart, and she had a way of talking and thinking that required a fella to stay on his toes. But, at least to Neil's way of thinking, he was no fool, either.

He watched her across the fire. Again, the light was hitting the gold in her eyes. She had a nice face. It was lovely and innocent, and as he stared into it, he felt his lips pull back into a wide smile.

It was a smile Katie quickly returned.

No, he would not stay just for the gold or because — despite himself and her craziness — he found this woman appealing. He would stay because he could tell just as sure as he was sitting there that Katie Burke was still not telling the whole story, and he had a real curiosity to find out why.

FIVE

Pepe began to bark at Katie and Neil as soon as they topped the ridge. He was a big dog with hair the same color and texture as the thirty dingy blots of stupidity he was charged with herding and protecting.

Neil didn't like sheep. They were the most ignorant four-legged creatures he'd ever come across. But the dog tending them was smart.

By the time he and Katie had loped down the hill and forded the thin trickle that was Lance Creek, Pepe must have recognized him, because his bark turned into a yip. He spun a couple of tight circles and started wagging his tail.

"Hey there, Pepe," Neil called out. "Where's Raf?"

Just as he said that, a wiry man barely five feet tall came up out of a ravine. He had a lamb tucked under each arm. With a laugh, he shouted, "I'm telling you a hundred time, but you never listen. That dog, he don't speak no English, eh?" He dropped the lambs, and they scampered off toward the flock. "He only speak *Euskara,* the mother tongue."

Neil came out of the saddle and ran to his friend. He shoved out his hand, but the little Basque slapped it away and gave Neil a hug instead. Neil returned the hug, but then he quickly stepped back. Holding up an index finger, he said in a stern voice, "Now don't you try to kiss me, damn it." He turned to Katie, who was still astride the sorrel. "If you're not careful, ol' Raf here'll slobber all over you before you know what's happening."

Raf seemed to see Katie for the first time. "Hey, who is this flower you travel with?" he asked.

"Her name's Katie Burke, and she is trouble through and through."

The little man grinned. "I'm see that." He shook his hand as if he had just touched something hot. "What is a beautiful woman like you doing with such a bum as this?" He jerked a thumb at Neil.

"I've hired him to take me into the Black Hills."

Raf clasped his cheeks with both hands. "Oh," he groaned, "I'm thinking you must not be so smart as you look, eh?"

Katie smiled. "You might be right."

Neil cut in. "Katie, this midget's name is Rafael Cossiga, and if you happen to be carrying a deck of cards, then this is your lucky day. Raf is the worst poker player in all the world."

Raf always wore a white beret, and he removed it and gave Katie a deep bow. "Is my honor to meet you, young lady." He rose and placed his hand to the side of his mouth as though trying to prevent Neil from hearing. In a loud whisper, he added, "And do yourself big favor. Never listen to this viper."

Katie nodded. "Something tells me that's good advice."

Raf turned to Neil. "There must be, in all this world, some man somewhere who plays the poker worse than Rafael." He shrugged and added with a smile, "But I never meet him."

"And you never will, neither."

"Don't matter," said Raf. "I'm don't play poker no more anyhow." He swept his arm toward his flock. "Raising the woollies is gamble enough for me."

"That's the truth," agreed Neil. "It'd take a fool to bring mutton into this country, which I reckon makes you more than qualified. The only smart thing you ever did in your life was to hook up with Lottie. How's she doing anyhow?"

Rafael beamed, touched his fingertips to his lips, and threw a kiss at the sky. "More lovely than ever," he said. "You and Katie Burke go to the house and see for yourself. Me and Pepe'll move the children up closer, and then we'll have us a fine supper." He lowered his head and gave Neil a hard look. "I'm betting you have some brandy stuck inside one-a them big ol' packs, eh?"

"Well, believe it or not, that's one bet you would win. I'd never be fool enough to show up at your doorstep without brandy."

Rafael tossed his head back and barked out a laugh that sounded as if it came from a man twice his size.

"Who's Lottie?" Katie asked as they rode the half mile to Rafael's house. "His wife?"

"Well, they call each other husband and wife, but I doubt they've ever gone so far as to request the blessings of the clergy. For all practical purposes, though, they're as married as anyone ever was."

"That's nice," Katie said a little wistfully. "Good for them. How'd they meet?"

Neil eyed the woman riding beside him and decided it would be hard to shock a mendacious faro dealer. "Lottie was working as a cook and an occasional whore at a place called Poker Alice's outside of where we were posted." When Katie made no comment, he asked, "Does that give you pause?"

She shook her head. "The world can be a harsh place," she said.

They came to a steep spot, and Neil had to give the headstrong roan a couple of good kicks to get him up it. Once they were at the top, he said, "That was back in '78, when they met. It was our last year in the Army. By then, Raf and me were at Camp Sturgis on the far side of the Hills from here. Raf was smitten with her the first time he saw her. We mustered out in September, and the very first thing he did was ask Lottie if she'd like to try out a new kind of life. They've been together ever since."

"Have they been over here in Wyoming raising sheep all that time?" Katie asked.

"Nah, Raf worked as a ranch hand about sixty miles east of here for a couple of years. Then a little more than a year ago, he located this deserted homestead and filed on it."

"He seems to be doing well enough," Katie observed.

Neil let out a half laugh, half snort. "If not being scalped by an Indian nor shot dead by some irate cattleman is the mark of how a fella's doing, then I reckon you're right. But I expect either one of those things could happen at just about any time."

Katie looked around at the rolling prairie and the huge expanse of sky. "It's a pretty remote place he chose, isn't it?"

"Not remote enough for sheep."

The Cossiga homestead was a small but well-tended place. The buildings — a two-room house and a barn — had been built by the original homesteader and were made of cottonwood logs and clapboards. Because cottonwood didn't grow as straight as pine, it wasn't as well suited for construction, but the builder had done a fair job, and since moving in, Raf had replaced all the loose chinking in both buildings and added two small corrals and a sty.

A brown-eyed Jersey watched them from one of the corrals, and a couple of pink pigs snorted in the sty. Fifteen or twenty chickens clucked and strutted about the yard, and along the side of the barn, Lottie had put in a large garden. The garden was doing well. The corn was tall enough that Neil was sure it had made it to Raf's knees by the Fourth of July, and had maybe made it to Lottie's.

He took it all in — the house, barn, corrals. Maybe Katie was right. Raf did seem to be doing well. It had been a while since

Neil had been here, and the place was looking better and more settled all the time.

"Hello in the cabin," he called out as they rode up. "Is anybody home?"

After a bit, the door opened, and an enormous woman stepped out onto the porch. She was almost as tall as Neil, even in his boots, and outweighed him by a good fifty pounds. Her thick, yellow-blond hair was piled atop her head, adding another four inches to her already imposing height.

Being myopic, she craned her neck and squinted. "Who's there? Is that you, Bancroft?" For some reason Neil did not understand, she never used his Christian name.

"It's me, Lottie. I swear, you're getting blinder every day."

"When it comes to looking at you, being blind ain't so bad. Get off that animal and come give me a kiss on the lips." She eased herself down the porch steps and came toward Neil with her large arms held wide.

After Neil had provided Lottie with her kiss, he introduced Katie and explained that they were passing through on their way to the Hills.

"Well, this is a fine surprise," Lottie said. "Just fine." She then took Katie by the hand and told Neil to tend to the horses while she and Katie had some buttermilk and flat cakes. "I just made a fresh batch this morning," she said. "Also there's beans in the pot and cornbread in the Dutch oven. Once that little Basque shows up, we'll have 'im kill us a couple-a chickens."

When visiting Lottie, suppertime was always a big event.

After they had eaten and the dishes were washed, they all went outside and sat on the porch. The ladies drank tea, and for the boys, Neil broke out the brandy and two fresh long nines.

There was a waxing gibbous moon, but it wasn't yet so bright that its light did much to erase the stars. They were sprinkled across the sky like gold dust on velvet.

"I always liked this place at night," Lottie said. "I doubt I've ever been anywheres I like so much as this little piece of prairie at night." She was sitting next to Raf, and she reached over and put her hand on his thigh. He covered it with his own hand and gave it a squeeze. "Of course," she added, "it can be a real eyesore in the winter, or when the crick floods, or when the hail beats down, or during a drought, or . . ."

"No, no," Raf interrupted, "is beautiful them hard times, too. Is always beautiful, this place."

"It is nice," Katie agreed. She was next to Lottie, and since there wasn't another chair, Neil sat on the porch's top step with his back against the rail.

"It's all right, I reckon," Neil allowed, "so long as you don't see a bunch of disgruntled Sioux come loping across the top of that hill over yonder." He pointed toward the northeast, the direction of the Great Sioux Reservation.

"Mister Lakota, he don't bother us none." Raf had been referring to the Sioux as "Mister Lakota" for as long as Neil could remember.

"Do you ever see any?" Katie asked.

"Oh, sometimes they come," Raf answered. "Some boys stop by just other day. I give tobacco."

"Were there six of them, by chance?" Neil asked.

Raf thought for a second and answered, "Six is right. How you know, eh?"

"We ran across a gut pile yesterday where someone'd killed an elk. It looked like there were about a half dozen unshod ponies in the group."

"They don't cause no trouble for us," Raf said. "Sometimes they just get lonesome for the old ways, and they leave the reservation."

89

"I hope they don't get lonesome for *some* of their old ways," Katie said.

Raf took a big puff of his cigar. "Euskal Herria is homeland of people who speak Euskara. Is been homeland of us since beginning of all times. We fight Romans and Visigoths." He shook a fist at the sky. "We fight Charlemagne. Now the French, the Spanish, they pretend they own us. They pretend they our master." Raf smiled. "But they are not master of us. And even with its army and with its reservations, in the end, America, she is not the master of Mister Lakota. Maybe, since chiefs stop fighting for Black Hills back in '77, the worst is over." He crossed himself. "I pray is over anyhow, but still America, she is not master." He gave Neil's upper arm a gentle, backhanded swat. "What you say, fast-gun, bronc-busting cowboy, eh?"

Raf always teased Neil, the New Yorker, about how he had taken to the ways of the West.

Neil took off his hat, hung it on his knee, and ran his hand through his hair. "Hell, Raf," he said, "I don't know. I try not to ponder such things. I figure we've been doing the red man wrong for at least as far back as the *Mayflower,* and it sure doesn't surprise me that he doesn't like it very

90

much. On the other hand, I reckon it stops being a moral question that I have much interest in right about the time one of them young bucks decides he wants to count *coup* by hanging my scalp on his belt. Don't get me wrong. I don't blame 'em for wanting to do it. We've been doing violence to them since the beginning. But even if he does have the right, I guess I'll do what I can to keep my hair just where it is."

Raf reached over and ran his fingertips over the crown of Neil's head. The hair there was a bit thinner than it had been a few years before. "Looks like," Raf said, "Mister Lakota, he better hurry."

Neil batted his hand away.

"Once, when I was a girl," said Lottie, "my momma and me was in a train depot in Chillicothe, Ohio — I never knew exactly what happened, whether the engineer lost control of his locomotive or maybe just went crazy — but for some reason, this train came barreling down the track, right into the station yard, and it crashed at full speed into the roundhouse. It was like the world was coming to its end. There was explosions and fire, and railcars flew off the track in every which direction. Dozens of people died that afternoon — men, women, and children — and at least a couple of hundred was injured. Neither me nor my momma was hurt none, thank the Lord, but, I swear, there was bodies everywhere. People was screaming. There was blood, and . . ." She hesitated, cleared her throat, then added, "Well, it was horrible. I was only nine, and of course I was scared, but I still remember, even as bad as it was, that it wasn't the bodies of the folks who'd been hurt and killed that was the scariest. What was the scariest was looking through the windows just before the crash and seeing the fear on the faces of the passengers as that train roared past. Even at nine years old, I understood that those people on that train knew that there was not a power on this earth that could stop what was about to happen." She gave Raf's thigh a pat and then took her hand away. Folding her arms across her ample middle, she said, "And I figure that's the way it is here. The whites're coming into the Indian country just like that train came into the Chillicothe station yard. I ain't saying we're right. If the truth was told, I expect we aren't. But still, there ain't a power on all this earth that can stop it from happening."

No one spoke for a minute or so. Finally, Raf nodded and said, "Is true. Is bad thing for Mister Lakota, and a few young, feisty

Indians might still fight for little while more, but nobody gonna stop it. Mister Lakota, he done his best, but he mostly give up now. Those boys I give tobacco the other day, they ain't gonna hurt Lottie and me."

Fidgeting with the golden Flying Swan attached to her shirt, Katie said, "I hope you're right about that." She didn't sound too sure that he was.

"He's right, I reckon," Lottie said. "Them young bucks don't mean us no harm. I expect there are some who come and go off the Reservation who'd rather kill us than look at us, but those kind are few these days. The batch that came by here just wanted to get out for a while to see what they could see." She looked through the dim light at her husband. "It's the damned cattlemen we gotta worry about."

"Have you had any trouble from anyone?" Neil asked.

Lottie sipped from her cup. "There's a couple of brothers who have a spread just to the north of here who have no fondness for sheep nor Basques, neither one. I doubt they much like portly ex-whores, either."

"Have they done anything?" Katie asked.

"Just made threats is all," said Lottie. "A week ago, Josh — that's the youngest one, Josh Becker — he come in and dropped a dead ewe right over yonder in the yard." She raised a hand and pointed. "I don't know how that dern sheep got away from Pepe in the first place — they rarely do — but this one had. Anyway, Becker rode in with her thrown across the front of his saddle, and he dropped her in the dirt. We could plainly see that she had a bullet hole in the top of 'er skull. When Raf asked him what was going on, Becker said he found the sheep on his property, and he'd better never find another one, or there'd be hell to pay. He said if we knew what was good for us, we'd get our asses off this land and take our stinking sheep with us."

"Doesn't sound neighborly, does he?" Neil observed. "I expect Raf here stayed perfectly calm and collected all through Mister Becker's visit."

"He did," said Lottie, "except for the part where he stormed into the cabin and dug his old Dance and Park out of the foot-locker, came back out, and said he was gonna start counting. Said if Becker wasn't gone by the time he got to five, he was gonna be laying on the ground next to that dead ewe."

"Damn, Raf," said Neil, "I thought you could only count to three."

The small man smiled and nodded. "Is

true, only three. But no matter. Becker, he gone by the time I get to two."

Neil and Katie both thought that was funny. Lottie didn't laugh, though. Instead, she gave her husband a hard look. "Raf's coming on to middle age, Bancroft," she said to Neil while she stared at Raf, "but he handles his temper like a teen."

"Hey," Raf said in his own defense, "I do better'n usual, eh? I didn't shoot him."

Neil thought that was pretty funny, too, but he didn't dare laugh.

Lottie went on. "It's getting bad, though. A couple of days ago, Norman Greasby, the biggest landowner around, came by for a visit. He don't like sheep, neither, but he's a good man, and we count 'im as a friend."

Raf added, "Mister Greasby, he say no more woollies than we run, it don't matter to him, but he say the small operators, 'specially Beckers, they want to see us gone."

"Well," said Lottie, "what they want is to see us dead, but I reckon they'd settle for gone. Mister Greasby's been able to hold the Beckers at bay up to now, but I guess ol' Wild Bill here," she jerked her head at Rafael, "waving that gun at Josh has got 'em pretty hot." She lifted her eyes, and for a moment she stared off at someplace far

95

enough away that Neil figured, with her eyes, she'd be unable to see it even if it weren't dark. "Bancroft," she finally said, "I was just thinking. When do you plan to leave for the Hills?"

"First light, I reckon, if I can get this one on her feet." He prodded the air in Katie's direction.

"First light, huh? I wonder if I could get you to change your plans and stick around for a couple of hours."

"Is not needed," Raf said, his back stiffening.

Lottie turned toward her husband. "Maybe not," she said, "but it couldn't hurt none."

Neil flicked the ash from his cigar. "What're you getting at, Lottie?"

"Mister Greasby and the Beckers're coming over here in the morning."

"Coming here?" asked Katie. "Why?"

"Mister Greasby says it's time we settle this bad blood before somebody gets hurt." She looked at Raf. "And I gotta agree with the man, 'cause I figure if anybody gets hurt, it's gonna be . . ." she paused, taking her lower lip between her teeth, "this one here."

"Rafael, he take care of hisself."

Lottie just shook her head at the little

man's boast. After a bit, she went on. "Anyhow, Mister Greasby figures since he's a friend of both sides, he could act as a go-between, so to say — kind of a referee."

"What would you want me to do?" Neil asked.

"I don't know. Nothing special, really. Just be here with Raf when the meeting happens. Help him talk to the Beckers."

Raf came to his feet. "I'm don't need no help to talk to no pigs." He threw his cigar into the bare dirt of the yard. It exploded in a spray of sparks. "I tell 'em bastards just what is. I tell 'em just what is gonna be." He drove his fist into the palm of his hand. "Rafael do his own goddamn talk. Rafael, he talk just fine."

Neil smiled. "Raf," he said, "by golly, you're right. Your way with words is pure inspiration."

Six

Neil did Raf's morning chores at the same time that he tended to his and Katie's horses. That allowed Raf enough time to move his flock to grass that was a half mile away from the house and get back in time for the meeting with Norman Greasby and the Becker brothers.

Lottie had awakened everyone long before dawn with her banging about the cabin. "We need to get breakfast done and have the place cleaned up before they get here," she said.

Neil had never seen Lottie so fussy.

He and Katie had slept on pallets in the front room. They both rose and took turns washing up. After changing clothes in Raf and Lottie's room, Katie came out pinning the Flying Swan to her fresh shirt.

"What can I help you with, Lottie?" she asked.

"Maybe you could whip up some breakfast

98

while I straighten the house."

To Neil's surprise, Katie proved to be quite a hand. It was one thing to stir a skillet of gravy over a campfire — something she did well enough — but it was still another to produce the sort of breakfast Katie put together. She fried up some of the salt pork they had brought on the trip and made a batch of flapjacks as fine as any Neil had ever had anywhere, including restaurants in Cheyenne, Denver, and even Chicago. She said the trick was a simple one — use milk instead of water, eggs if any were available, which today there were, and if there was something tasty sitting around, add it to the batter. They'd picked a bagful of wild raspberries on Box Creek the day before, and Katie tossed them in with everything else. Covered in molasses, the cakes proved a treat.

After breakfast, Neil heard someone ride up, and he went to the window for a look. "Got us a visitor," he said. "But there's only one, not three."

Raf opened the door and gave the man flipping his reins around the porch rail a smile. "Mister Greasby," he said. "Come in. Come in."

"Mornin', Rafael. Fine day, ain't it?" The

man climbed the steps and came into the house.

Norman Greasby was a man in his early fifties whose size fell about halfway between Raf's and Neil's. He had on jeans that were clean but worn. The jeans were stuffed into the tops of boots so scuffed that Neil expected a toe to pop through at any minute. The man's shirt was made of tow linen, over which he wore a vest of brown cloth. His hat, which he now took off, was cream-colored and had lost most of what shape it might have once had. A two-inch-high sweat stain made its way around the crown's circumference.

On the whole, Norman Greasby was a friendly-looking sort but didn't, at first glance, appear to be the prosperous land-owner and rancher that Neil knew him to be.

"Morning, all," Greasby said, taking everyone in. His hair was white and curly on top but trimmed so close on the sides that Neil could see his pink scalp shining through. The man's eyes found Lottie's, and he smiled and said, "How're you, Missus Cossiga? My, but don't it smell fine in here."

"We had breakfast a while ago," Lottie said, "but there's still a couple of tasty flapjacks left if you're interested, and we're all having us some coffee."

"No thanks on the flapjacks," said Greasby. "I've already et." He had a ruddy face and blue eyes, and the smile he offered Lottie showed a gap between his two front teeth. "I'll sure take you up on some of that coffee, though, if it ain't any trouble."

As Lottie poured him a cup, she asked, "Where's the Beckers?"

Raf pulled a chair out from the table, and Greasby sat down. "Oh, they'll be along directly," he said. "I talked to 'em last night, and they said they was coming."

Lottie placed the cup on the table in front of the man and said, "Pardon my poor manners, Mister Greasby. This here fella is Neil Bancroft, and the young woman is his friend, Katie Burke."

Neil wasn't so sure Katie qualified as a friend, exactly, but polite behavior required that he let Lottie's remark stand.

Katie smiled at the rancher and nodded. Neil shook his hand. "Nice to meet you," he said.

They all sat down, and Greasby watched as Neil scooted his chair up to the table. "Bancroft?" the older man said as he scratched the pink scalp above his right ear. "Neil Bancroft? How come that name sounds so familiar?" He looked at Raf, but

101

before Raf could answer, Greasby snapped his fingers. "This must be the fella you told me about."

"Yes," Raf said. "Is him, my friend from Army."

"Well, I'll be switched," Greasby said. He came to his feet and grabbed Neil's hand and gave it another hard shake. "This is quite an honor, Mister Bancroft, it truly is. Raf here's told me all about you."

Neil allowed his hand to be pumped a couple of more times, and then, as gently as possible, he pulled it away. He must have had a perplexed expression on his face, because Greasby added, "He's told me about your army days together. Your years with Custer."

Now Neil understood. "Oh," he said, "that." He gave Rafael a stony look.

Greasby dropped back into his chair, but his smile was just as wide as before. He leaned forward, his forearms resting on his knees and excitement covering his face. "You know, I've dragged about as much of the story out of ol' Raf here as he seems willing to tell. I sure wish I could visit with you about it some."

Katie looked at Neil and asked, "Custer? You served with General Custer?"

"*Colonel* Custer," corrected Greasby.

"*Lieutenant* Colonel Custer," corrected Rafael.

Greasby laughed. "Yes, sir, that's right. Lieutenant Colonel Custer. He mighta wore an eagle and a star in his younger days, but he never saw 'em again. Thank heaven for that. To my way of thinking, except for Bill Sherman, George Armstrong Custer was the lowest snake ever to come out west. What he done down on the Washita was shameful. And, by God . . ." he smacked the table with his fist, "as far as I'm concerned it was a crime, assuming that the murder of women and children still falls within the boundaries of criminal behavior."

He started to say more but stopped himself and gave Neil an embarrassed expression. "I hope I ain't talking out of turn, Mister Bancroft. I sometimes get carried away. There ain't many who share my feelings regarding Colonel Custer, and I know he was your commanding officer. If I've offended you, why then, I apologize."

"I'm not offended, Mister Greasby. What happened on the Washita was before Raf and me were a part of the Seventh, but there were many among us who'd served down there. Most kept it to themselves, but there were a few who told us the story — the whole story, I expect, and not just what was in the papers."

"Hell, all that was in the papers was from that pack of lies Custer filed with Phil Sheridan and that bastard Sherman." When he realized the curse had slipped out, he looked to Lottie and Katie and said, "Sorry, ladies. I forget myself." But without waiting for them to accept his apology, he returned his attention to Neil. "It was from Custer's report of the incident to his superiors that the newspapers got their story."

Neil nodded but didn't say anything.

Greasby went on. "What Custer done was as bad as what John Chivington done down on Sand Creek, only folks never really questioned Custer's actions. He claimed to've killed better'n a hundred Cheyenne braves, but from what I've heard, it weren't no more than maybe ten or fifteen. The remaining eighty or ninety was women, children, and a few old men."

"Yes, sir," Neil agreed. "I've heard that as well."

"But they counted it as a great victory in the press."

Neil knew that what Greasby said concerning the attack on Black Kettle's Cheyenne camp at the Washita River was mostly true. It was a dark spot, to be sure — a disgrace — but the man seemed a little too passionate about an event that had taken place more than a dozen years before.

Neil took a sip of coffee, then pointed out, "You seem to have strong feelings regarding the matter, Mister Greasby."

"Well, sir, Mister Bancroft, you're right about that. But I reckon if the truth was told, I'd have to admit to a certain prejudice against William Tecumseh Sherman and any activity in which he played a part. Custer was a skunk who done what he done, but we all know it was Sherman who was running the show. And it was Sherman who covered up what really happened and allowed Custer's lies to stand."

"Could it be that you're from below the Mason-Dixon line, Mister Greasby?" Neil already knew the answer to that question. It was clear from Greasby's drawl.

The older man nodded. "I know what you're getting at, Mister Bancroft, and it's true. But I'm more than just from the South, sir. I was born and raised in Georgia, and you might say that I have seen the effects of General Sherman's tactics up close. But still, my prejudice don't change the facts. What Custer done on the Washita River was a horror for which all Americans oughta feel shame."

"I'd have to agree," Neil said.

"And," Greasby went on, "he tried the same thing yet again just up north of here a ways." He smiled. "But, of course, you two fellas know about that much better'n me. Even as awful as your ordeal was, it was your lucky day to be with Reno and Benteen instead of that buckskin-wearing fool."

"Excuse me, Neil," Katie interrupted, her forehead wrinkled. "Am I understanding Mister Greasby right? Were you and Raf with Custer in Montana?"

Neil nodded. "Yes, under his command, assigned to Marcus Reno."

"My God," said Katie in barely more than a whisper, looking to Raf and then back to Neil. "Then you two were at the Little Bighorn?"

"They were," said Greasby. "They were among the group who fought the first battle in the valley along the river. Custer ordered Reno and his men to attack the village, and then Custer went around so he could come at the camp and reinforce them from the other side. But he never came to help, did he? When he spotted about three thousand warriors down there instead of a hundred women and children, like he'd run across at the Washita and like Chivington had at Sand Creek, he decided to run back up the hill

106

rather than come to the aid of his men down below."

Neil thought that comment was a little unfair.

"By then, we was running, too, eh?" Raf said to Neil. "We come out of trees on the charge, and then we see Indian tepees stretching as far as horizon."

Neil stared into his coffee. "Even if not quite so far as the horizon," he corrected, "it was sure far enough for my tastes, I reckon. I doubt there've ever been so many damned Indians gathered in one spot."

"Is for sure," Raf said. "Even with all them Indians, though, Major Reno, he led us to charge. But down there by the river, we getting whipped bad." He tapped himself beneath both eyes with the index and middle fingers of his right hand. "I see for myself when Bloody Knife, one of our Arikara scouts, get shot in head. He was right next to Major Reno, and major get splashed with Bloody Knife's brains. That is when Reno calls retreat. Was crazy time, eh?"

Lottie gave the little man a hard look. "You could maybe leave out the details, Raf, if you don't mind. There is ladies present, you know."

Raf shrugged and smiled. "Was not many brains. Bloody Knife, he was not so smart."

"Everybody knows the story of what happened next, I guess," Greasby said. "At least as far as Custer and the men who were with him is concerned. They met a speedy demise."

"Those boys fought for better than an hour before the last man went down," Neil said. "And they fought brave. George Custer did as well."

Greasby shook his head. "I know they did. I didn't mean to imply nothing else. If it sounded like I was, well, sir, then I sure apologize. That was not my intent. And, as far as I know, Custer, though a fool, was as brave a man as he ever needed to be. From what I hear, he was more than courageous during the War Between the States." He looked to Lottie and Katie. "But the real bravery came later, over the remainder of that day, all through the night, and most of the following day."

Neil stood and crossed to the coffee pot. He refilled his cup, and Lottie, seeing that the pot was close to empty, said, "I'll put on some fresh."

"What happened?" Katie asked. "I mean, I know that Major Reno and his men made a stand at the top of some hill overlooking the Little Bighorn River, but I never heard the details."

"You ain't told your friend here the story, Mister Bancroft?"

Neil gave a quick shake of his head and sat back at the table.

"I reckon that don't surprise me none. Seems to me that you're much too modest a fella, sir, if you don't mind me saying it." He turned to Katie. "Major Reno and the men who survived the battle at the river retreated to the high ground, but they got pinned down on the ridge without hardly any cover at all. They fought the Indians off and held 'em at bay, but they were surrounded, and them braves just hid in the tall grass and behind rocks and such, and they started picking the soldiers off, one by one.

"Major Reno asked for a volunteer for picket duty, and who should stand up?" He nodded across the table at Neil.

"As the hours ticked by, the number of dead and wounded climbed. They'd set up a makeshift field hospital in the center of their perimeter, but even the boys whose wounds weren't necessarily fatal was starting to die because of the heat and the lack of water.

"Reno asked for volunteers to make their way through all them Indians and go down that hill to the river to collect water and bring it back." He leaned toward Katie and asked, "And who do you think was among the first to volunteer?" Again, he nodded at Neil.

"From all I read about it, and from what Raf here's told me, them red men put up one hell of a fight trying to stop Mister Bancroft and them others from getting down to that river, but they got there just the same. And then, not only that, but they got back up the hill toting as many canteens as they could carry."

He picked up his cup, but he didn't take a drink. He just held it. "Mister Bancroft here put his own life at risk against huge odds in order to save the lives of his friends. To my thinking, going after that water was the bravest deed in all the Indian wars. I expect it's as brave as any deed ever done in any war. A willingness to die for your comrades — well, young lady, that's just what bravery is."

He lifted his eyes to Katie's. "Them boys who faced all them Indians in order to get down to the Little Bighorn River to fetch water for the wounded was awarded the Medal of Honor, our nation's highest award. Only there was one of them courageous young men who for some reason known only to himself never claimed his medal."

He paused before asking, "Do you know who that fella was?"

When Katie didn't answer, Greasby, for the third time, turned to Neil and nodded.

They heard riders come into the yard, and Greasby said, "That'll be Artie and Josh. I'll go out and have a word with 'em before we get started." He pushed himself up from his chair and went outside.

Neil crossed to the window and saw four men climbing off their horses. The two in front were unmistakably brothers. They were both lanky, lean-jawed types in their early to mid-twenties. There was very little to distinguish them one from the other except that beneath the line of their hats, Neil could see that one's hair was more red than blond, and the other's was more blond than red. The blond had sideburns that reached below his ears almost to his jaw, and the redhead had a thick mustache whose ends drooped past the thin mark of his mouth. They both wore side arms, as did their two companions, although they all wore them like cowboys, not like gunmen.

Greasby shared some words with the brothers, and the one with the sideburns seemed to grow a bit agitated. Whatever it was that Greasby said to cause the agitation, he apparently said it again, and after a bit, with scowls on their faces, the brothers unbuckled their gun belts and hung them on their saddle horns.

The one with the mustache said something to the two men who had ridden in with them, and then Greasby and the brothers stepped onto the porch.

Once they were inside, Greasby introduced Katie and Neil. Arthur was the mustached one, and now that Neil could see them closer, it was clear that he was the older of the two by a couple of years. The younger one, Josh, wore a mean pouty expression, but both men had a look of unpredictability, and Neil figured they both bore watching. Neither looked very smart, but it was plain that it was Arthur Becker who was the boss, and in the end it would be Arthur who would have to be reckoned with.

"Of course," Greasby said, continuing with the civilities, "you boys know Mister and Missus Cossiga."

"Have seat," said Rafael, and all the men pulled up chairs to the table. Katie found a spot in the corner. Lottie poured coffee all around and then joined Katie.

Greasby took a big slug of coffee and then said in cordial tones, "I want to thank you gents for agreeing to this get-together this morning. I hate to see hard feelings growing in our little community here, and I hope there's some agreement we can reach to work things out."

Neither Raf nor either one of the Becker boys responded, and by the tension, Neil could tell right away that this meeting was every bit the doing of Norman Greasby and no one else.

"Now you Beckers have a sip of them coffees and stop looking so damned mean." With an air of authority that left no doubt as to who was in charge, Greasby pointed a finger at the cups in front of the brothers. "Lottie Cossiga brews as fine a cup of coffee as anyone ever, and it's foolish to allow it to cool."

The boys looked at the older man and then did as he said.

Nodding toward their cups, Greasby asked with a broad smile, "Now ain't that good?"

Arthur didn't answer the question, nor did he return the smile. "Me and Josh're here out of respect for you, Mister Greasby, and for no other reason. There ain't any agreement we're willing to make with this sheep man here other than maybe agreeing to help 'im load all his shit onto his wagon so he can get outta this country a little faster than if he was to load it by hisself."

"See?" said Raf to Neil. "See how is? This is waste of time."

Greasby sat up straighter. "Hold on, Raf," he said, "and you too, Artie. This is the very reason I thought we oughta have this pow-wow. You fellas can't say two words without getting all het up. Damn, it's frustrating even being around you. Why d'ya gotta be that way for, anyhow?" There was a faint note of pleading in Greasby's voice.

"I'll tell you why, Mister Greasby," said Josh. "You know as well as we do what them damned sheep does to the land. They come in and eat every blade of grass in sight. Hell, much of the time they even pull the shoots up right by the very roots. What's more, if there *is* any grass left after sheep've been at it, a fella can't get his cows to graze it. I don't know why that is for sure. Maybe it's something in their piss. But whatever it is, it ruins the ground and makes it useless for anything else, ever."

"I know," said Greasby. "I've heard that said a hundred times, but I ain't sure it's the truth, and neither are you."

"It's true," said Artie. "You can take a bullwhip to a cow, and you can't drive 'er across ground that's been grazed by sheep. It's a known fact."

It was already clear to Neil that these two fellas had no intention of working anything out with Rafael. Part of him even had to agree with them. He'd heard the same thing about sheep ruining the ground for cattle, but as far as he could see, that had nothing to do with why they were there. "You know something," he said, "I reckon there's only one fella sitting at this table who has a fondness for the woollies. Just like you boys — and you, too, Mister Greasby — I work with cows myself. Cows and horses. But the fact of the matter is, this land we're sitting on belongs to Raf. It's his place. He's worked long and hard to make this a going operation."

"Who're you?" asked Josh.

As he spoke, Neil had been dividing his attention among the four other men at the table. Now he focused on the younger Becker. "Weren't you paying attention a minute ago, son, when Mister Greasby introduced us?"

"I heard your name. What I want to know is what's your business here?"

Arthur Becker addressed Greasby. "Josh has a point. Him and me came over here this morning expecting to talk with Cossiga. We didn't know the meeting was going to be opened up to strangers."

115

"It's all right, Artie. Mister Bancroft's a friend of Raf's, and if Raf wants him here, why that's sure fine by me." To Neil, he said, "Go on with what you were saying, Mister Bancroft."

"It's Raf's property," said Neil, "and I figure he has the right to raise anything he wants on it, whether it be sheep, alligators, or Bing-gal tigers."

"Well, sir," said Artie, "I guess that's where you and me differs. I don't think some newcomer, 'specially some foreigner, should be able to just come in here and run something across this ground that we know is harmful to the land. You say he's worked long and hard. Hell, me and Josh grew up out here. Mister Greasby and our pa come out to this country not long after the damned war. They fought Indians and rustlers and blizzards and droughts. Don't you tell me how hard this goddamned Spaniard has worked."

Neil cringed. He knew that Arthur Becker had just made one very big mistake, but before he could do anything about it, Rafael was out of his chair and flying across the table, his hands clawed and aimed at Becker's throat.

"You call Rafael a *Spaniard,* you son of a bitch." He hit the older Becker hard enough to knock him backwards out of his chair, and they both crashed to the floor. Rafael's hands were so tight against Becker's windpipe that his knuckles were white.

Josh Becker started to go after the little Basque, but before he could leave his seat, Neil clasped a hand on Josh's shoulder and held him down. "Sit right there, young fella," Neil said.

It was Greasby who stood and pulled Raf off. "Hold it now, Rafael, goddamn it," he shouted. "There'll be none of that. Stop it." Greasby was able to get control of Raf but not without some effort.

Once Greasby had him on his feet, Raf shrugged the old rancher's hands away and said, "Is okay." He stared down at Becker, who was still on the floor, gagging and sputtering. "Is okay now, Mister Greasby." He then aimed an index finger at a spot between Arthur Becker's bulging eyes, and in a quiet, even voice he said, "My advice to you is don't never again call Rafael no stinkin' Spaniard. You do, you have bigger worries than sheep pissing on grass."

Artie pushed himself to his knees and then threw an arm over the table to lever himself to a standing position. Still holding his throat, he croaked, "Let's get outta here, Josh. There ain't no talking to this —" He

117

stopped before he finished his statement.

Neil doubted Becker was going to say the word "Spaniard," but whatever harsh name he was about to call Rafael, he apparently thought better of it and instead staggered from the cabin without saying a thing.

SEVEN

Josh followed his brother and slammed the door on his way out.

Greasby watched them leave, and then he turned to Raf and said, "You got a real talent, Rafael, for bringing a conversation to a close."

Rather than respond, Raf glanced at Lottie, who gave him a none-too-pleased expression.

"You boys stay here," Greasby said in a weary tone. "I'll try to catch 'em before they leave."

Once Greasby was out the door, Lottie came to her feet. "Rafael," she said, her lips as thin as string, "you ain't never been accused of being smart, but that was about the dumbest damned thing I have ever seen you pull."

Without meeting her eyes, Raf mumbled, "Sorry."

Lottie started to say more but stopped

herself before it came out. Instead, she went to the table and began collecting the dirty cups.

Neil gave some thought to scolding Raf himself but decided it wasn't necessary. The man already looked like a whipped pup. Raf would never stop giving in to his natural impulses, but in all the years Neil had known the feisty Basque, Lottie was the one person he'd ever seen who could get Raf to consider the consequences of his behavior. The problem was, Raf considered the consequences only after the fact, never before. Neil figured Raf was doing that now and needed no chastisement from him.

Curious as to what was taking place in the yard, Neil went to the window and peered out. Greasby talked to the brothers while the two men who had arrived with them looked on. Artie still had a hand to his throat, but he seemed to have stopped sputtering. Josh had taken the gun belt from around his pommel and held it as he listened to what Greasby had to say.

As Neil watched, Katie came up beside him and placed a hand on his arm. They hadn't touched since she'd blotted blood from the wounds he'd received from the corporal back at Fetterman. Neil had to admit that the feel of her was pleasant.

Leaving her hand in place, she asked, "What happens now?"

"Who can say?" he answered. "The Becker boys didn't have any willingness to settle this matter peaceably in the first place, but they at least had to pretend to be reasonable. Now ol' Raf's given 'em an excuse to do their worst."

He turned to look at his friend, who had moved across the room and now stood next to Lottie. Neither spoke to the other, but Raf was helping her clean things up.

"I know," Neil went on, "that Raf's not the easiest fella to get along with. It doesn't surprise me at all that he went for Artie's throat just now. What surprises me is he didn't shoot Josh last week when Josh killed that ewe and dropped 'er in the yard. In case you haven't noticed, Rafael sometimes acts in haste."

"It's the truth, though," said Katie, "what you said about Raf having the right to raise whatever he wants on his own land."

"Oh, I figure even as hot-headed as he is, in this situation, Rafael's got right on his side." Neil turned back to the window and watched the cattlemen in the yard. "But then again," he added, "being right doesn't make a fella bulletproof."

Neil could tell by Greasby's gestures that

he was again telling Josh to drape his gun belt over his saddle. There was clearly reluctance on Josh's part, but he did it, and once he had, Greasby led the brothers back into the house.

"Let's try this again," Greasby said as they came through the door. His manner showed frustration, and his tone sounded gruff.

Raf and Lottie turned to face the men coming in.

"Rafael," Greasby began, without sitting down, "the Beckers here've decided to make you an offer."

"Offer?" Raf looked confused. "Offer for what?"

"Your place here. The whole shebang — lock, stock, and barrel. Every bit of it — ground, buildings, animals. You keep your wagon, horses, and personal effects, and they'll take the rest."

Rafael said nothing. He just stared at the man, transfixed.

Neil cleared his throat, and Greasby's attention shifted to him. "How much are the Beckers willing to pay?" Neil asked.

"They're willing to give fifteen hundred dollars cash money. They can have it to him and do the deal by the end of the day."

"Fifteen hundred dollars?" Raf repeated.

Greasby nodded. "And that ain't negotiable, Raf, which is all right because we all know that's a damned sight more'n the place is really worth."

Raf said nothing, and Greasby looked to Lottie. "It's a fair price, Missus Cossiga. Much more than fair. I mean, you folks've only been here a year. Them's damned fine wages, I'd say."

For once, Lottie was at a loss for words, and it was Raf who spoke up. "You want our home?" He said it with the same disbelief he might've had if he'd asked, "You want our hands?" or "You want our eyes?"

Not understanding, he looked to Lottie. "Is our home they want to buy, Lottie?" When she didn't answer, he turned to Neil and gave him a questioning look.

"It only makes sense, Raf," Greasby said. "Look at the situation. The Beckers can't abide you raising sheep here along Lance Creek. It's just as simple as that. And you ain't willing to stop raising sheep and go to raising something else that your neighbors find to be less offensive. The only way for everybody to come out of this thing is for them to buy you out."

Rafael looked lost, and Neil stepped forward and said, "Give us a minute, would you, Mister Greasby? Maybe you gents could wait outside."

"Why, sure. Not a problem. C'mon Artie, Josh, let's give these folks their privacy." Greasby shuffled the Beckers out the door and closed it behind them.

Because he knew Raf as well as he did, Neil directed his first comment to Lottie. "Greasby makes some sense," he said.

Lottie shook her head. "It ain't up to me. It's up to my husband." She took Raf's hand in her own. It seemed that Lottie ruled the roost on the little things, but on the big things, it was Rafael who made the decisions.

Neil looked at his friend. "What do you say, Raf?"

"You think we should do this thing, Neil?"

"I think you oughta consider it. I fear what these Beckers might do. They're dumb, and they're mean, and that's a dangerous combination. They want you out of here at any cost, and if they can't buy you out, then they're likely to shoot you out. The only law around here is vigilante law, and I wouldn't count on a vigilance committee made up of cattlemen to be too sympathetic to the plight of a sheepherder, even if the sheepherder's just been shot."

"You say these Beckers can kill us and no one do nothing?" Rafael asked.

"It looks like a real possibility," Neil said.

"I don't know that for sure, of course. Greasby seems like an honorable enough fella, I guess, but who can say? In the end, he's a cattleman, and he's known these boys all their lives, and he knew their father before 'em. I'd say there's a good chance that the Beckers could do whatever they want in this, and when it got down to it, there's not much anyone would do."

"Is not right," said Raf.

"No, it's not, but what's right and what's wrong rarely have anything to do with what is. I'm guessing that's a fact that you're as familiar with as I am."

Rafael nodded. "Is true. The Spanish, he taught me what's right don't matter nothing at all. The French, he taught me that, too. I come to United States of America, and I see USA, he is teaching very same lesson to Mister Lakota, eh?" He turned to Lottie, and they looked into each other's eyes. After a bit, the little Basque said to his wife, "Rafael, he is tired of over and over being taught same old lesson."

"Then what are you saying, Raf," Lottie asked. "That we'll stay?"

Tears budded in Lottie's eyes, and Neil couldn't tell if they were tears of sadness or joy. Was she frightened for her husband, or was she proud of his willingness to take a stand? Maybe it was both, or maybe it was something else altogether. Neil had never had any skill at determining what wellspring produced a woman's tears.

"Yes," Raf answered. "We stay. Is okay, Lottie?"

Lottie let out a sigh. "Rafael, Rafael," she said as though she were saying the obvious and had said it a hundred times before, "I am wherever you are, and I always will be."

"Then is settled. We stay."

Lottie draped her heavy arms around the little man and pulled him close. She held him that way for a long moment, and then, with just a shadow of a smile, she said in a soft voice, "Damn, but you are one stubborn Spaniard."

"Hey," Raf whispered, "don't call me no Spaniard."

"Neil," Rafael said as they stepped out onto the porch. "Rafael do talking, but you stay close by."

"Don't you get crazy now, Raf," Neil warned. "You check that temper."

"Will be okay."

Raf and Neil walked out into the yard where Greasby, the Beckers, and the two men Neil figured to be the Beckers' hired hands stood smoking cigarettes.

"Mister Greasby," Raf said when they got to the group, "thank you for help. I think you good man and good neighbor. You work hard to keep peace."

Greasby shrugged and said, "I do what I can."

"Mister Arthur Becker," said Raf, "I'm sorry for what happened inside cabin. Rafael, sometimes his temper explodes, eh? Is bad thing."

Becker said nothing.

"I wish we could be friends. We neighbors. We worry about same things. Too much sun, too much snow. The wind, she's always blowing. The coyote, he gets your calves, he gets my lambs. I wish we could be friends, but that is not to be, I reckon. Even so, we could still be good neighbors. Your fifteen hundred dollars is a fine offer. More than old place is worth, for sure. But like you boys, Rafael, he and Lottie make this home." He paused and then added, "And home, she cannot be for sale, eh? Not ever."

Raf's answer to their offer hung there for a bit while everybody took it in. It was clear the Beckers were surprised that he'd turned them down.

Finally, Josh threw his cigarette butt into the dirt and shouted, "You're a goddamned fool, Cossiga."

"Hold on a second, Josh," Greasby said. "Mister Bancroft, is there no turning this thing around?"

Neil shook his head. "I reckon not. Raf here seems to've made up his mind. I don't see why this has to mean trouble, though. Hell, most of the time he's only running about fifty head. It's not like he's some damned sheep baron or mutton-aire or something."

Arthur Becker spoke to Neil, but he stared at Raf when he said, "They's a damned pox." He reached over and pulled his gun belt from his saddle and strapped it on. His brother did the same. "They's like a disease, sheep and sheepherders are, and if we don't stop it right here and now, it'll spread. More of 'em'll move in, and pretty soon the whole land'll be covered with 'em."

"That's ridiculous," said Neil. "Raf's only one man trying to make a living out here on the plains. He can't hurt you none, nor your operation, neither."

Arthur rotated himself a quarter turn so he was facing Neil head-on. "You know something, Mister?" he said. "This is none of your business, and you had best back off." To Rafael, he said, "And you, Cossiga, I'll ask you one last time. Do you wanna take our offer or not?"

Raf fixed his dark eyes on Arthur Becker, and Neil could almost hear Raf's temper bubble up. To his credit, though, Rafael restrained himself and simply answered, "Not interested."

"All right, then," Arthur said, "suit yourself, but that's a decision you'll soon regret." He looked at his brother and their two men. "Mount up," he said, hooking a boot into his stirrup. "Let's get the hell outta here. There's work to do." They all spurred their animals and rode off to the north in the direction of the Becker ranch.

When they were gone, Norman Greasby pulled his own reins from the porch rail and climbed on his horse. "Rafael," he said as he settled into his saddle, "I fear what them boys'll do. You watch yourself, you hear me?" He turned to Neil and said, "It's been my pleasure to meet you, Mister Bancroft. You were a fine soldier and a true hero — and meeting a hero is not a thing a fella often gets the chance to do. I wish we could've visited more. I have an interest in history and the relivin' of adventurous times. I take particular joy in the stratagems of politics and the tactics of war. One of the few pleasures available out here on the prairie is giving thought to such things." He touched the brim of his dirty hat, turned his horse, and left.

Neil, too, feared what the Beckers might do, and he asked Katie if she objected to staying one more night.

"I have no objection," she said. "I think we *should* stay awhile longer." They were in one of the corrals, and Neil was pulling a steel comb through the roan's mane. "But I have to ask," she added, "you being my employee and all, is it your intention, as Mister Greasby called it, to risk your life for a comrade?"

Neil was sorry that Greasby had brought up his and Raf's days with the Seventh Cavalry. He was especially sorry the man had brought it up in front of Katie Burke, and he avoided a direct answer to her question. "The Beckers'll do something," he said. "I think it'd be good if I'm around when that happens. Whatever they're going to do, they'll do it soon, while Artie Becker can still feel Raf's hands around his throat."

Katie was not going to let him change the subject. "That was quite a story Mister Greasby told about what you did at the Little Bighorn," she said. "You must be courageous."

"I figure what people call courage is nothing more than just doing what most anyone would do if they're put in a bad situation. At times like that, people stop thinking about what *might* happen if they do something and start thinking about what *will* happen if they don't. It's a common trait, and most folks do it without even giving it a second's thought."

He hit a snag in the roan's mane and gave it an extra little tug. The horse snorted and jerked his head. "Easy, roan," he said. "Easy now."

"Does that horse not have a name?" Katie asked.

Neil shrugged. "If he does, he never told it to me." He thought he might get her to laugh with that one, but she didn't. She had a nice laugh, and he liked to hear it.

"You're a strange one, Mister Bancroft."

"I believe I've heard that before."

"You have a horse that you're clearly fond of, yet you don't bother to give him a name. Why's that?"

"Never saw any need to, I guess."

"Have you always been that way?"

He paused and thought back. "I suppose. I had a dog once when I was a kid. I didn't name him either."

Her eyebrows went up. "You didn't even name your own dog?"

"Well, he answered to Dog. I guess he

131

figured that was his name. He always came when I called him."

Katie took the horse's muzzle in her two hands and looked him in the eyes. "Are you like that old dog?" she asked. "Do you think your name is Roan?"

Neil stepped back from the animal, pulled a tangle of horsehair from the comb, and let it drift away on the wind. As he returned to his combing, he said, "Considering all the trouble he gave me when I was trying to get him broke, I'm guessing he thinks his name is Shit Head."

She still didn't laugh, but he saw from the corner of his eye that he did make her smile.

EIGHT

Most nights, Pepe guarded the flock alone, but that night, Neil and Raf split the duties. It was decided that Neil would take the first watch, and Raf would stay at the house. Raf was to take over at midnight, but, as they did in the Army, Raf relieved him fifteen minutes early — which was good. The lower part of Neil's back throbbed, and the ground had grown a lot harder as the night wore on.

"No excitement?" Raf asked as he climbed the small rise to where Neil sat guarding the sheep. Raf had his Dance and Park shoved into the top of his britches and a Roper revolving shotgun cradled in the crook of his arm. Both were notoriously poor weapons. Many times Neil had tried, without luck, to convince Rafael that he needed to get something decent.

"Nothing going on here," said Neil. "There was a bobcat skulking around a couple of hours ago, but Pepe chased him off. Other than that, not much happening. How about back at the house?"

"Quiet as can be. Maybe them fellas do nothing, eh?"

"Maybe," said Neil, although he didn't believe it. One way or another, the Becker boys intended to rid themselves of Rafael Cossiga. There was not a doubt in Neil's mind about that.

Neil sat leaning against a rock, and Rafael dropped down beside him. Together, they looked out over the pasture where the sheep grazed. The bright moon turned it silver, and Neil could see why Raf had a fondness for the place. Lance Creek flowed off to the left, and then, in the shape of a wide horseshoe, it meandered back to the right. A thick line of tall cottonwoods grew along the creek's banks.

Frogs croaked a constant chorus, and from time to time, there was the soft hoot of an owl.

"Here," Raf said, pulling Neil's bottle of brandy from his jacket pocket. There were just three or four fingers left. Neil had hoped that the three bottles he'd purchased at the sutler's back at Fetterman would get him all the way to Custer City, but he knew if he hung around with this little Basque much longer, there was bound to be a shortage.

Neil took the bottle, aimed the neck in Raf's direction, and said, "Here's to your health." He drank a third of what was left and handed it back to Rafael, who, in a wink, polished off the rest.

"I think," Neil pointed out, "that you might've taken more than your fair share just then, Rafael."

"Hey, has been long, hard day." He tossed the empty bottle into the weeds.

"How're the women doing? Anybody getting any sleep back at the cabin?"

"Yes, I think so. Lottie, like always, she wake up when I'm leaving, but Katie, she asleep on her pallet as I tiptoe through front room." His eyebrows jumped a couple of times when he added with a smile, "That Katie, ooh, she is pretty one, eh?" He grabbed his forehead with the palm of his hand and rocked from side to side as though he were dizzy. "She make poor Rafael's head spin and spin."

"She's beautiful to look at, all right," Neil allowed, "but so's a cougar."

Raf shook his finger at Neil. "Don't you say bad things. Katie is nice. Rafael, he thinks she is much too good for the likes of you. What job she hire you to do anyway?"

"She told you. I'm taking her into the Black Hills."

"Must be more to it than that."

"Well, she seems to think that her husband hid some gold somewhere around Custer City before he was murdered."

"Murdered?"

Neil told Raf the story Katie had told him three nights before at Archie's Café.

"So Katie Burke, she is beautiful, rich widow. Sounds too good to be true."

Neil went on to tell Raf of the gunfight the morning he and Katie had departed Fetterman, leaving out the part where he'd discovered — through talking with the silhouette cutter — how Katie had neglected to tell him she was being chased by her husband's killers. Neil also left out how he figured she was still lying to him. *He* knew it was crazy to get involved with this woman, but his pride demanded that his friends not know.

When he finished the tale of the gunfight, Raf said with disbelief, "You had some fella drawing down on you, and you shoot him in his foot?"

Neil nodded.

"And you did this on purpose?"

Neil nodded again.

"Does not sound like you to be so fool-ish."

"I thought I could avoid killing him."

Raf rolled his eyes toward the gray swatch of Milky Way that spanned the broad sky. "This from man who I watch for years practice shooting? Didn't you always say most important rule of gunfighting — something every gunfighter knows — is you put first bullet into chest just to slow 'em down, and you put second bullet into head to stop 'em?"

Neil smiled. "As far as rules go," he said, "that's a basic one, as I understand it."

"All them years you was trying to get good with gun, you never once talk about shoot-ing someone's foot."

"I took a dangerous risk, I admit, and it proved to be a mistake, since as soon as I turned my back, the son of a bitch tried to kill me."

Short supply or not, Neil wished for a couple of reasons that Rafael had brought along one of the full bottles of brandy. His back was killing him, and the talk was head-ing in an uncomfortable direction.

"Why you do such silly thing?"

"I don't know," Neil said. "Guilty con-science, I guess."

"How you mean?"

"A while back, when I was working as a range detective, I got into a scrape with a couple of boys over by Whiskey Mountain. I figured they had about a half dozen heifers that belonged to someone other than themselves."

"Rustlers, eh? One good thing about sheep, nobody rustles 'em."

"I located these men one afternoon and mentioned my suspicions. They were wild bastards, and as soon as I told them who I was and why I was there, they started shooting. It ended up with me killing them both, but come to find out, I was wrong. Those two fellas had done a lot of bad things in their lives, and I still don't know why they felt a need to draw on me like that, but as it happened, those six cows belonged to them all along. They even had a bill of sale from Tom Sun's place over by Devil's Gate."

Rafael shrugged. "So you made mistake, but they are shooting at you. You gotta to kill 'em, eh. You have no choices."

"I guess, but it was enough to get me out of range detecting and send me back into the bronc-busting business." He looked out across the pasture. "Life's dirt cheap these days, Rafael," he said matter-of-factly. "I don't know, maybe it's that way because of the damned war. Folks fighting them big battles and seeing thousands upon thousands of men die in a single day's time, that does something to a nation, I reckon — turns it kind of cold." He pulled a shoot of grass out of a clump that grew next to where they sat, stuck the tip of it in his mouth, and began to chew. "I was too young for that war, thank God, but the Indian Wars taught me that life is cheap — both the lives of whoever we happen to be fighting and our own lives as well."

Raf gave him a bewildered expression. "Did you become Quaker when Rafael not looking?"

Neil smiled. "No, Raf. I'm still the same hopeless sinner I always was."

"Is good. I begin to worry about you. You sound like maybe the old fight you always have is gone."

Neil shook his head. "Nah, it's like I said about the Sioux. If some fella's trying to take my scalp or perform some other unpleasantry, I expect I'll do whatever I can to stop him. I fear that a hard life has given me the ability to be a hard man, but I wish it could be another way." He looked across at his friend. "It's my hope someday to leave these dusty trails for good, find a woman as fine as Lottie, and make a peaceful life somewhere."

Raf extended his hand toward the sheep and the pasture, the trees and the creek beyond. "Like here?" he asked. "This is Rafael's peace."

Neil smiled again. "Yes, sir, Raf, but I might like somewhere even farther from the trail than this. Your place has a peaceful look about it, but I doubt that's the case."

They sat for a bit without speaking, listening to the croak of the frogs. Finally Raf asked, "You figure we have to kill them Beckers?"

Neil made his answer brief. "I expect we will." He turned to his friend and added, "There'll be a fight. I'm certain of it."

"Is okay. We have been in many fights before, you and me, and we have always been lucky, eh?"

He and Raf had often discussed their good luck on the Little Bighorn. Neither of them had understood it. Those Indians could have made short work of them just as they had done Custer's detachment, but for some reason that no one could understand at the time, they hadn't, and even after five years, the reason remained a mystery.

"I've never understood our good luck, Rafael, but let's just hope it holds."

Raf had walked the half mile from the house, but Neil had ridden the roan, and, with a groan, he pushed himself to his feet and ambled stiff-legged to the horse, rubbing his aching back as he went. He had taken a hot bath that afternoon, and that had made his back feel better, but now it was screaming again. It was his plan when he got to the cabin to take another slug or two of brandy.

He pulled the reins free from the short bush where he'd tied them and said, "I stacked a few sticks and some kindling against that rock over yonder if you'd like to build up the fire." He nodded toward some dimly glowing coals four or five feet away from where Raf sat. "I let it die down because sitting next to it made me feel a little like a target." He looked skyward. "But hell, the moon's so bright it probably doesn't make much difference." He turned toward the horse. "Anyhow, the wood's there if you want a fire. See you in the morning."

He started to climb aboard the roan but stopped when Rafael said, "Thank you, Neil, for helping."

"You don't need to thank me, Raf. Helping is what friends do."

"Sure, I know. Still, you stay . . . even when you think Rafael, he make big mistake."

"I don't think you're making a mistake. Of course, the safest thing would've been to take those fools' money and get out as fast as possible. But the safe road isn't always best. Hell, if it was, neither one of us'd be in this violent country in the first place. I'd probably be busting my hump chopping down hardwood trees in the Illinois forests, or worse yet, pulling fish out of Lake Ontario back in Oswego. I never found neither one of those choices appealing — that's why I left. I figured the West'd be different. Out here, a fella oughta have the freedom to do whatever the hell he wants. Maybe that's not the way it is, but that's sure the way it oughta be."

Rafael gave him a toothy smile. "Let freedom ring, eh?"

"Damn tootin', by God," Neil said with a chuckle. "Let 'er ring loud and clear."

Just as he said that, Pepe started to bark, but the barking stopped with the crack of a rifle. The dog let out two quick, high-pitched yelps and then fell silent.

"Pepe," Rafael shouted, and before Neil could say a word, Raf was on his feet. He tore the reins from Neil's hands and jumped atop the roan. The roan, not liking the sudden commotion or the feel of an unfamiliar rider, whinnied, took the bit in his teeth, and began to buck, but the little ex-cavalryman would have none of it. He slammed a fist down hard between the surly horse's ears, jerked the bit tight to get the roan's attention, and then gave him a solid kick with his right boot. The horse headed in the direction of the gunfire, and Raf had him at a dead run in fewer than a dozen steps.

Before Raf took off, Neil made a grab for the Marlin, which was tucked into his saddle scabbard, but he was too late.

"Goddamn it, Rafael, wait up," he screamed, but the Basque paid him no mind. He held his shotgun in one hand and the reins in the other, and he was kicking that horse for all he was worth.

Between them and where the shot was fired, the cottonwoods curved around, and Raf aimed the roan in that direction.

Neil ran down the hill toward the flock and a stand of rocks, which was the only cover around. It was his hope to find a posi-tion so that if Raf started getting shot at, maybe Neil could return the fire. The problem was that the angle was bad, and so was the range, and all he had was his short-barreled Colt. He cursed Raf again for leav-ing before they could devise a plan.

Neil hunkered down behind a large rock

and watched Rafael ride into the trees. Some moonlight filtered through the leaves, but not enough for Neil to see what was happening from this distance. He watched as Raf and the roan first faded into a shadowy outline and then disappeared altogether. He could still hear the pounding of the horse's hooves, and it sounded as if Rafael had not slowed the animal down at all. Even if Raf avoided getting shot, there was a good chance he'd break his neck riding like that through the trees.

That thought had just skimmed through Neil's mind when he heard a crash and a scream from both the horse and rider. Neil waited and listened, holding his breath. After a minute, the roan trotted out from the same spot in the trees where Raf had ridden in. The horse seemed okay, but his saddle was askew, and Rafael was nowhere in sight.

Neil heard movement in the brush, and then there were voices, but he couldn't make out what was being said.

After a bit, someone called out, "Bancroft, we've got your *amigo* here." Neil recognized the voice as Arthur Becker's. "Why don't you do us all a big favor — yourself, too — and come out from behind them rocks?"

"You'd be smart to listen to him, Mister."

The voice came from behind, and Neil spun to see the larger of the Beckers' men holding a revolver leveled at his chest. The man jerked the gun's muzzle, indicating Neil should raise his hands.

"I got him, Mister Becker," the man called out.

"Fine. Bring 'im into the open."

"Get goin'," the man said, and they both stepped from the rocks and pushed their way through the bleating sheep toward the sound of Becker's voice.

Neil walked with his hands raised, and when he and the man behind him had covered half the distance to the trees, Rafael came into the open, followed by the two Beckers and the other hired man. Arthur held what looked in the moonlight to be the Colt single-action .38-40 Neil had seen hanging from his saddle horn earlier in the day. As they came out, the hireling led four horses, and Josh coiled a hemp rope that trailed behind him as he walked.

"You picked a bad time, Bancroft, to pay a visit to your friend," Josh said with a laugh. He walked with the same jaunty gait he might employ if he were taking a stroll down Main Street.

They met in the clearing, and Arthur said to the man behind Neil, "Good work, Hoke.

I thought Bancroft might give you some trouble, but it looks like you got 'im caught without a hitch." He dropped his eyes to Neil's holster. "Josh, take his gun."

The younger brother pulled Neil's piece.

"Sorry, Neil," Raf said. Raf's beret was gone, and a sheet of blood covered his face. He kept trying to wipe it from his eyes with the back of his hand. When he spoke, his voice was hoarse and strained.

"How bad are you hurt, Rafael?"

"Hell, he's all right," Josh said with a giggle. "His voice box ain't working so good, though. Me and Darryl here stretched a rope about eight feet high across that deer path through the trees back yonder. We figured if we killed that dog, this one'd come riding through there lickety-split, and sure enough, he done just that." He turned to Rafael and said, "You being a hot-headed fool and all makes it easy to predict your behavior." He reached over and grabbed Raf by the hair and pulled his head back so that Neil could see the purple line forming across Raf's throat. "You shoulda seen it," Josh went on. "When this Spanish nigger hit that rope, he went flying off his horse like a little brown birdie."

All four of them seemed to think that was pretty funny.

Neil had to admit, their plan to capture Raf was a clever one. They had to have known that when they shot Pepe, Raf would come galloping through the trees, and the path of least resistance through those trees would be the deer trail. They also must have figured that Neil would head to the stand of rocks, which was the closest place where he could provide Raf any cover at all.

Although he found it hard to believe, Neil guessed that these boys had more brains than he'd given them credit for. That possibility did not cheer him up.

"Are you okay, Raf?" Neil asked.

"I'm'll live," Raf croaked.

"I wouldn't bet on it," said Josh.

Judging by the way they guffawed, Hoke and Darryl thought that was pretty funny, too, but Arthur didn't seem to see the humor. "Shut up, Joshua," he said. He turned to Neil. "We don't aim to hurt you boys if you behave yourselves. But if you give me any reason at all to kill you, I'll do 'er, and I'll do 'er with a smile. Is that clear to you?"

He fixed Neil with a cold stare. Neil returned the stare and didn't answer his question. It was a face-off, and he could see in Becker's eyes that there was a part of the man that knew he should press the matter, but there was another, larger part that made him reconsider. Instead, he looked away and said to Josh and the others, "All right, boys, get started. I'll stay here and watch these two."

Josh said, "Hoke, you and Darryl mount up. I figure that low spot over there next to them rocks'll do." The two hired men climbed on their horses, and Josh tied the other two animals to a bush.

"What you do?" Raf demanded.

"Shut up," said Arthur, jabbing the muzzle of the .38-40 a couple of times into the small of Rafael's back. "You'll see soon enough."

Nine

Hoke and Darryl herded the sheep down into the low spot, then dismounted and tied off their horses.

"This is gonna be fun," said Josh, pulling his Winchester from his scabbard and jacking a round into the chamber.

The two hirelings drew their rifles as well, and all three men positioned themselves around the flock.

"No," Rafael shouted. He hurled himself in the direction of the three men with rifles, but before he'd taken a step, Arthur Becker brought his Colt down hard on the back of Raf's head. Raf went to all fours. He was not unconscious, but he appeared to be stunned.

Neil made a move for Arthur, but the man swung around and shoved the pistol in Neil's face. Their eyes caught, and this time Becker didn't look away. The Colt between them gave him more sand than he'd shown a few moments before.

"You wanna die for this, son of a bitch? Is that what you really want, to take a bullet for a bunch of sheep?" Arthur's lips pulled back over uneven teeth. "I *will* kill you."

"Why are you doing it, Becker?" Neil shouted. "This man's few animals aren't hurting you, and you know that. Why are you doing this?"

" 'Cause this is our country, and we don't have to abide his kind coming in ruining things. We give 'im a chance to go off peaceful, but he wouldn't take it. That was his choice. Now he'll see what happens." Without pulling his eyes from Neil's, he called out, "All right, Joshua, get it done."

The three men opened fire, and the roar of their rifles and the screams of the sheep were deafening. The whole thing could not have lasted for more than a minute, but it seemed as though it would never stop.

It did stop, though, finally, and once it did, the summer air lay thick with gun smoke and an eerie silence. Even the frogs and the crickets and the owls were quiet.

Rafael was still on his hands and knees, glaring into the dirt. He made no sound, either, nor any move to stand.

Josh and the two men stared down at their handiwork. Every so often, they fired another round into the mass of dead and dying sheep. After a bit, they turned and walked back over. Josh wore a broad smile. "I killed most of 'em myself," he boasted to his older brother. "I was cockin' and firin' faster than both-a these two loafers put together."

"The hell you say," said Hoke. "I outshot you two to one."

Josh laughed and shoved Hoke's shoulder.

"Shut up, both of you," Arthur said.

"Aw, now, Artie," said Josh, "why're you being all serious? We been wanting to kill them woolly bastards for months, and now we finally got 'er done." He poked the toe of his boot into Raf's ribs. "The question now is, what're we gonna do with this one?"

"You're not doing a thing with him," said Neil. "You've had your fun, and you've done what you came for, now get the hell off Raf's land."

"Damn," said Josh with genuine surprise in his voice, "he talks tough for a man with an empty holster."

"Don't he, though?" said Arthur.

"Maybe we oughta just kill 'em both," suggested Josh, "and toss 'em in with them sheep." He nudged Hoke with his elbow.

"Well," said Artie, smiling for the first time, "we don't really have us a quarrel with

151

this one." He jerked the Colt toward Neil.

"That's true," allowed Josh, "but, on the other hand, I was counting on getting to kill Cossiga." He drew back his boot and kicked Rafael in the ribs hard enough to lift him off the ground and spin him onto his back. Raf gasped, clutched his side, and clenched his teeth.

"And," Josh went on, his smile still wide and bright, "if we kill the little one, common sense says we gotta kill Bancroft, here, too, don't it? What do you think, boys?" He turned to Hoke and Darryl.

"Sounds reasonable," Hoke said, joining in the game.

Neil fixed Josh with a stare and held it until he saw the young man's smile flicker. He turned to Arthur. "Like I said, Becker, your mischief here is finished."

Arthur took a step toward Neil and through thin lips said, "Mister Greasby told me all about you, Bancroft. He says he figures you're a fellow to be reckoned with. Is that true? Are you a fella to be reckoned with?"

Neil didn't answer.

Arthur took another step forward. "Mister Greasby says he figures you're one tough customer. Is he right about that? Are you a tough man, there, Bancroft?"

Still, Neil didn't answer.

Holding his side, Rafael pushed himself to his feet. "You have fight with me, Becker, not Neil Bancroft."

Arthur ignored Raf and moved in even closer to Neil. "Say, for instance, if I was to do this, what would you do?" He continued to hold the .38-40 in his right hand, and he put his left hand in the center of Neil's chest. Gritting his teeth, he gave a hard shove, pushing Neil back three steps.

Neil felt his anger rise but didn't react.

"That ain't enough to get you going?" Becker asked. "How 'bout this, then?" He pulled back his fist and drove it into Neil's jaw.

It landed hard enough to drop Neil onto one knee, but it wasn't much of a punch — nothing compared to what the big corporal back at Fetterman could dish out. It did put a small cut on his lip, though, and Neil watched as a half dozen tiny drops of blood spotted the dirt next to his left boot.

Becker leaned down and asked in a soft, taunting whisper, "Did that hurt, Mister Bancroft?"

Neil raised one eye toward the man leering down, but he didn't answer his question. He blotted the blood with the back of his hand and stood.

"Hell," Arthur said with a laugh, "I've always figured Mister Greasby to be a smart fella, but it seems he's got you wrong. You ain't tough. Why, you're a damned woman. I push you, and you don't do nothing. I hit you square in the mouth, and *still* you don't do nothing. Tell me something, Bancroft . . ." his smile disappeared, "what would you do if I done this?"

He put the muzzle of the already-cocked Colt flush against Neil's forehead, and Neil could see, by the light of combined fear and excitement that shone in the man's otherwise dull gray eyes, that he was about to pull the trigger. Neil's mind scrambled for a way out, but there was nothing he could do, and with a sinking feeling, he knew it.

It would end right here, murdered by a young, dumb cattleman who presumed he could make the world be just the way he wanted it to be.

To Neil, the saddest thing of all was that he had no respect for his killer. There had been others over the years — both white men and red — who'd tried to kill him, that Neil had respected. It was a shame it had to be a man like this who got the job done. But even with that, there were worse places and worse ways for a man to die.

He steeled himself, took in a breath, and

held it, accepting that it was the last one he'd draw.

"Becker," Rafael said, "I have run across many bastards in my life, but you is one huge pig bastard." Raf hawked up something thick and wet from deep in the lower regions of his lungs and spit it squarely into Arthur Becker's left eye.

The little Basque gave Becker a wide, contented, and defiant grin when Becker turned and shot him through the head, blowing out the back of Rafael's skull.

Neil screamed, and in a reflexive action, he smashed his fist into the side of Becker's face, knocking him out and sending him flying so hard into his kid brother that they both tumbled to the ground.

While Josh's arms were flailing in an effort to get untangled from his unconscious brother, Neil spun and made a dash for the trees.

"Shoot that son of a bitch," Josh screamed. His words sounded strained from the weight of his brother across his chest.

There was a shot, and Neil heard the insect-like *ffft* of a bullet zip past his ear. He veered in order to put the Beckers' two horses between him and the men doing the shooting, but before he could get there, there was another shot, and he felt the bullet take him in the left upper arm.

He was in a dead run when the bullet struck, and he almost hit the ground, but he held his footing and made it to the other side of the horses, where he continued his sprint for the trees.

"Artie, goddamn it," Josh screamed, "get offa me. You two assholes, why're you just standing there? Get Bancroft. Don't let him get away."

Neil made it to the trees that lined Lance Creek and headed downstream without slowing down. He ran for all he was worth and didn't stop running until he thought his lungs would explode.

It was dark in the trees, and the brush was thick enough that Neil couldn't see the men, but over the babble of the creek, he could hear them calling back and forth to one another.

Neil slipped down to the water, took a drink, and checked his wound. The bullet had passed through without hitting the bone, but it had torn out a chunk of meat from the outer portion of his upper arm just below the shoulder. The wound was half an inch wide and four times that long, and it bled heavily. Blood sheathed his arm and dripped from his fingers. He wore no kerchief, so he pulled out his shirttail and tore a piece from the bottom. He wadded it up and poked it down into the gouged-out hole. He then tore a longer strip from his shirt and wrapped the wound as tightly as he could.

He took another drink and listened. They were coming. Arthur Becker had regained consciousness, and Neil could hear him barking orders, but his voice was muffled and sounded full of pain. Neil hoped he'd busted the bastard's jaw.

The image of Becker's turning and killing Raf leapt into his mind, and a gasp came from him that he could only half stifle. With effort, he pushed the thought aside and told himself he couldn't think of that now — there was no time.

He needed a gun. Without a gun, he was dead.

He made his way to the edge of the trees and looked out across the clearing. The roan was grazing a couple of hundred yards away, and Neil could see the dark shape of the butt of the Marlin sticking up above the horse's shoulder.

Even as bright as the moonlight was, there was a chance he could make it to the roan without being spotted, so long as the Beckers and their men stayed in the trees. It was a risk he might have taken with any other horse, but even at the best of times, it was a chore to catch the pigheaded roan when he was enjoying grass in an open pasture. There was no way Neil could do it without detection.

There had to be another way.

Neil thought back to what Katie had said that first afternoon in Dick's saloon after he'd passed her damned test. She wanted to hire a man who was clever enough to get out of a bad situation by taking advantage of whatever was at his disposal. The problem here was that four armed men were moving in on him, and there was nothing at his disposal to take advantage of.

Unless . . .

A thought struck him, and he looked again across the pasture. The roan was there, eating the grass Raf's sheep had missed. A couple of hundred feet on the other side of the roan were the rocks Neil had hidden behind when Becker had first called him out. From there, he traced a line back past the horse to where Raf, the Beckers, and Darryl had emerged from the trees. He made a mental note of where that spot was and again ducked into the cottonwoods and scrambled back to the creek. He crossed the creek as quietly as possible, and once on the other side, he headed upstream.

The brush was as thick on this side as the other, so there was little fear of being spotted. The Beckers and their men were moving downstream on the opposite side of the creek. Arthur Becker led the way, and the others followed at hundred-foot intervals. Josh brought up the rear. Neil felt his blood chill when he came even with Arthur. He could hear their confident chatter back and forth along the line. They had to figure he was wounded and trapped, and it was just a matter of time before they found him.

Not wanting to run the risk of making any noise, he stopped and waited for them to pass. When they did, he moved on. After another hundred yards, he crossed the creek and made his way to where the trees opened onto the pasture. Once he was there, he looked out and again found the rocks where he'd hidden when Raf rode off. There was the roan, and even closer than the roan were the Beckers' horses. Those horses were tied, but their scabbards were empty.

He might be able make a dash to one of those animals and ride back to the cabin, but the Beckers were sure to follow, and all that would accomplish would be to put Katie and Lottie in needless danger.

No, he had to deal with these men here.

Again, he got his bearings. The Beckers

had brought Rafael out of the trees only fifty feet to the right of where he now stood. He slipped back into the cover of the trees and headed in that direction, avoiding the deer trail and keeping to the bushes.

The place he looked for was easy to find. When Josh and Darryl strung their rope and knocked Raf from the roan's back, the roan must have gone down, too, because the ground was torn up, and the smaller bushes were crushed. It was pure luck that the horse had not been injured, but that would be small consolation to Neil unless he did something fast.

He searched the deer path, but the thing he sought wasn't there. Again, he pushed into the bushes and continued to look. After a couple of minutes of groping about in the dim light, he felt his heart speed up. There it was. In the bushes at the base of a large cottonwood was the Roper revolving shotgun. Earlier, when they'd come into the clearing, Neil had seen Raf's Dance and Park jammed into the front of Arthur Becker's jeans, but no one had been carrying the shotgun.

Neil picked it up and brushed it off. It held four twelve-gauge shells in an internal cylinder. He had little experience with this weapon, but he knew its reputation, and it wasn't good.

He slipped his thumb over the big hammer and pulled the long breechblock partway back. Pulling it all the way back would eject a spent round and bring the next shell in the cylinder up. Pulling the trigger would push the shell into the breech and fire the gun.

It all seemed very complicated to Neil. Lots of things could go wrong. But Raf had loved this particular gun. He'd sworn by it and said it had never let him down.

We'll see, Neil thought. We will see.

Neil knew he could not meet these four in a head-on gunfight. There was no way he could cock and fire the shotgun fast enough for that.

He needed a plan.

Again, he pushed his way through the brush to the edge of the tree line as close to the Beckers' horses as he could get. He picked up a medium-sized rock and chucked it at the nearest horse. It hit the horse's rump, but the animal just flicked a muscle and swished his tail as though he were shooing a fly. Neil found a rock that was a little heftier and threw it. It hit with a solid thump, but all the horse did was snort and sidestep a bit.

This animal seemed as mild in temperament as the roan was nasty.

Neil searched the ground for something else to throw. He located a clump of prickly pear, kicked a piece loose, plucked off the thorns at one end so he could get a good hold of the thing, and fired it at the horse's backside like a baseball pitcher sending a strike across home plate. The cactus hit and stuck. When it did, the horse let out a scream that might well have been heard in Nebraska.

Downstream, Arthur Becker called out, "What's that? Was that one of the horses?"

Josh called back, "Yes, it was. I'll go check it out — make sure he ain't doubling back on us."

Figuring Neil was unarmed, the younger Becker must have felt safe enough running in the open. He left the trees and headed straight for the horses. When he was ten feet away from the animal Neil had pelted with cactus, Neil stepped out from his hiding place. Josh saw him, and his mouth dropped open. He tried to skid to a stop, but his boots slid in the loose dirt, and he went down on his ass hard enough to rattle his teeth. "Goddamn it," he yelled. From his sitting position, he lifted his rifle in Neil's direction, but he was much too slow. Neil pulled the trigger on the old Roper, sending the hammer down on one of the big twelve-gauge shells. The buckshot caught Josh Becker right at the mouth, blowing away everything from the center of his nose to the top button of his shirt.

There was no question about it. Josh Becker was dead.

Neil crossed over and retrieved his short-barreled Colt, which Josh still had tucked in his belt.

Looking down at the shotgun, Neil pulled the hammer back, and just as it was designed to do, the spent reusable cartridge popped out, and the cylinder brought the next shell around.

Josh's rifle lay on the ground next to his body. Neil considered taking it. It would be a handier and a more trustworthy weapon than the shotgun, but when he saw the rifle's magazine tube was mangled by the shotgun blast, he decided against it.

He bent, picked up the spent cartridge that had just killed Josh, and tucked it into his pocket.

The shotgun blast had brought about considerable commotion down the line. Neil could hear screaming and cussing. Arthur Becker, who was still farther downstream than the others, called out to Josh and shouted for Hoke and Darryl to get back to the horses and give his brother some help. Neil could hear them coming — one leading the way, the two others trailing behind.

Even though their number was now at three, Neil still could not face them all at once, so he found a hiding place in some thick brush away from the deer path. He settled in and waited.

Despite his makeshift bandages, the blood still came from his arm in a steady flow. He tore another strip from his shirttail and wrapped it around what was already there.

When he was first shot, he'd been surprised by how little it had hurt, but whatever it was that caused the absence of pain then was no longer working. His arm felt on fire.

A tumbler of that brandy would sure hit the spot. A little while ago he'd wanted brandy in the hope it would ease the pain in his back. Now, sitting in these bushes bleeding like he was, he could no longer feel the familiar throb in his lower spine. It seemed a bullet tearing a chunk out of a fella's arm was a miracle cure for backaches. That thought brought a sad smile. It was the sort of comment that always gave ol' Raf a chuckle.

The smile didn't last long, though. Someone was coming. As the man moved in a little closer, Neil could see that it was Hoke, the one who had gotten the drop on him over in the rocks.

Hoke was a little smarter than Josh. He wasn't running out in the open but was coming down the deer path. While he was still out of range, he moved to the edge of the trees and peered out. He didn't have to go all the way into the clearing to see the truth.

He gasped and shouted, "He got Josh. He's deader'n hell. The son of a bitch damn near blowed his head off."

The running Neil had heard coming from downstream slowed to a walk. Becker and Darryl were no doubt considering what to do next. Neil could be anywhere, and it seemed they did not want to rush into anything too risky.

While Hoke stood staring into the clearing at what was left of Josh, Neil rattled the bush where he hid. Hoke spun around, and as he did, Neil rattled the bush again, then eased backwards toward the creek. Once he was to the water, he made his way along the bank where the ground was soft and the grass damp and quiet to walk on.

He could hear Hoke running from the edge of the clearing deeper into the trees.

In a crouch, Neil scuttled back up the bank and moved to within fifteen feet to the rear of where Hoke knelt behind a cottonwood for cover.

Neil expected that with surprise on his side, he should be able to break out of the bushes and be on top of Hoke before the man had time to react. And even if he did, Neil could use the long barrel of the shotgun as a club, knock Hoke out, and avoid killing him.

Neil was giving that prospect some thought when Hoke pulled the hammer back on his Winchester and fired a shot into the bush where Neil had been hiding. While the sound of that shot was still ringing in Neil's ears, Hoke levered another round and shot into the bush again.

This man was quick to shoot. Neil put aside any thought of taking on additional risk in an effort to keep from killing him.

He leveled the Roper's barrel and pulled the trigger. This time, the sound of the shotgun did not provoke the same screams and curses that it had when Neil had killed Josh Becker. This time, after the big gun's blast, things were very quiet.

Although Neil had known he couldn't use the Roper to take on four men at the same time — or even three — he figured he might be able to handle two. But whether he could or not, he was ready to try. All this skulking was not to his taste.

Neil cocked the shotgun, and the spent shell turned a lazy flip as it came out. He caught it before it hit the ground and put it in his pocket with the shell that had killed Josh.

When he heard Becker and Darryl approach, he stepped out of the bushes. Like Hoke, they, too, sneaked along the deer trail.

They came into view about twenty-five feet away, and both carried their rifles across their chests at port arms. Neil pointed the shotgun at them and said, "Hold it, boys. No need to come any closer." He shook his head and added, "As foolhardy as it was, I guess I can see why Rafael rode down this deer path. The brush is too thick to bring a horse through here any other way. But it's a wonder to me why in the world all you other fellas keep walking down the thing like it was a damned boulevard. It's clear you've never fought Indians."

The two men stood shoulder to shoulder — Becker on Neil's left, Darryl on his right. Neil had the Roper aimed at the narrow spot between them.

Arthur Becker said in a mumble, "You

kinda got us at a disadvantage here what with your shotgun aimed like that and us with our rifles pointed up." The right side of his face, where Neil had hit him, looked like he had a billiard ball stuffed in his mouth.

"That's true, Arthur, I do have the advantage, and that's just how I like it." Neil figured whichever one moved first would be the first to die, and with a smile, he pointed that out.

When he did, both men swallowed hard.

Neil did not point out that as close as they were to each other, the one who didn't die would surely take a few pellets. It was Neil's hope that taking some pellets would slow the remaining man down enough that Neil could get the long draw of the big shotgun's hammer cocked, and its trigger pulled, before he got killed himself. That was nothing more than his hope, however, and not a thing he was sure would be the case.

Darryl looked at Becker and then back to Neil. "Say, Mister," he said, "I'm just a hired man." There was a quiver in Darryl's voice that Neil found appealing. He had taken a real dislike to these men. "I only worked for the Beckers a little more than a month."

"So what're you getting at?"

"I don't care to die for 'em."

"I can see how you might feel that way," Neil allowed.

"How 'bout I just drop my rifle here? I'll go get on my horse and ride away, and you two can settle this on your own." With a nervous smile, he added, "I expect you'd rather face one gun than two, am I right?"

"Yes, sir, you are right about that," agreed Neil.

With both hands, Darryl held his Winchester out, ready to let it fall.

"You're a chickenshit if I ever seen one," Arthur Becker said.

Darryl shrugged. "That may be, but this ain't my fight, and you know it."

"It may not be your fight," said Neil in a cold, even voice, "but you were quick to kill one man's livestock, watch that same man be murdered, and then help his murderer to hunt another man down. You do what you think's best, but my advice would be not to drop your rifle."

Darryl blanched and pulled the Winchester back into his chest.

"You call this a fair fight?" Becker shouted as best he could through his swollen jaw. "You standing there all prepared like that?"

"I'm not calling it anything, Becker. You boys make a move or die standing still. I'll only wait so long."

It was Darryl's knees that gave him away. They twitched just the tiniest bit before he swung the Winchester's barrel. But even as slight as the movement was, it telegraphed to Neil what was coming. He moved the muzzle of the Roper an inch to the right and pulled the trigger. The big gun roared and slammed a load of buckshot into the center of Darryl's chest. It knocked him down the same way a locomotive would knock down a man who was foolish enough to stand between the rails. Darryl's rifle went flying, and so did Darryl, but even as quick as it was, Neil could see death in the man's empty eyes.

The sound of the shotgun was still bouncing off the trees, and Darryl was still in the air as Neil turned his gaze on Becker. It was difficult to see in the poor light, but Neil could just make out a half dozen tiny black spots in Becker's left sleeve and the front of his shirt. They were holes made by pellets from the blast that had killed Darryl. Whether they did anything to slow Becker down was hard to say.

Neil crooked his thumb over the shotgun's hammer and pulled back at the same time as he swung the muzzle to the left. He stopped it level with Becker's stomach, but before he could squeeze the trigger, Becker brought his rifle around and fired.

The bullet split the air next to Neil's head, and when it hit the cottonwood behind him, Neil felt the tree bark explode onto the back of his neck. The moment the bullet hit, Becker brought down the Winchester's lever to jack in another round, but before he could get the lever back up, Neil fired.

The blast hit Becker in the belly, just to the left of center, nearly cutting him in two. Gore exploded from the wound, and Becker spun a perfect pirouette that was graceful despite the man's already being dead.

It was over, and Neil let out the breath he'd held since he'd seen the twitch in Darryl's knees. He looked back on the moment when Arthur Becker had first placed the muzzle of the .38-40 against his head, and on everything that had happened afterwards, and he had to admit that he was surprised he had survived.

That surprise was a feeling he'd felt before.

He pushed his hat back a couple of inches, and with his right sleeve, he wiped sweat from his forehead. He then leaned against the tree and took in a few deep gulps of Wyoming air.

Many times over the years, Neil had been wrong about things, and Rafael had been right. It had happened again. Neil had often voiced his doubt about the quality of Raf's Roper, but the little Basque had always given it praise.

Neil cocked it, and the last of the Roper's reusable steel-cased shells spun out and landed on the ground next to the one that had killed Darryl. He picked them up, held them for a moment, and stuck them in with the ones he'd used on Josh and Hoke. They settled into his pocket with a faint clink. Four killers. Four shells. Neil liked the economy of that.

Holding the Roper closer so he could better see its action in the dim light, he pulled the trigger for the last time. When he did, the breechblock slammed home with a satisfying snap.

TEN

Lottie insisted on burying Rafael by herself. Although Neil's arm ached, he was capable of digging, but Lottie would not have it. She wanted to do it alone.

As for the others, Neil had tied their bodies to their horses and scared the horses off. He figured they'd either end up back at the Becker ranch or they wouldn't. It didn't make much difference to him either way.

Lottie buried Raf overlooking the creek at a spot she described as a special place. She didn't say why it was special, and neither Neil nor Katie questioned her on it.

"What'll you do now?" Katie asked Lottie as they walked to the house after they'd said some words over the grave.

Lottie didn't answer, and Katie didn't press.

It was midmorning by the time they arrived back at the cabin. Without speaking, Lottie retreated to the cabin's bedroom.

"I feel for her," Katie said once they were alone.

Neil nodded. Finding each other was the best thing that had ever happened to either Lottie or Raf.

Just thinking about Raf's murder made Neil's fury rise again. He wished he could kill the Beckers and their men all over again. Killing them only once was not enough.

"Take off your shirt," said Katie. "It's time we look at that arm. We should've done it hours ago." There was water heating on the fire, and she poured some into a pan. "I saw some pieces of cloth here earlier. I can use them for bandages if I can remember where they were." She rummaged through a cupboard. After a bit, she said, "Here we go," and pulled out a handful of fabric scraps that Neil assumed had been saved for such times.

With a wince, Neil removed his shirt. His makeshift bandaging was now blood-soaked and filthy. He tossed the torn and bloody shirt into the corner and took a sip of the brandy he'd waited until now to pour.

Despite how much he'd craved the liquor earlier, it had seemed pretty low on the scale of things once he'd returned with Rafael's body.

Carrying the pan of water and a pair of

shears, Katie came to the table where Neil sat. She cut away the strips of shirt he'd used for bandages and gave a quick grimace as she lifted out the red-soaked wad of cloth Neil had stuffed down inside the hole. She took the gory rags to the corner and dropped them on top of Neil's bloody shirt.

Dipping a washrag into the water, she cleaned the discolored flesh. She then held a towel under his arm and poured water from the pan into the wound. Neil's stomach clenched with the pain of it.

Katie put the pan back on the table and blotted his arm with the towel. "I wish we had some iodine," she said, "but I guess this'll have to do." She took the glass out of Neil's hand and dumped its contents directly into the open hole. As far as Neil could tell, she might've also dropped in a shovelful of hot coals.

"Good sweet God," he screamed, and he came out of his chair. "What the hell're you doing?"

"Oh, just sit," said Katie, shoving him back down. "If you're going to be a crybaby about this, you can bandage yourself."

"You could at least provide a man some warning before you do something like that." He sloshed another finger of brandy into the glass and tossed it back.

He could see what he thought was a flare of compassion spark in Katie's eyes, and she gave his wounded arm a gentle stroke. Her touch was soft and cool. Like the rest of her, her hands were beautiful.

"You're right," she said. "I'm sorry, Neil. It wasn't my intention to be so rude and uncaring."

"Well, you were," he answered, but there wasn't much force behind his words.

She offered him a quick, embarrassed smile. "Forgive me?" She brushed a wisp of his hair away from his forehead.

He gave her a sneer, but then he returned her smile.

She still stroked his left arm, so he reached for the bottle with his right.

"Here," she said, "let me pour that for you." She took the brandy and gave him a bigger, less awkward smile this time. It was that same beautiful smile that always made his insides flutter.

This woman was crazy, and her acquaintance with the truth was casual, but, he told himself, in her own way, she was only trying to help.

He let her take the bottle. "All right," he said, "thanks." He pushed his glass toward her.

Katie lifted the brandy, but instead of

pouring it into the glass, she poured more of the liquid fire directly into the center of his wound.

Again, Neil shot straight up out of his chair. "Goddamn it, woman," he screamed. "Jesus Christ, what's wrong with you?" He jerked his arm from her. "Get the hell away from me."

She put her fists on her hips, and her eyes turned to slits. "That wound you have is a gaping hole, Neil Bancroft. It's wide, and it's deep. The bullet blew out a chunk of the muscle. It's already filthy inside there, and because there's so little flesh left around it, it's pointless to even try to stitch it back together, which means it'll collect even more dirt. We have to get it as clean as possible right now and keep fresh bandages on it, or it'll get infected. It may already be too late." Her expression stayed hard, but her tone softened. "If your arm does get infected, then where'll you be?"

The largest part of him figured her to be one damned poor nurse. His arm felt far worse now than it had before she started ministering to it, but in the end, he knew she was right, and he sat back down.

"Are you going to behave yourself?" she asked.

"The Sioux could learn a few torture

tricks from you, I'd say."

Again she asked, "Are you going to be-have?" She gave him a fiery stare.

He wiggled for a bit under the heat of that stare, but finally he muttered, "Yes," and put his arm back on the table.

"That's better," Katie said.

"Go ahead and work your evil," said Neil under his breath. "I figure I can take your worst."

Katie had just finished bandaging his arm when they heard riders come into the yard. They shared a quizzical look.

"Who could that be?" she wondered.

Without putting on a shirt, Neil went to the door. There were more than twenty men on horseback in the yard, and in the center of them was Norman Greasby. By the look on the men's faces, Neil doubted they were here to wish him well.

"Good morning, Mister Greasby," Neil said, stepping out of the house onto the porch.

"Mornin', Neil."

"I'd offer you gents some coffee, but I'm afraid we don't have enough cups."

"We're not here for coffee," Greasby said.

"I doubted that you were."

"We're here to talk to Rafael, and I expect

we'll need to visit with you some, too, before we're done."

"Oh? What was it you wanted to visit about, Mister Greasby?"

"It so happens that I rode over to the Becker place this morning right about the time Arthur and his two hirelings came riding in tied to their horses."

"Is that so?"

"Yes, it is, and it seems them fellas was a little bit on the dead side."

"I guessed as much, them being tied to their horses and all."

Greasby stood in his stirrups and stretched his legs. "Joshua wasn't with 'em. I sent a couple of men out roaming around the countryside to see if they can find him. They ain't returned yet, but I gotta real hunch young Josh's out there somewhere tied to his horse as well. What're your thoughts on that?"

"You might be right. Those Becker boys're real close. What one does, the other seems to wanna do, too."

"I'll be straight with you, son. We're here to hang Rafael. We figure he killed them fellas, and because I respect you as much as I do, it pains me to say it, but I'm guessing there's also some blood on *your* hands. I'd

179

say there's a chance we'll also be hanging you."

"Do you have any proof that Raf killed those men or that I had any part in it?"

Greasby gave a world-weary laugh. "You're brave, Neil, but I guess you ain't too smart. What you see before you is a vigilance committee. I'm here to tell you that it ain't exactly a court-of-law standard of proof that a vigilance committee is after. Our requirements aren't quite so stringent." He shook his index finger in the air for emphasis. "But our justice is speedy, which, to my thinking, more than makes up for it."

"Yes, sir, I expect your requirements for proof are pretty low. All you fellas are after is someone's neck to fill a noose, nothing more."

"Well, that's putting a little sharper edge on it than it deserves. What we want are the men who killed the Beckers, and I figure that'd be Rafael Cossiga and you. Now, if you'd be kind enough, I'd appreciate you telling me where Raf is."

"Be happy to." Neil pointed past the group. "He's down yonder by the creek."

Greasby said something Neil couldn't hear, and a half dozen men turned their horses to leave.

"If you're sending those boys off to fetch

180

Raf," Neil called out, "they'll be needing to take along a shovel."

The men reined in and turned back to face Neil.

"Are you saying he's dead?" Greasby asked.

"He seemed to be when his wife buried him this morning."

"Do you want to tell me what happened here, Neil?" Greasby asked.

"No," Neil said, "not particularly. I figure it's none of your business."

A man sitting on a bay next to Greasby said, "Let's do send a couple of boys down there with shovels and make sure if there's a grave that Cossiga's in it." The man looked again toward Neil. "And while they're doin' that, let's string this son of a bitch up from a rafter inside that barn over yonder."

Greasby jerked a thumb toward the man on the bay. "This here's Frank Crawford. Frank was a constable down in Austin, Texas, for better than ten years before he moved up here. As you might expect, with all that experience, Frank here feels passionate about law enforcement." Greasby took off his hat, looked up at the morning sun, and scratched his head. "I'm hoping to get this matter cleared up as quick as possible, Neil. It's a fine summer morning, which means, of course, there is considerable work to be done." He handed his reins to Frank Crawford and swung a leg over his horse. He dropped to the ground, started walking toward the house, and motioned for Neil to come down off the porch.

When Greasby called him down, Neil glanced at Katie, who stood beside him, and with her eyes, she told him to stay right where he was.

Lottie, who by then had come outside, said, "Don't go down there, Bancroft. You stay close, do you hear me?"

"It'll be all right. You and Katie go inside."

"Like hell we will," said Katie.

Neil gave her a frown but knew from her harsh language that it was pointless to argue. He came off the porch and met Greasby at a spot between the house and the riders where they could talk without being overheard.

"Thanks for coming down, Neil," Greasby said in a low voice. "I'll be honest with you, son. These boys want some blood. I've tried to slow 'em up, but I figure that's about all I can do."

Neil gave Greasby no reaction.

"Now, if you'll allow me a moment's speculation," Greasby went on, "I would guess that Rafael did not kill them boys. He was a good man, but my money says he'd be incapable of such a thing." His eyebrows went up. "You, on the other hand, are a different breed of pup." He gave Neil a big smile, leaned forward, and asked in a whisper, "You killed 'em, didn't you? I'd even wager that you got 'em all, and that Raf didn't kill even a one. Ain't that right?"

When Neil didn't answer, Greasby continued.

"Come on, Neil. It's all over now anyhow. You might as well tell me. I can understand how you felt. You and Raf watched the Beckers and their men shoot all of Raf's sheep, and you just lost your reason. It made you furious. I can appreciate that. It would affect any man the same damned way."

As he looked into Greasby's wide, understanding face, something clicked inside Neil's brain. It was almost audible — as distinct as the snap of the Roper's breechblock — and when he heard that sound, all that had happened made sense.

Neil looked at the friendly Norman Greasby, and he had to smile. It wasn't much of a smile. It was as small and brief as any smile could be and still register at all, but it was there, and Greasby saw it.

"Go on, Neil. Tell me the story. What happened out there? Maybe I can convince these fellas not to hang you. Hell, since Raf's already dead, maybe that'll be enough for 'em after all. I can make 'em believe that it was all Raf's doing. Everyone knows Raf had a hard time checking his impulses. I can convince 'em that Raf did it all, and they'll be willing to let you go. But first, please, tell me what really happened."

"What's the matter, Greasby? Weren't you watching it all from the trees?"

Greasby's face went blank. "What?"

"How about letting me do a little speculating, too? I'll speculate that despite all your pretending, you never wanted Rafael and the Beckers to settle their differences. Just the opposite. I'm thinking that you kept the fire between Raf and those boys stoked pretty high. You hated Raf, and you hated sheep, and you wanted them out of here, and you didn't care how it was done. You couldn't run Raf off, and you couldn't buy him out, so there was only one thing left."

"Why, that's crazy. I was Raf's friend. You know that. Hell, ask Lottie. She knows I was Raf's friend. I tried my best to smooth all this over."

"How'd you know the Beckers had killed Raf's sheep?"

That question stopped Greasby short, and a couple of deep lines formed in the space between his bushy white eyebrows. After a bit, he opened his mouth to speak but then closed it without a word.

Neil went on. "I never mentioned anything about any sheep killing, and I doubt that when you ran into Artie this morning that he did much talking, either. So you had no way of knowing about the sheep unless maybe it was you who told the Beckers to do it in the first place."

Neil hooked his thumbs in his gun belt and took a casual stance. He enjoyed the nervous look that had settled into Greasby's eyes. That look convinced him he was hitting on the truth.

"How about killing Pepe, Raf's dog? I bet that was your idea, too. The Beckers weren't clever enough to come up with that on their own. But you are. You knew when that dog was shot that Rafael would come a-running, and when he did, he'd have to go through those trees along the creek — the perfect place to grab him. You also knew that I'd be taking to those rocks trying to give Raf cover, and you had them position their man down there. Maybe I was wrong about you being in the trees watching — that's why you're so curious to know all the details —

but I'm right about you putting the whole plan in motion, aren't I?"

Greasby gave a half smile and a quick nod. He leaned toward Neil and tapped himself on the temple. "You're a little bit smarter than I thought, aren't you?"

"I don't see what was in it for you, though. Besides getting rid of Raf and his few sheep, what did you stand to gain from all this?"

"Not so much, really. Both Raf's place and the Becker place border up against mine, and if one or both of 'em was out of the way, I could get their property easy enough. But that wasn't —"

"One or both of them?" Neil interrupted. He had to think for a second before he understood what it was Greasby had just said. But then it came clear. "Oh," he nodded, "I get it. This ended up with the Beckers being dead, so you collected your posse and came over here to hang me and Raf. If the Beckers had killed us, then you would've taken the same posse to the Beckers' place and hanged *them*."

"Oh, I doubt it'd been the same posse exactly. I don't expect that I could've rounded up more than five or six men to hang the Beckers. You gotta remember, Raf was a sheepherder. Lots of boys're willing to hang a sheepherder." Greasby gave a

186

chuckle. "Some'd rather hang sheepherders than eat fried chicken."

Neil chuckled, too. "You're something," he said. "You really are."

"Why, thank you, son." He sounded proud of himself. "You pretty much have it figured out, except for the part about doing it to get Raf's and the Beckers' land. Oh, there *is* that, but that's just a bonus — a way to kinda keep score. Mostly what I wanted was just the doing of it. You know what I mean?" He smiled. "The planning and the plotting it all out and putting 'er into action. You gotta admit, it's all pretty fine how it fit together. The trick to it, of course, is knowing the people you're dealing with and just what it is they're 'fraid of. That's how you get folks to do what you want. You figure out their fears. The Beckers, for instance, were afraid of anybody who was different than they was. Ol' Rafael fit into the Beckers' fear just like he was made to order."

"How about you?" Neil asked. "What're you afraid of, Greasby?"

Greasby dug his pinky into his ear and gave a close inspection to whatever it was he fished out. "I ain't afraid of much, I reckon."

"How about dying? I figure a man like you has a real fear of dying."

"Hell," Greasby allowed, "we all have some qualms about dying, but I don't expect it bothers me any more than it does the next fella. How I feel about dying, though," he added as he pulled his watch from a vest pocket and popped it open, "don't matter nearly so much as how *you* feel about it, 'cause I predict, Neil, that you'll be swinging from a barn rafter here in less than, oh, let's see . . ." he checked the time, "maybe ten, fifteen minutes tops." He snapped the watch shut and dropped it back in his pocket. He then waggled an index finger in Neil's direction as though a thought had just come to him that had been causing him some concern. "Before you go, though, how 'bout satisfying my curiosity and telling me why in all the world you chose not to receive your Medal of Honor? I find that behavior most peculiar. Why would any man do that, I wonder?"

Neil ignored the question. "When we met the other day, you said Raf had told you all about me. Did he ever tell you how, for years, even way back in our army days, as silly as it might've seemed at the time, I worked real hard to acquire certain skills?" Neil gave his holster a pat. "I don't know why I did it. I never even held a handgun until I was in my twenties, but it got to be like — I don't know — an obsession. It turned into a kind of sickness, I guess you might say. Did Rafael ever tell you about that?"

Greasby shrugged. "He mighta mentioned it."

"You say you can predict the next fifteen minutes, Mister Greasby, but I say this time you've got 'er wrong."

"How's that?"

"I may die. I expect you're right about that part, but I'll not hang. That's where you're mistaken."

"Wanna bet?" Greasby raised his voice. "Frank, get a rope and make a noose."

"My pleasure, Mister Greasby." Frank Crawford untied a rope from his hornstring and built a loop.

Behind him, Neil heard Katie gasp.

"He can noose up a dozen ropes, Greasby, but I'm not going to hang, and do you know why?"

"No, why?"

"Because if I die this morning, it'll be because all of them cowboys you got lined up behind you there are going to pull their guns and shoot me instead." He did a quick count of the posse. "Hell, with that many hands, I figure I could easily have a couple of dozen bullet holes in me before I even hit the ground."

"We could do it that way, I reckon," Greasby allowed, "but personally, I'd rather see you swing. That way it's more legal and a hell of a lot more fun."

"No." Neil shook his head. "They're going to *want* to shoot me."

"Now, why would they want to do that?"

"Because they'll feel like it's their duty once I've put a bullet right between your eyeballs."

Greasby blanched, but his expression didn't change.

Neil leaned in so close to Greasby's face, their noses almost touched. "My prediction, Mister Greasby, is that in about thirty seconds, I'm going to back up five steps, draw my trusty shooter here, and kill you right where you stand. As soon as I do that, your boys'll open fire. There's not much I can do to stop it, but I do have the comfort of knowing that the last thing I'll see on this good earth is your glassy eyes staring up at nothing."

"You're bluffing."

"Bluffing? Come on, man. I got nothing to lose by killing you and plenty to gain. The thought of hanging does not appeal to me."

Neil took one step backwards. "You're

wearing a sidearm," he said. "I suppose you could maybe regain control of what's just turned in to a nettlesome situation by pulling yours before I can pull mine."

He took two more steps back.

"Yes, sir, Greasby, I'd predict that we're both 'bout to say howdy-do to Jesus."

He took step number four.

"What's going on here, Mister Greasby?" Crawford called out. "Why's he backing up like that?"

Though the day had not yet turned warm, tiny balls of perspiration popped out on Greasby's forehead.

The distance he'd put between himself and Greasby now looked just about right, and in a cold voice, Neil said, "You, friend, are exactly one footstep away from dead."

Greasby's eyes shifted, and the puffy flesh along his jawline quivered. He looked at Neil, who stood straight, both feet planted, his right hand softly touching the outside of his holster.

Then the old rancher blinked twice, coughed, and called back over his shoulder in a voice that sounded like a dry, rusty hinge. "Put the rope away, Frank."

"What?"

"You heard me, goddamn it. I said coil up that rope." He tried to swallow, but it looked like there was a lump in his gullet that he couldn't push aside. "Bancroft didn't have nothing to do with the killings." Greasby tore his eyes away from Neil's, looked back at his men, and ordered, "You boys get on home. There ain't nothing for us to do here. It was the Basque who killed the Beckers, and the Basque is already dead."

Once Greasby and his men rode off, Neil, who had lost a considerable amount of blood and who had not slept at all the night before, went to the barn, climbed into the loft, and lost himself to the world. When he awoke nine hours later, the women had most of Lottie's possessions loaded in her wagon.

"What's this all about, Lottie?" he asked as he came into the cabin. Katie was boiling a couple of chickens in a large pot as Lottie packed into a trunk what few items remained. He jerked a thumb back over his shoulder toward the wagon in front of the house. "Are you leaving?"

Both women looked up when he came in. "Neil," Katie said, crossing the room. "I was just about to come check on you." She touched the bandage on his arm. It was soaked with blood. "We'll change that, and then we'll eat. You have to be starved."

Neil sat at the table, and Katie went to collect fresh bandages.

Answering Neil's question, Lottie said, "Leavin' is best. I don't know nothin' about runnin' a place like this." She stopped her packing and looked around. "Besides, there ain't nothin' left for me here anyhow except for a bunch of memories." She folded one of Rafael's shirts and placed it in the trunk. "And I reckon memories're moveable things."

"Katie and I are headed over to Custer City if you'd care to tag along."

"No, thank you, Bancroft. I'm done with Dakota. I had enough of them Hills to last me a whole lifetime."

"Where'll you go then?" Neil asked.

"They're putting in a rail line about thirty miles south of here, and they're headed west. From what I hear, they'll be buildin' it at least as far as the Wind River, and they's always lookin' for a decent cook. I'll work for them awhile and see some of Wyoming that I ain't never seen."

"I don't know, Lottie. A rail camp's a rough place."

She stopped her packing and squinted, eyeing him as close as her weak vision would allow. "Are you thinkin', Bancroft, that I'm incapable of handlin' myself around a bunch of rowdy men?"

Neil smiled. "No, Lottie. Now that you mention it, I reckon you'll do fine."

That night, Neil killed, butchered, and salted the two pigs. He got filthy with his butchering, and while Katie and Lottie finished up a few of the little things, he washed himself at the well.

His arm hurt like hell, and when he cleaned it, he noticed it was getting red and puffy around the edges. He hated to do it, but he guessed when Katie put on a fresh bandage, he'd let her waste a little more of his brandy by applying it to the wound. He was of the opinion that the brandy would do the bullet hole just as much good if it got there by way of his stomach, but Katie didn't agree.

After his bandage was changed, he grabbed a couple of hours' sleep as best he could, considering the throb in his arm, but he was out of bed again well before sunrise. The lowest part of the eastern sky was just turning pink by the time he'd finished loading the wagon and had his and Katie's horses ready for travel.

"Thanks for what you done, Bancroft," Lottie said as they stood outside the cabin preparing to leave.

"Hell, I didn't do much, Lottie. If I had,

Raf would still be with us."

"No," she said, "it's just like we was saying the other night about the train coming through the Chillicothe station yard. There was no stopping it. This was a thing that was bound to happen. It's good that his best friend was with him when it did."

She put her big arms around Neil and pulled him to her. They held each other for a bit, and then Lottie cleared her throat, pushed herself away, and crossed to Katie. "You take care of this rascal," she said. "I know he can be a handful, but do your best." She then pulled Katie to her as well. "You two get along now. I just have one more thing to do, and I'll be leaving myself."

Neil and Katie mounted up and watched as Lottie crossed the yard to the back of her wagon. She hefted down a large can of coal oil, carried it to the house, and sloshed half of its contents across the porch and outside walls. She then produced a match and popped it alight with her thumbnail.

Neil stood in his stirrups and started to call out for her not to do it. It was a good house, and what she had in mind seemed a waste. He caught himself, though, before he spoke.

Who knew about such things? Certainly he didn't. It could be that what she was doing made sense. He no longer tried to apply reason to everything that happened. Some things just needed doing. Despite the waste, maybe this was one of those.

He sat back in his saddle and watched in silence as Lottie Cossiga put a match to the home that she and her husband had made.

ELEVEN

Neil and Katie set off that morning, making their way back to the Dakota trail between two points of bright, golden light — before them glowed the rising sun, and behind them, the Cossiga cabin.

As they rode away, Neil looked back only once. He stopped at the top of a rise and turned toward the homestead. The house's dry logs and clapboards made for quite a blaze. Now that he'd given it a little more consideration, he decided maybe he could understand Lottie's logic in setting it afire after all.

Norman Greasby might end up with the land, but the cabin would be hers and Raf's forever. That thought made Neil feel better. His arm ached from the wound, and his heart ached for the loss of his friend, but he pondered that thought for a moment, and it eased at least one of those pains a little. After a while, he turned the roan and gave the horse some spur.

If he and Katie rode hard, they could make Custer City in a couple of days, and with that in mind, Neil kept them to a steady trot.

Around noon, they came to a small stream and stopped to rest and share a can of peaches.

"How does your arm feel?" Katie asked.

His first inclination was to inform her that, since she asked, it hurt like one giant son of a bitch, but he caught himself before that came out. "It's felt better," was all he said.

"Let me see it." Katie pushed herself from the rock where she sat and started in his direction.

"No, it's all right. I don't want to take the time to mess with it now. We'll tend to the bandages tonight after we've made the Cheyenne River." He held out the can for her to take the last peach and then drank what juice was left. "Let's head out, girl," he said, tossing the empty can over his shoulder. "We lost some time on Lance Creek, and we need to make some tracks."

Katie gave him a wary expression. "Maybe we should slow the pace down some," she suggested, "and give you a chance to mend a little."

Neil did a quick check of the loads on the pack horses and climbed aboard the roan. He winced when he pulled himself up. It felt like a bolt of lightning had struck inside his arm, but he didn't let on. He knew if he did, Katie would nag him until he finally let her fuss with it. In his opinion, a nagging woman was the only thing in all the world that was worse than an oozing bullet wound.

"We can't slow down," he said. "I expect over in Dakota we got us a whole territory full of evildoers just itching to kill you for your treasure map. It'd be rude to keep those eager boys waiting."

She slipped a boot into her stirrup and swung into the saddle. "You're a smart aleck, Neil Bancroft. I'll never understand it, but the truth is that even when you're bleeding, you insist on being a smart aleck." She said this without a smile.

Neil knew her statement to be at least partly wrong. He was no longer bleeding, and despite the pain, he figured that to be a good sign.

"And you, Katie Burke, when you get all sulky like that, your mouth puckers up just like an ol' prune. It makes you look years older than your actual age."

Her eyes narrowed, but before she could

respond, he gave her a grin and kicked the roan.

The afternoon was a long one. By five thirty, Neil guessed they were well into Dakota and the Great Sioux Indian Reservation. It was his hope when they left that morning to get to the river by the end of the day. They were only about five miles away, but it was clear he couldn't make it.

Earlier he'd believed that since the wound had stopped bleeding, it had improved, but he knew now that he'd been wrong. With every step the roan took, it sent an arrow into Neil's shoulder. He tugged at his left sleeve in an effort to loosen it. It had grown so tight around his upper arm that he expected the cloth might tear.

"Whoa, horse," he said and reined in, bringing the roan to a stop. His head started spinning, and he had to grab the pommel just to stay in the saddle.

Katie rode up beside him. "Are you all right?" she asked. "You don't look so good."

"I'm thinking we better call 'er a day."

Katie nodded. "I think you're right."

In an effort to clear his head, Neil clenched his eyes and squeezed the bridge of his nose between his thumb and index finger. "I hate to stop, though," he said. "It'll have to be a dry camp." When he opened his eyes, things were no less fuzzy. "We're still a ways from the river, and there's sure no flowing water around here."

He preferred not to camp in the open, but there wasn't much out there. The grassy plain was treeless. "I can hang on a bit longer, I reckon, if we take 'er slow. Maybe we can find a likely spot a little farther on."

"Are you sure?"

"Let's give it a try." He nudged the roan, and when the horse started up, Neil had to strengthen his grip on the saddle to keep from tumbling off.

"I don't know about this," Katie said. "You look like you might drop. I'll ride as close as possible so I can at least make a grab for you if you start to topple."

She brought the sorrel up next to Neil, but the roan would have none of it and took a bite toward Katie's horse, causing the sorrel to flinch, sidestep, and spin.

After riding a painful half hour, Neil spied some breaks and an outcropping of rock that at least provided some long, late-afternoon shadows. He veered the roan in that direction, and when they got there, he dismounted, leaned against the rock, and slid to the ground.

"This'll do for the night," he said. "I could

use a breather." As much as he'd wanted to keep to the trail, he knew that even if someone placed a gun to his skull, he'd never make the Cheyenne River — not today anyway.

He took off his hat and wiped sweat from his forehead with the back of his hand. "It's sure a scorcher, isn't it?" His voice sounded old, as though he'd aged a couple of decades just since leaving Lottie at dawn.

Katie dropped from her saddle and came to him. She placed her palm on his cheek, and her hand felt like snow.

"You're burning up," she said. "Let me see that arm."

He allowed her to unbutton his shirt and pull it off. When she brought the tight cloth across the wound, he let out a gasp. It was an embarrassing little sound, but at the last second he turned it into a cough — a kind of casual clearing of his throat — which he hoped covered it up. He guessed it was silly and prideful, but it was bad enough to be forced to make an early camp — he didn't want to cry out and have Katie question his mettle.

"My word," she said, once she had his shirt off.

He looked at her and then followed her wide gaze down to his arm. The sleeve had been so tight that when she took it off, it had twisted the bandage away, exposing the wound. Although it was no longer bleeding, it still had the appearance of raw meat. Except for that, it looked nothing like it had the day before. A flame-red puffiness circled the blown-out flesh, and on the wound's lower edge, there was a mottled red and white swelling about half again the size of a toddler's fist.

"Damn," he whispered in amazement. "That's quite a lump there, isn't it? It looks like my arm's just swallowed a gopher."

Exhausted, he leaned his chin against his chest and drifted off into something close to sleep.

The night was filled with dreams. In one, he was with his comrades on the hill above the Little Bighorn River. They were surrounded by the very Indians who earlier that day had routed them from their village. Less than a mile to the north, many of these same Indians had killed, stripped, and mutilated George Armstrong Custer and everyone in his immediate command.

In this dream, Neil lived again the sporadic flash and pop of gunfire ripping through the Seventh's perimeter. Sometimes the shots did no more than kick dirt into the stifling summer air, but often there would be the *whomp* of a bullet finding its mark.

In another dream — in some ways, for Neil, a dream that was even more frightening — he felt the winds of Lake Ontario tousle his hair as he and a half dozen other young men wrestled nets on a rocking boat. He relived all the doubts he'd suffered in his youth. He despised fishing and everything about it. It was mindless, grueling work, yet at the same time he had a real love for the boats and the long blue lake. As he grew to manhood, the life of a fisherman was expected of him, but he wanted nothing to do with it. To Neil, it was a prison that teased its inmates with the cool breezes of freedom.

And all through what seemed like an endless night, the dreams and nightmares were broken by Katie whispering soft reassurances. Or lifting his head and giving him water. Or bathing his face when the sweats came. Or holding him close to her warm body when he shivered with the chills.

At daybreak, through a thick fog, he heard her say she was riding to the river for water.

"I'll be back, Neil. You have to hold on while I'm gone. Do you hear me?"

He thought he had answered her, but he must not have. She put her hands on either side of his head and shook him until his eyelids fluttered. She was down in his face and shouting, their eyes not two inches apart. "Neil, listen. We're almost out of water. I'm going to the river. I'll be back as soon as I can. You have to hold on. Do you understand?" She shook him again. "Can you hear me?"

In a rasp, he finally answered, "Of course I hear you." And even in his fog, he had the urge to make her smile. "You're screaming in my face. Do you think getting shot makes a fella deaf?"

She stared at him with frozen features.

He frowned and added, "Damn, but you're a hard woman to amuse."

"I've put the water we have left here beside you. Try to make it last if you can. I'll be back before noon."

"I'll be right here," he said, "unless a trolley happens by. If it does, I'll go on ahead, and we can meet up again in Custer City."

Still no smile.

He tried to look down at his arm, but she'd covered him with a blanket. "Lift this off me, would you?" he asked.

"You don't need to see it." This was said in her usual, stubborn tone, and instead of removing the cover, she pulled it higher and tucked it under his chin. "Just take my word for it. It's not something you want to look at."

He was never one to take someone's word for anything he could just as well see for himself. With effort, he pushed up onto his right elbow, and when he did, the blanket slid away. What he saw caused a moan that he thought at first had come from someone else, but which he then realized had risen from his own fever-parched throat. Even if he had thought to try, there was no masking this sound with a forced cough as he'd done before. This was a sound of pure despair, and there was no pretending it was anything less.

The lower edge of the wound had turned a sickening gray, and the abscess had grown even larger. The blotchy, red-streaked skin was stretched so tightly that it looked as though it might rupture like an overstuffed sausage.

The pain, which had been excruciating all night long, was even worse now that he'd seen what was causing it. He felt his stomach roll over, and he thought he would retch. Katie was right. He didn't need to look, and he should've taken her at her word.

Without speaking, he dropped onto his bedroll, and she pulled the blanket over him. As he slipped again into sleep, he felt the soft stroke of her hand caress his forehead.

Before she left for water, Katie piled their gear around him and draped a blanket across the packs to block the morning sun. Even so, the air was thick. At first, it was thick with just the heat and flies. Later, it was thick with voices and faces.

People came to him as he lay alone on that Dakota prairie. Both friends and strangers came. Both the living and the dead. Some would speak to him, while some only stared. Some he would talk to, and to some he didn't dare say a word, but only watched as they skulked about his camp.

He had no idea how long he drifted in and out. His sleep was shallow, and at some point a sharp sound brought him to the surface. When his eyes blinked open, he saw the tarnished-copper skin and squared face of an Indian standing above him. His first thought was that this was just another of the dream people, but he couldn't be sure. This surly Indian looked real enough, but so had the boys on the boat, and so had the bullets singing through his regiment's perimeter above the Little Bighorn.

He rubbed his eyes and looked again. Still,

the Indian stood above him.

Neil had lived in the wild country long enough to have learned to always sleep with his gun nearby. It was his habit to keep the short-barreled Colt next to his head whenever and wherever he bedded down, and a bedroll on a remote prairie was no exception. He wasn't sure whether this red man hulking over him was real or a nightmare, but either way, Neil figured he couldn't go wrong by shooting the son of a bitch.

Mustering what little strength he had left, he moved for the gun. If this was real, then the intruder wouldn't be alone, and if that was the case, Neil was a dead man. He resigned himself to losing his scalp, but judging from the nasty turn his wound had taken, he figured he wasn't long for this world anyway, and fighting Indians was a fine way to go. He'd known many good men who had fallen doing the same. Because of his condition, at best, he'd get only one before they got him, and this scowling bastard standing over him seemed the likely choice.

Neil brought his right hand over to the holstered Colt, but there was no speed in his movement. The Indian stepped on Neil's wrist with the same easy deliberation he might use to squash a caterpillar.

"Goddamn it," Neil said. He struggled to free himself, but he had very little fight. He watched as the Indian slipped a broad-bladed knife from the waistband of his buckskin breeches and then knelt and threw back the blanket.

"Do your worst, you son of a bitch," Neil shouted, "and then be damned."

With that last bit of defiance, the bright day again darkened. Neil slid into blackness as he watched the red man lift his knife.

It was night when he awoke, and a large, crackling fire lit the camp in hues of amber. A canteen lay beside him, and he pushed himself up to reach it better. When he did, he heard Katie call his name.

"Neil, you're awake," she said, "and just when we were about to call it a day. Here, lie back down." She knelt beside him. "Let me get that for you." She brought the canteen to his lips and gave him a sip. The water was sweet and cool. "You seem to've slept better this time," she said. "Not nearly so much tossing and turning." She brushed his hair away from his forehead and lay her palm on his brow. "You're still warm," she said with a smile, "but you're not so hot as you were. I think you're doing better." There was a hint of surprise, even disbelief, in her voice. "You had me worried." Her hand lingered on his forehead longer than was necessary to check for fever.

"There were dreams," he said in what sounded like someone else's voice.

She nodded. "Yes, I could tell. Not pleasant ones, either, from the sounds you made."

"No." He couldn't remember much detail in the long parade of nightmares, but his recollection of the last one was vivid. He could still see the sun glinting off the blade of the Indian's broad knife. That was a vision that would stay with him awhile.

Again, he was exhausted. The simple act of swallowing water seemed to have taken everything he had.

This time, as sleep trickled in, he thought he could hear the muffled sounds of chanting.

Katie woke him the next morning by holding a steaming cup of broth beneath his nose. He realized as soon as the smells hit his nostrils that he was starved.

"What is it?" he asked, not that it mattered.

"Antelope."

That was surprising. It smelled too good to be antelope. His first couple of sips were hesitant, but then he gulped it down.

"You probably ought to take that a little slower," Katie warned. "It's been two days since you've had anything to eat."

"Two days, huh?" That meant it had been five days since they'd left Fort Fetterman. A lot had happened. "We're not setting any records getting to Custer, are we?"

"We'll make it," Katie said, "although for a while I was thinking maybe we wouldn't." She nodded toward the cup he held. "Care for more?"

He handed it to her, and she crossed to the fire and ladled in more broth. As she came back, he noticed patches beneath her eyes as dark as paint.

"You look like you haven't been getting much sleep," Neil said. He took the cup from her and drank. He sipped slower this time, savoring the taste. Until then, antelope had never been one of his favorite meats, but he couldn't remember ever tasting anything better. "I'm sorry for causing so much trouble."

"You're a chore all right," she said. "But on the other hand, you're much more like-able when you're in a coma."

Neil thought he was dreaming again. "Did you just make a joke?" he asked.

"What makes you think I'm joking," she

said, but she smiled when she said it.

"I admit," Neil said, "that the last two days've been kind of blurry, but it seems I do recall at some point in all of this that you crawled right into my bedroll. I know I have many irresistible qualities, but it was awful cheeky of you to take advantage of me like that in my time of sickness."

Her smile disappeared. "You were freezing with the chills. You needed to be warmed, and that seemed the most efficient way to do it."

"Efficient? You're sure right about that." Neil smiled. "Very efficient. I expect the reason my temperature ended up getting so high was because you wiggled up against me like that. It's a wonder in my weakened state that you didn't kill me."

"You had me scared to death, Neil Bancroft, and it's just like you to make fun of it."

He threw back his blanket. "I'm feeling some better now. How 'bout climbing in here again, and let's see if I can give *you* a fever."

She jerked the cover back over him. "That day will never come." She took the empty cup out of his hand and rose to leave.

"I could use some more of that," he said, "and scoop a little meat into it this time if you please."

She seemed to ponder the wisdom of that, but after a bit, she turned and walked to the fire.

As she refilled the cup, Neil said, "Good job on bringing down the antelope. I recall your boast about being a sharp shot when we bought the rifles back at Fetterman."

She still seemed miffed at his teasing. "I'll have you know that was more than a boast." She returned and handed him the cup. This time there were a couple of tasty-looking chunks of meat mixed in with the broth. "I'm as true a shot as you or any other man." She sat on the ground next to him. "But as it happens, I'm not the one who killed this antelope."

Neil was confused. "You're not? Who did?"

"The Colonel." She showed a flicker of a smile. "It could be that the Colonel's the one man who *is* a better shot than I am. That antelope was more than three hundred yards away when he killed her."

Neil was even more confused now. "What are you talking about?"

"When I went to the river for water, I ran across three men who were on a hunting expedition. One was the Colonel." She paused for a second, then added, "The other two were Indians."

"Indians?"

She nodded.

"You're telling me that out here in the middle of nowhere, you ran across a white man and two Indians roaming around hunting together?"

"Yes, the Colonel says that he's so busy the rest of the year that he likes to spend as much of the summer hunting as he can. He says it's his favorite pastime."

As he considered what Katie was telling him, Neil heard the sound of approaching horses. He looked up to see three men, a white man and two Indians, riding toward the camp. The younger of the two red men carried a couple of sage chickens by the feet, and the white man had what appeared to be a yearling deer draped across the front of his saddle.

They rode into camp, and the white man let the deer drop to the ground. He then came off his horse, and as he crossed to Neil and Katie, he wore a wide, handsome smile.

"Well, would you lookie here," he said. "Our wounded brother seems to be comin' 'round. You had us concerned, sir, I don't mind tellin' you, real concerned."

The Colonel was a man of about Neil's age who wore thigh boots that showed a glossy black sheen beneath their patina of dust. Atop his head was a broad white hat, which, as he came toward them, he pulled off. When he did, the long hair he had rolled up and tucked inside the crown fell to his shoulders. The hair was mostly dark brown, but a few strands of gray ran its length, and it looked as though, in time, the gray would win out.

He bent, and taking Neil's hand, he gave it a hearty shake. "The name's Cody, Mister Bancroft. William F. And I'm pleased to make your acquaintance."

TWELVE

"Cody?" Neil said, returning the Colonel's handshake. "Bill Cody?"

"One and the same."

"Well, I'll be damned. Buffalo Bill, right here in our very camp." Neil couldn't get over it. "I will just be damned," he repeated. "I heard you were back east doing plays."

"I am, or at least I was until a few weeks ago. The show's on hiatus."

"High what?" Neil asked.

"Oh, that's just a fancy word they use in New York City. What it means, at least for me anyhow, is that I'm free to put a couple of thousand miles between me and that no-'count Judson."

"Who's Judson?"

"Judson's the real name of Ned Buntline. I reckon he feels it's advisable to use an alias." He let out a laugh. "In his case, I figure he's right. The man's a scoundrel and a fool. I separate myself from him every chance I get."

Neil had always heard that Buffalo Bill Cody was the best of friends with Ned Buntline, the famous dime novelist and playwright. He guessed he'd heard it wrong.

Cody eyed Neil's arm. "How's the wound doin'?" he asked.

"He just woke a few minutes ago," Katie said. "I haven't looked at it yet. He seems to be feeling better, though. He's returned to his usual obnoxious behavior."

Cody laughed again and gave a tug to his billy-goat beard. In a manner that revealed a flirtatious nature, he said, "If a man can cause a girl as pretty as you a little vexation, why, I'd say that's a sure sign of health. Let me have a look at that thing."

He squatted beside where Neil lay and drew back the blanket. The cloth that Katie had taken from the cabin, and had been using as bandages, was now replaced with a swatch of buckskin held by a couple of leather thongs. Cody untied the thongs and lifted the buckskin away.

Neil was pleased to see that even as bad as it was, it was much better than it had been the last time he'd had enough of his senses about him to take a look. The abscess had been slit and drained, and the moldering flesh he'd seen around the edges had been neatly trimmed away. The wound was painted with a rank-smelling mixture of something unknown to Neil, but whatever it was, it seemed to promote healing and take away most of the pain.

Cody turned toward the Indians. The younger man was dragging the small deer out of the sun while the older man tended to the sage hens. "Sees Ahead," he called out, "ask the chief there if he'd take a look at this, would you?"

The young man spoke to the man with the chickens, and they both came over. Cody backed away while the older one examined Neil's arm.

Neil realized as the Indian knelt beside him that the last nightmare had not been a nightmare after all. There really had been a red man coming at him with a knife, but it wasn't to lift his hair. It was to lance his abscess and tend to his wound. "So you're the fella who fixed me up." Neil stuck out his hand, offering to shake.

Sees Ahead translated, and the old man gave Neil a nod but made no move to shake his hand. Instead, he took the small piece of buckskin from Cody and reapplied it. He said something to Sees Ahead and then stood and returned to the chickens.

"Chief says you will not die."

"Well, that's some good news," Neil allowed.

"Ain't it, though?" said Cody. He jerked his head in Katie's direction. "Lucky for you, this little dumplin' ran across us over along the Cheyenne yesterday morning. When she got us back here to take a look, I figured you to be a goner for sure."

"I had that thought myself," said Neil.

"The chief, though, is a man of many skills. If anyone could drag you back from death's door, he's the fella."

"He's a medicine man," Katie said.

"That's right. Course, bein' a medicine man don't mean he's a doctor exactly. He's more of a priest. But it's clear that he's got some talent in the healin' arts."

Katie agreed. "He sure has proved that. It's like a miracle."

"But I reckon if you was to ask him, he'd tell you that drainin' the poison and applyin' the poultice had less to do with Mister Bancroft's gettin' better than his chantin' and prayin' did. The chief here's the leader of the Hunkpapas and is considered the holiest fella in the entire Sioux Nation."

"Well," Neil said, "whatever he is, he sure knows his business." He pushed himself up from his bedroll, and though his legs wobbled, he headed for the pot simmering on the fire. "I think I'll have me some more of that tasty antelope soup."

Bill Cody and the Indians left with their rifles again that afternoon but came back empty-handed, which was just as well. Cody said they mostly went out for the ride. There wasn't much left of the antelope, but with the chickens and deer, the camp was well stocked with meat.

"Hell, this ain't so much, though, not really," Cody said that night as he shoveled a plateful of chicken bones into the fire and sliced his second slab from the venison roast sizzling on the spit. "When I was shootin' buffs for the railroad down in Kansas, every man among us was eatin' steak mornin', noon, and night. A fella could hammer spikes twelve hours a day in the broilin' sun and still get fat around the middle if he wasn't careful."

Neil was coming to realize that Bill Cody's conversation was about ninety percent horse apples, but it came out in such a good-natured banter that Neil didn't mind. The ex-scout and Indian fighter had hundreds of stories filled with adventures of olden times when the West truly was a wild and woolly place. Even though it was clear that large chunks of these tales were bald-faced lies, Neil doubted that it made any difference to either Buffalo Bill or his listeners.

Earlier in the evening, Cody had produced a bottle of whiskey, and he and Neil were sharing sips as they ate. They had offered some to the Indians, who were eating across from them, but they had declined. Neil got the feeling that Sees Ahead would have been glad to partake, but the chief had given the young man a harsh glance, and that was the end of that.

"I expect I've killed better than four thousand buffalo over the years. It ain't necessarily somethin' I'm proud of, but it's a fact. I couldn't even guess how many hunts I've been on — couldn't begin to say. For sure, the most fun I ever had shootin' buffs, though, was the time ol' Sheridan assigned me and Custer to take the son of the Czar of all the Russias, Grand Duke Alexis Alexandrovich, out on a huntin' expedition. I tell you, that Russian was the poorest damned shot I ever did see. Smith and Wesson built him a special-made, engraved revolver as fine as any handgun on Earth, and I took him within fifty feet of a big ol' fat bull. That man fired twelve shots at that animal and never hit him once. Me and the boys was bustin' a gut tryin' to keep from laughin'. George Custer had so much trouble containin' hisself he had to ride off about a quarter of a mile so's he could do his guffawin' without insultin' the Russians. It probably would've caused a war if the Grand Duke had seen how that man was laughin'." Bill washed down some meat with a hefty gulp of whiskey.

"Finally, I told Duke Alexis to put away that dern pistol, and I give him my huntin' rifle. We moved up to within ten feet of that poor beast, and the Russian finally got him shot. As soon as the buffalo hit the ground, all them Ruskies started celebratin' to beat the band. They broke out champagne, and every last man in the huntin' party got his very own bottle. Once we was all finished, we chased down another buff, and the Grand Duke shot him as well. The animal hadn't hardly stopped twitchin' before out came another round of champagne, and once again, each of us got his own bottle. It turned out to be quite a shindig." He took another jolt of whiskey and added, "Hell, before we got back to camp, I was rootin' for the Duke to shoot hisself five or six more."

He paused to suck a piece of meat out of a molar, leaned back, and looked at the stars. "Look at all them sparklers, would you? If I had my druthers, I don't reckon

I'd ever go any farther east than the Missouri." He dropped his gaze to Neil. "Sometimes, though, things just sort of drag you along without you havin' much to say about it."

He took another pull from the bottle and another bite of venison. "My, ain't that good, though? My happiest days by far've been on the prairies, huntin' game."

"How long've you fellas been out on this hunt?" Neil asked. He wanted to ask how the great Buffalo Bill ended up on a hunting trip with a couple of Sioux, but he figured that was none of his business.

"We started out a day before we run into Katie. The chief's been holed up in Canada. He sneaked down to the reservation for me and him to get together."

"Why was he in Canada?" Katie asked.

"Well, the chief here is somethin' of a renegade, if truth be told. For a while, the government was goin' to a whole lot of trouble to locate him, so he gathered a couple hundred of his people together and skedaddled up north to hide out."

Neil took the bottle out of Cody's hand and helped himself to a sip. "Is the Army searching for him still?" he asked, wiping his mouth.

"Not really. There's an amnesty offered if

he'll turn hisself in. On the other hand, I reckon if they were to run across him, it'd be a feather in some officer's cap to haul him into the nearest fort. The chief's been known to raise some hell from time to time, especially back in earlier days." Cody reached over and reclaimed his bottle. He was pleased to share his whiskey, but it seemed he liked to keep it on a short lead. He threw back a drink and then continued his conversation. "I've known the chief ever since my tour of duty scoutin' for the Fifth Cavalry. I always kind of admired the fella myself. A while back, I wired some people I know in Canada and asked them to get word to him so we could meet here on the reservation this summer. I wanted to visit with him if possible."

"About what?" Neil asked.

"I'm givin' some real consideration to startin' up a show of my own. It may take me a year or two to get 'er done, but it's my ambition to do it as soon as I can. There's real money to be made in the show business if a fella did it right."

"How do you mean?" Katie asked.

"All the impresarios I've run across believe that every show's gotta be up on a stage with footlights and painted scenery, but when it comes to a show about the West, it seems to me that these eastern boys are thinkin' way too small. That's exactly what the West ain't — small." He spread his arms, taking in the sky, the prairie, and every point beyond. "The West is big. Everythin' about it's big." He looked again at the stars. "Now that is one sky worth starin' at, ain't it? They ain't got no sky like that back east. We got us wide spaces out here where big things happen, and you can't confine somethin' like that to no wooden stage on Manhattan Island. It just can't be done, not if you want to let folks see what it's really like. I tried to make Judson and the others understand that, but there's no tellin' them fools a thing, so I reckon I'll just have to do 'er myself."

"That sounds interesting, but what's that got to do with the chief?" Neil wondered.

"I'd like to give him and some of his people a job. Can't you just see it? Instead of a show with walls and curtains, we could have us a show in the great outdoors, kind of like a rodeo." He pronounced the word "rodareyo," but Neil knew what he was talking about. He'd heard it pronounced that way before by some of the old-time plainsmen. "We could have us a few Conestogas and show what life was like on a wagon train. Maybe have the Deadwood stage roll

by, and let the chief here and a few of his
boys attack it. It'd be great fun with guns
blazin' and arrows flyin'. I bet people'd be
more than glad to pay good money to see
somethin' like that."

"I think they would, too," agreed Katie.
"In fact, I'm sure of it. It sounds wonderful."

"There you have it." Cody laughed. "The
public has spoke." He had another drink,
and Neil thought the man's eyes were going
a little glassy. "Have a snort," he offered,
handing Neil the bottle.

Neil was quick to oblige. He took a couple
of swallows and this time handed it back.

Cody went on. "We could even mount
some battles. The people'd be standin' in
lines to see my old pal, G. A. Custer, meet
his demise above the Little Bighorn." He
turned to Neil. "By the way, Katie here tells
me you was at that battle . . . served with
Reno."

"That's right."

"How'd you like to have a job, too? I'll be
hirin' lots of cowboys and such once I get
goin'."

"I don't know. I doubt that I'm much of
an actor."

"Neither was I at first."

From some of the things Neil had read,

Bill Cody still wasn't much of an actor, but politeness kept him from pointing that out.

"Besides, since you was at the battle, I'd cast you as the great Yeller Hair hisself. If you're playin' George Custer, all the actin' you'd need to do is at first pretend to be a pompous ass and then a little later pretend to be dead." He added with a smile, "I know from personal knowledge that Custer had a real knack for bein' an ass, and I expect by now he's got that dead part down pretty good, too."

Katie thought that was funny. It seemed to Neil that lots of folks were better at making her laugh than he was.

"Also," Cody went on, "if you was to come to work for me, you could help me stage the battle, you havin' been there and all."

"Well, I never really saw what was happening with Custer. While that was going on, we were pretty busy in the village trying our best not to end up the same way he did."

"Yes, sir, I heard about what you boys went through. How many men did you lose down on the river?"

"Maybe a quarter."

"And plenty more once you retreated to the hill where they spent a couple of days pickin' you off one by one. Katie said you was a hero — won the Medal of Honor but never bothered to collect it. How come?"

Neil shrugged.

"You ought to write the adjutant general's office a letter and have 'im send it out to you. If the United States of America wants to give it to you, it's purely foolish of you to turn your back on it. That's my opinion anyhow. I got me a Medal of Honor once, and I tell you, havin' one of them things is like havin' money in the bank."

Sees Ahead and the chief stood. "Cody," Sees Ahead said, "we will sleep now. The chief says we will leave for the north in the morning."

"All right, young fella. You boys have yourselves a good rest." To the chief, he said, "You still planning to do what Sees Ahead is suggestin'?"

Sees Ahead relayed Cody's question, and the older Indian nodded and said, "Yes." He then added something in Lakota, which Sees Ahead interpreted.

"He said our people are starving in Canada, and he will take the amnesty. We will surrender at Fort Buford before the next full moon."

"That's good news," said Cody, clearly pleased. "I figure that's a wise decision. What's he say about goin' back east once I put a show together?"

Sees Ahead spoke to the old chief, and Neil could tell by the man's demeanor that the Indian had no more intention than Neil had of participating in Bill Cody's escapades.

"Chief says he is not interested. It would not be seemly for *Tatanka Iyotake* to do such a thing, but he wishes you good fortune." The two men headed toward the place away from the fire where they slept.

As they walked away, Cody called out, "Tell him I'm sorry that's how he feels, but thank him for the good wishes. I sure do hate to see you fellas head off tomorrow, but we'll get us in one more good hunt before you do."

Neil, Katie, and Cody watched as the two red men left the light of the fire.

"It may take me a while," Cody said, "but I promise you before I'm done, I'll put a headdress on that old Injun and have him ridin' in a parade."

"What's this *Tatanka Iyo* — whatever you call it — that he was talking about?" Neil asked.

"That's the chief's given name in Lakota. Tatanka stands for bull, and Iyotake stands for sittin'." He winked and took a big slug of whiskey. "I reckon you two fellas must-a crossed paths up in Montana a few years back."

After breakfast the next morning, Neil helped the three men load their gear. None of them would be returning to camp. The chief and Sees Ahead would go north to Canada, and Cody would head down to Cheyenne, where he was to meet some bankers from the East. They had hired the ex-scout to lead them on a hunt in the Snowy Range Mountains west of Laramie. Neil suspected that not only would Cody guide their hunt, but he would also point out how wise it would be for the bankers to invest in a thrilling new kind of show that depicted the great Wild West.

"It's been an honor to meet you, sir," Neil said as he and Katie watched Cody saddle his horse.

"Same here, Neil." He turned toward Katie, and his bushy eyebrows went up. "And you, too, Katie." With a smile, he added, "Who'd've thought we'd run across a beauty like you out here on the plains of Dakota? The odds were stacked against it, that's for sure." He finished with his cinch and then said, "I plan on havin' lots of women in the show, too, if you're interested."

"Well, I just might be," Katie said, returning Bill's smile. "What do you think I'd be suited for?"

Neil figured the glib showman would have a clever answer to a question like that, but before he could give it, Neil said, "I'm going to say good bye to Sees Ahead and the chief while you two talk business."

He still had no talent for telling when Katie was lying, but he suspected that was just what she was doing now. Acting in shows would never appeal to her. She got enough of that in real life. Besides, Neil figured that once they found the gold, Katie Burke would do little more than sleep until noon on satin sheets in the finest hotels around.

"Sees Ahead," Neil called out as he crossed the camp to where the Indians were watering their horses and preparing to leave. "I wanted to thank you and the chief for all your help. I figure by now I'd be either dead or close to it if it weren't for the two of you."

Sees Ahead smiled and nodded. The chief reached over and untied the thongs that held the buckskin and smelly poultice onto Neil's arm. He examined the wound and then said something to the young Indian.

"Chief says that he has given salve to your woman. Keep the wound salved and covered for one week, and then take buckskin off

231

and let the air get to it."

"All right," Neil said, "I sure will."

The chief said something more, and Sees Ahead interpreted. "You will have thick . . ." He searched for the word. "I don't know what you call it," he said. "Crust over wound."

"Scab?" Neil suggested.

"Yes, scab. You will have a thick scab over the wound that will be there for a long time. When it goes away, you will have a scar that will be there forever."

"I figured that much, but it doesn't matter. I've accumulated plenty of scars over the years."

Sees Ahead went on. "He says before you travel, you should eat good and rest for one, maybe two more days." The old man shook his finger at Neil and added something more that caused Sees Ahead to laugh. "He says you should avoid bullets. Bullets are very bad for you."

Neil also laughed at the old chief's joke. "That sounds like fine advice, and I'll try hard to follow it." The chief smiled, too, for the first time, and a thousand lines creased his weathered face.

Neil looked to Sees Ahead and asked, "I'd like to pose a question to the chief if I could."

The young man nodded.

"Tell him I was with the Seventh at the Little Bighorn."

Sees Ahead spoke to the chief, and the old man's features froze.

"I've always wondered why you didn't kill us all." Neil looked at the chief as he spoke. "Your boys had us surrounded on that hill. There were only three hundred of us, and you had a couple thousand braves. Why didn't you come in and kill us like you did Custer? There was little we could've done to stop it."

After Neil's question was delivered, Sitting Bull gave his reply, but Sees Ahead paused for a bit before he related the answer. Finally, the young Indian translated. "The chief says that Gall was the war chief at the Battle of the Greasy Grass." Sees Ahead nodded toward the older man. "Tatanka Iyotake was in the village making medicine so that the warriors would have victory. Chief says that Gall was a fierce talker. In those days, Gall hated the whites, and he had some successes in battle, but mostly, he just talked. The chief believes that in his heart, Gall is an old woman, and because of that he did not force the battle on the hill to its end." Sees Ahead paused again and then added, "Tatanka Iyotake says that if *he* had been the war chief in that battle instead of Gall . . ." he lifted a hand in the direction of Neil's injury, "you would not have lived to receive this wound."

Neil almost laughed again, thinking the Indian was making another joke, but he was stopped short by the man's steely glare.

His and Sitting Bull's gaze held for a long moment, and Neil could feel the old man's despair. It was there, and it went deep, but Neil could also feel the man's anger and contempt for him and for every white who had ever ventured into this country, and Neil was glad it was Gall who had been the war chief. Very glad.

Neil wished Rafael were here. After five long years, they finally had an explanation for their good luck on the hill above that Montana river.

THIRTEEN

Once Bill Cody and the Indians were gone, Neil tried to nap, but he was restless. Katie had moved her bedroll to the shade of the rocks and was thumbing through a dog-eared issue of *Ladies' Home Journal.* As she did, she ran her thumb over the gleaming Flying Swan pinned to her shirt and hummed a pleasant enough rendition of the old ditty "Little Brown Jug."

Neil watched her awhile as she read. Katie was a mass of contradictions. She was a feminine woman, but on the trail she was as competent as any man. She sat a horse like a *vaquero,* and Neil expected that if the truth were told, she could ride farther in a day than he could have even before he had a chunk blown out of his arm.

But as able as she was, it was clear that the trail was not her natural locale. Katie Burke was a woman best suited for fancy salons and fine restaurants. That creamy skin demanded to be swaddled in silk and chiffon, not denim and leather. And despite her scuffed boots, faded jeans, and old canvas cap, watching her flip through a magazine written for women brought home that this was a creature meant for finer things.

"What are you staring at?" she asked without looking up from her magazine.

Neil was lying on his side, and he lifted his head and cradled it in the palm of his hand. "Why, I'm staring at you," he said without guile.

"Well, stop it."

"You are a puzzle, Katie Burke."

"I'm a puzzle who's going to smack you in about two seconds if you don't stop staring at me like that. It's rude behavior, and I'll not tolerate it." She licked her fingertip and flipped another page. After a bit, she stopped her reading and lifted an eye toward him. "What's that supposed to mean anyway — I'm a puzzle?"

"You have the elegant looks of one of those pampered females in that magazine you're holding, but even out here in the wilderness, you're able to accomplish whatever needs to be done, whether it's riding fifty miles or keeping a dying man from dying."

"I didn't keep you from dying," Katie said. "What was wrong with you was way beyond my skills to fix. It was that old warrior with his knife and magic poultice who kept you alive — against his better judgment, too, I imagine."

Neil didn't argue about that.

"Go to sleep," she said. "You need to rest. If that infection comes back, I doubt you'll be so lucky next time."

Neil pushed himself up, crossed to their food supplies, and pulled out a burlap bag of dried apricots. "You mean, if I get infected again, you won't fetch me another medicine man to chant away my fevers?" The apricots were cut in halves, and he sat down beside her and bit into one.

"I've rounded up my last medicine man for you or anyone else. If you get sick again, you're on your own. The next Indian we run across might not be so accommodating."

Neil smiled and held out the opened sack. She reached in and helped herself.

"We're almost to the Hills," he said, jutting his chin toward the northeast. "You can see their tops right out there on the horizon."

Neil watched her as she turned in the direction he indicated. The sculpture of her face was smooth and firm — her cheeks high and her nose thin and straight.

"You can't see it from here," he said, "but the Red Canyon leads right up into the high country. Once we get there, the threat of Indians'll be slim, even from the crazy young bucks who're still running wild."

"I thought the Red Canyon was the most likely spot for an Indian attack."

"It was a few years back, because it has lots of good places for an ambush. But it's not anymore."

"Well, that's good news," Katie said.

"The Hills might be their sacred ground, but the Sioux like the plains a whole lot better than they do the mountains."

"Why's that?"

"With all the trees and rough country, the mountains are too confining. Mister Lakota likes to see what's out in front of him. They haven't raised much hell in the Black Hills since '77, and even then it was mostly down in the lower elevations, especially here on the southwest side up through the first stretch of the canyon. Also on the east side around Buffalo Gap, and on the north up around Spearfish and Rapid City."

"If he likes to stay on the plains, then I say the quicker we hit the mountains, the better." She finished off the last bite of an apricot and returned to her magazine.

"I figure we could be well into the canyon by this time tomorrow, and all we'll have to worry about up there," Neil added, "are bandits and cold-blooded killers." She turned to face him, and he bit the inside of his lip in an effort to slow the smile he could feel beginning to crack. "The Black Hills," he added, "can be an inhospitable place."

She closed the magazine and tossed it aside. "If you're amusing yourself by trying to scare me, Mister Bancroft, you can just forget it."

He couldn't hold his grin back any longer. "No," he said, "I reckon you're not one to scare so easy. It took some courage to ride down to that river and fetch water all alone. Thank you for that."

"It wasn't much. Unlike the time you went for water, I didn't have a couple of thousand Indians shooting bullets and arrows at me." She pulled her knees up to her chest and wrapped her arms around her legs. "Why didn't you get your medal, Neil? I'm with Greasby and Colonel Cody on that. I just don't understand why you wouldn't."

"The ceremony where they presented them was held the month after I mustered out. I was already gone from the fort by then."

"But didn't you know your name had been put in and that it was coming?"

"Oh, sure. Earlier that year when the folks in Washington decided to give it to us, they telegraphed the camp, and we were told. Everybody had been talking about it for a while. It was even in the newspapers."

"And didn't they tell you when you got out of the Army that they were making the presentation the following month?"

"Yes."

"You could've gone back for it, couldn't you?"

"I reckon so."

"I bet some of the others who'd already been discharged went back."

"I expect."

Neil could tell she'd wanted to ask these questions for a while, and now they were all coming out. "Or since that time, you could've done like Bill Cody said and written the adjutant general's office and had them mail the medal to you."

"I could've done that. I could've done all those things, I guess, but I really don't want it, Katie."

"That's what I don't understand. Why don't you want it?"

It seemed she was not going to let it go, so he took in a deep breath and said,

"Because when you get right down to it, those things aren't so much for the people they're given to as they are for the people doing the giving. I figure it's been that way for all time. Old men always send young men off to die, or to do horrible things, or both, and so to feel better about the whole mess, those same old men create these ornaments and give them out to the young men, and by doing that, it calms the old men's demons."

Katie didn't respond, but he could tell she didn't agree with what he was saying.

"Look," he continued, "I guess I can't speak for everybody, but I feel sure that nobody going down that hill that day was thinking about any medal. We all did what we did because we had to. Our wounded friends needed our help. They were dying, and we had no choice. It was just that simple. As far as I was concerned, that was the only reason I went for water. It wasn't for those old men in Washington or because I thought the cause we were fighting for was so grand. My feelings that day were not complicated or noble. I did it for the boys on the hill."

Neil could tell he hadn't convinced her. He didn't blame her. He doubted many people would agree with him. She looked at him now as though he were a bit of a fool, and maybe he was, but he couldn't control how he felt about the thing. All he could do was keep it to himself, which is what he always tried to do. Most folks would let him do it, too, but not Katie. She could never just let something lie there. She always had to poke it to see if it would twitch.

She sat there now with her chin on her knees, staring at him.

After a bit, Neil said with a little shrug, "Besides, it really wasn't so much. Like I told you before, most anyone would've done the same. For certain, you would've done it. You've proven that in the last few days."

Katie shook her head. "No, I'm a lot of things, but heroic isn't one of them."

"Nonsense. You keep your head about you, Katie, that's for sure, even when things're dire." After a pause he went on. "I appreciate all you've done for me. I really do."

She lowered her legs and sat up straight. "All right," she said, eyeing him with a dubious expression, "let's have the joke. You're bound to have your fun, Neil Bancroft, so go ahead. Come out with it."

He smiled. "No, I'm serious."

"You might've been serious when you thanked me the first time, and you might've been serious when you were talking about old men and young men, but all of that lasted at least two minutes, and you're never serious for more than two minutes at a time. I've gotten to know you pretty well over the last few days, and two minutes is just about your limit. So let me have it. I'm all set."

"You are?"

"Yes, sir, I am."

"All right then. That's good." And with that, he leaned forward and kissed her. It was a soft kiss — little more than a brushing of his lips against hers. He was jittery about doing it, but something came over him and he couldn't resist, even though he knew she was an unpredictable woman and her reaction could go either way. She was apt to pick up the nearest rock and clout him with it — but she didn't. And counting that a success, he dared to kiss her again. This time, he showed a little more determination, but not too much. He was still leery. She hadn't clobbered him so far, but that didn't mean she wouldn't. To Neil's surprise, though, Katie drew herself in closer, and when she did, he kissed her in earnest. It was a deep, long, and thorough kiss. After a bit, their lips separated, but she didn't pull away. She left her hand on his shoulder and lay her head against his chest.

"I do thank you, Katie."

"I know."

He pulled her even closer. "I've wanted to kiss you," he admitted into the dark folds of her hair, "ever since I first saw you staring at me at the Fort Fetterman corrals."

Her only response was to nestle herself against him, and as she did, his insides hummed. It was a warm, pleasant feeling, one he had not felt in a very long time.

"Of course," he added, "my urge to kiss you eased up once you hired that soldier to beat me into unconsciousness."

"I'm sorry," she whispered and lifted her head. This time it was she who kissed him. When they came apart, she looked up and said, "And I've wanted to kiss you even *before* you caught me staring."

"You have?" That was a shocker. Apart from a few exceptions, Neil had discovered over the years that women found him pretty resistible.

"I've wanted to kiss you ever since I watched you climb onto that stringy Army bronc and let him buck 'til he was finished."

"Is that so?"

She smiled. "Hard to believe, I know."

She was even more of a puzzle than he had imagined.

"Well, like you said in the saloon that

afternoon, it's rare you see a man my age willing to do that sort of thing. Could it be you have a soft spot for fools?"

She looked away and gave a quick, almost inaudible little laugh. "That thought has crossed my mind," she admitted.

Neil considered exploring the headwaters of that comment but decided against it. Instead, he said, "If we've both spent all this time wanting to share a kiss, then how do you account for it taking so long to come about?"

"It's hard to say. I feel like I've made myself available, but I guess you didn't notice my subtle messages."

"Well," Neil allowed, "I've never had much of an eye for detail."

"That's for sure. You're not very perceptive."

"Nice of you to point that out."

"But then again, there have been some distractions, like the Becker brothers, lynch mobs, and high fevers."

"That could explain it."

She leaned against him, and again he felt that pleasant hum.

"I could do with less adventure from here on out," she said, "if it's all the same to whoever it is who decides such things."

"Oh, I don't know." He lifted her chin and

looked into the blue of her cornflower eyes. "I figure it's the adventures that makes it all so much fun."

He kissed her again, and when he did, she lay back on the bedroll and pulled him down beside her.

They spent the rest of the day making love and dozing and making love again. Finally, after dark, hunger forced them to leave their blankets and fix a meal, but once they had eaten and cleaned up, they went back to their place beside the rocks and continued their talking and dozing and lovemaking.

Once during the night, Katie's cries of pleasure grew loud enough to set off a chorus of coyote howls.

Neil stopped his caresses and looked over his shoulder, past the campfire, and out onto the dark prairie.

Katie, who lay beneath him, brushed the hair from her eyes and asked in a plaintive tone, "What are you doing? Why did you stop?"

Listening to the howls, Neil said, "I hope what we're hearing out there is coyotes."

"What do you mean?" Katie asked, following his gaze into the darkness. "What else could it be?"

"I just had the disturbing thought that we might be putting on a show for a bunch of snoopy Indians."

"What?" Katie placed the palms of both hands on his chest and gave him a hard shove, sending him sailing off her. She grabbed a blanket and wrapped it around herself from neck to ankles and then hopped to the fire and kicked dirt into the flames until there wasn't even the faintest glow. She then made her way through the dark back to the bedroll and lay down, still cocooned in the blanket. "I knew we should've put out that fire when the sun went down. It was one thing to have a fire like that when Mister Cody and those Indians were camped with us, but it's another thing entirely to have one when we're all alone."

Neil reached for her, but she slapped his hand away. Lifting her head, she looked out into the night. "I will not be a part of anyone's entertainment," she said. "Least of all a tribe of howling Indians."

"Oh, Katie, I was just talking. I'm sure it was nothing but a few coyotes baying at the moon." He again moved his hand in her direction, and it received another smack.

"The moon has set," she reminded him, "in case you haven't noticed." She dropped her head back to the bedroll and pulled the blanket up to her chin.

He could have kicked himself for ever saying a word, but he knew when he was beat, and he didn't reach for her again. Instead, he rolled onto his back, laced his fingers together, and rested them on his chest.

He stared up at the broad dome of stars. The Milky Way's familiar gray arm traversed the sky, and he considered what Cody had said about the West and its being a big place where big things occurred. Even through all his bluster, the showman was right. Neil sometimes missed the forests of New York State and the blue lake of his boyhood, but he was a Westerner now. There wasn't much a man could be sure of in life, but the wise man knew where he belonged, and Neil was certain that he was now a citizen of this vast, new country. For now, he could not imagine being anywhere else, but should the day ever come when he did go back east, he knew he'd take these plains and mountains with him.

These comforting contemplations were still whirling about his head when his covers lifted, and he felt the tips of Katie's fingers trace a soft line up the inside of his thigh.

"The Hills *are* black, aren't they?" Katie said as she stood in her stirrups and looked

248

up through the long red-walled canyon toward the slopes ahead. She sounded a little amazed.

"Well, they do seem to be," agreed Neil, "but what it is are all the dark-colored fir and pine trees packed in so tight that when you're back aways looking up at 'em, they just appear to be black. In truth, the Black Hills aren't black — or hills. Neither one. They're a lush green, and they're the tallest mountains east of the Rockies."

"Well, whatever causes it, the rich black's pretty splendid. I can see why people are attracted to the place."

Neil laughed. "What attracts folks is the rich color, all right, but that color's not black . . . it's gold."

They had kept late hours the night before but had risen early, washed, doctored Neil's arm, and got loaded and gone before sunrise. Once they crossed the Cheyenne River and left the prairie, they started a steady climb but traveled the trail used by the Deadwood stage, and despite the rough country and the rising elevation, they made good time.

Neil took in a deep breath, and the pungent scent of evergreen played at his nostrils. It was proving to be a fine summer's day. The weather was clear, and the horses were rested. Even the nasty roan was in a better-than-usual mood. He allowed the sorrel to come up close enough that Neil and Katie could share the occasional kiss or even ride awhile holding hands.

Neil had to admit that riding holding hands was silly and awkward, but for some reason that he couldn't quite understand, he didn't feel the least bit foolish doing it. This young, blue-eyed beauty had stolen his heart, and, to Neil's surprise, it seemed she felt the same.

"Do you think we'll get to Custer by sundown?" she asked.

"With the kind of time we're making, I figure we will for sure."

It was because of the quality of the road that they made such good time, and to Neil it seemed a real luxury. When he first entered the Hills with the Seventh back in '74, except in the few places where the trees thinned out into natural parks, they were forced to struggle through thick forests, over craggy rocks, and up and down steep gulches. It was hard, slow travel. He wasn't foolish enough to think that civilization had actually arrived in this wild place, but at least some of the trappings of civilization had, and this fine trail was one of them. There were other fine trails in the Dakota hills as well, but none better than the one to Deadwood.

"It'll be wonderful to get to town," said Katie. "A real bath, a good meal, and a feather bed are just what I need." She edged the sorrel in even closer. The roan gave her a wary eye but made no move to kick or bite. Katie leaned across and nuzzled against Neil's shoulder. "We'll need to get two rooms at the hotel, but we can get them on the same floor."

"Maybe even next door to each other," Neil suggested.

Katie looked at him from the corner of her eyes. "Maybe even adjoining." The girl had a way about her, that was for sure. "I say we sleep in late tomorrow. What do you say?"

As a rule, Neil was an early riser, but he supposed he could be convinced to loll about just this once. He gave her his answer with a kiss.

"Is there a theater in Custer City?" she asked.

"I don't know. Could be." He wasn't sure about Custer, but he knew there was one in Deadwood. From time to time, some pretty well-known performers made their way to the rowdy mining town. "Why do you ask?"

"Well, it's been a long, tiresome trail. I

251

thought tomorrow that we might sleep through the afternoon, have us a leisurely supper, and then afterwards attend a play or perhaps a music recital if there's anything around."

She sat back in her saddle but didn't release his hand. She fixed him with a sultry gaze, and there was the promise of a thousand various pleasures, both physical and otherwise, in those soft blue eyes. He expected this was a girl who was accustomed to getting whatever she wanted, and the word "no" was not something she often heard. He smiled and acknowledged to himself that she wasn't about to hear it now, either. Not from him.

"How does that sound?" she asked.

"I'd say that sounds like just the thing."

"Fine." She squeezed his hand. "It sounds like just the thing to me, too, especially the part about lounging around the hotel room all day long."

His pulse quickened.

She retrieved her hand, looked down at the sorrel's mane, and told him in a whisper, "There's nothing I'd rather do than spend the day doing nothing with you." She turned back and found his eyes. Her playful teasing was gone, and her voice took on a matter-of-fact tone. "You make me forget everything else, Neil."

His pulse grew even faster. She had a knack for bringing that about.

"Everything else?" he asked with a smile. "Have you forgotten that we rode this dusty trail in order to search for hidden gold?"

Her playfulness returned, and she batted her long lashes. With a provocative gleam in her eye, she asked, "Gold? What gold?"

Neil threw back his head and barked out a laugh that ricocheted off the high canyon walls.

Katie laughed, too. She then leaned across the space between them, clutched the back of his neck, and kissed him long and hard, snuggling her velvet tongue between his lips.

She had the looks and demeanor of a finishing school graduate, but there was just a touch of wanton in this young woman, and it was a touch that Neil liked just fine.

When she finally let him go, he had to clench his saddle horn and gasp for air.

FOURTEEN

They loped out of the deepest portion of the canyon and onto a wide plateau. It was a large place, bare of trees except for around its perimeter. A few miles ahead, Neil could see rocks bigger than Chicago buildings as the canyon once again cut its way into the rougher country. Here, the going was easy, and the climb steady but gentle.

At one point along the way, Katie said, "I rode a camel once." This was a comment that came out of the blue. They had not been discussing camels — or any other animal, for that matter — but Katie's conversation often took unexpected turns.

"Is that so?" said Neil. "From what little I know, a camel is a peculiar beast. I've read about them, but I've never had the chance to see one up close." He considered that for a second and added, "Or from a distance, neither, come to think of it."

"You haven't missed much," Katie said.

"The one I encountered was dreadful. It was always spitting. It smelled like a polecat. And, if you can believe it, it had a disposition worse than the roan's. It liked to bite just for the fun of it. One of the Panhandle ranchers had the idea that camels would be perfect for riding around the drier regions of West Texas."

"Makes some sense, I guess."

"It did to me, too, right up to the time that I actually met one."

"Was it hard to ride?"

"When I first climbed on," said Katie, "it seemed like it would be easy. It was one of the two-humped varieties, and I thought I could just slide in between those big ol' humps and it would be as comfy as a rocking chair."

"Was it?"

She rolled her eyes. "It was more like trying to straddle a tree branch in a cyclone. I was tossed around, thrown backwards and forwards. Finally, the camel went one way, and I went the other, and the drop from the top of that tall creature was far enough that when I landed, I broke my arm. I heard it snap. It sounded just like the crack of a bullwhip." She rubbed her left forearm as she recalled the event. "Not only that, when he saw me rolling around on the ground, he went out of his way to come over and step on me — did kind of a little camel dance right on my leg. I swear the thing was evil — meaner than a bull."

"I hear the sheikhs ride them in the desert all the time."

"Well, the sheikhs can have them. That was both the first and last time I ever climbed aboard anything with humps. Until then, I thought I could ride whatever was out there. When I was a kid, I once tried to ride a deer." She frowned. "Now that I recall, that didn't work out so well, either."

They left the open place and entered a long, winding valley where the going started to get steep again. Trees grew right up to the road — the same sort of fir and pine they had seen at the lower elevations, only this time there were also a few aspen thrown in the mix.

"I figure we're less than ten miles from Custer City," Neil said. "It won't be too long now."

They rounded a bend, and Neil was about to resume their earlier conversation and ask how in the world she had ever got close enough to a deer to even consider riding it, but the words lodged in his throat.

Up ahead, in the narrow ditch beside the road, sat a large stagecoach. It did not bear the usual markings of the Black Hills Stage and Express Company. It bore no commercial markings at all, but it was one of the ironclads, the kind of stage that carried no passengers but was used solely for the purpose of transporting cash and gold. Its matching six-horse team was still in harness. The lead horse was down, dead in its traces, and the rest were agitated and scared.

"Oh, my word," Katie said, the fingers of her right hand flying to her mouth. "What is it? What's happened?"

"Stay here," said Neil. He nudged the roan forward, but the horse balked, not liking what he saw and smelled. Neil gave him a good kick and forced him on. A half dozen black crows hopped about, but they scattered as Neil approached. So far, no buzzards were around, but he figured they'd fly in soon enough.

A stiff, claw-shaped hand stuck up from the space beneath the driver's seat, and it was plain even from fifty yards away that its owner was no longer among the living. On top of the stage were the bodies of two guards. One still held his shotgun. The other's shotgun lay in the dirt forward of the left rear wheel. Like the driver, both of these "shotgun messengers," as they were called in the Hills, were clearly dead. The shirtfront of the one who had dropped his gun was riddled with a half dozen bullet wounds. The other had been shot only once. A perfectly round hole loomed like a third eye in the spot between his eyebrows. The men's blood ran over the sides of the coach like spilled paint.

Neil unholstered his short-barreled and thumbed back the hammer. Still approaching at a walk, which was about all he could get from the roan, he called out, "Hello inside the stage. Is there anyone there?"

There was no response.

The left-side door stood open, and Neil came up close enough to peer inside. The late afternoon sun was edging below the treetops, but through the gloom, Neil could make out the dark shape of two more dead guards.

Between these two sat an opened strongbox that had been relieved of its contents.

Whoever the men were who had pulled this robbery were not only cold-blooded killers, they also knew their business. They had overcome five men and left them dead. Four of them had been armed and supposedly prepared for danger.

Thievery and killing were not uncommon in the Black Hills of Dakota, and neither was the robbing of stagecoaches, especially right around the town of Deadwood itself, but to Neil's knowledge, the Cheyenne-to-Deadwood line that drove this particular route had been robbed only once. It was back in 1878, and even then, most of the stolen loot had been recovered.

Neil doubted that whoever owned this stage would be able to count themselves as lucky. Even though murder had been done in the '78 holdup, there were a couple of witnesses left who could describe the bandits. This time, that was not the case.

Neil was now close enough that the smell of death was as thick as fog. The jittery roan's ears lay back, and his eyeballs bulged.

"It's okay, boy," he said, rubbing the horse's neck. "Everything's all right." Neil could hear the lie in those words and figured the roan could hear it, too.

Katie called from down the road. "Are they . . . are they dead, Neil?"

Neil scanned the trees on both sides of the road. The forest was dense enough that a dozen men could be watching from spitting distance, and he'd never know it. Judging by the still-wet blood, the holdup had occurred less than an hour earlier — maybe a lot less — but he doubted anyone was still around. At least that was his dearest hope.

"Yes," he answered. "They're dead. Come

on up and give me a hand."

He backtracked and met her thirty feet from the stagecoach. He handed her his reins, and as he dismounted, he told her to tie the horses in the trees. "I'm going to unhitch the team, give 'em some water, then tie them as well." He turned and looked again at the two dead guards on top of the stage and the grisly hand that rose from beneath the seat. "I also want to get the bodies of those three men inside the coach with the other two before the birds do them any more damage."

"What happened here?" she asked. "Was it a robbery?"

He nodded and told her about the empty strongbox.

"Do you think the robbers're still around?"

"I doubt it. They wouldn't've had any reason to stay. I'll take care of things here, and then we'll get into Custer and let the sheriff know what we've run across."

Katie took their animals off the road, and Neil went back to the stage.

Working the team out of its harness proved to be more of a chore than he'd counted on. The horses were thirsty and spooked and had no desire to cooperate.

When he finally got the animals and dead

men tended to, he crossed the road and returned to where Katie waited.

"Let's get out of here," she said. "I want to put some distance between us and this place, and I want to do it now."

She didn't have to tell Neil twice. He threw a leg over the roan, grabbed the lead to one of the pack horses, and applied his spur. Katie had already taken off, and Neil fell in behind.

On this last leg of their long journey, they made even better time than they had earlier in the day. They rode to Custer City at a gallop.

Custer Avenue, the city's main street, was laid out wide enough so that it would be possible for a wagon and six yoke of oxen to turn around, and when Neil and Katie hit town, moving as fast as they could go, leading a couple of pack horses, and riding in side by side, the pedestrians needed that much space just to get out of the way.

"Say, slow down there, you two," a voice called from the boardwalk. "D'ya wanna kill somebody?" An elderly man wearing a narrow-brimmed town hat and side whiskers came into the street, shaking a fist. "We got us women and kids around here."

Neil reined in and slowed but didn't stop.

261

Looking down at the man, he shouted, "Where's the sheriff's office?"

"What's that?" The old man cupped his ear.

"Where can I find the sheriff?"

"The jail's located one street over on Crook. Go up past the new courthouse about five blocks and make a left at the Kleemann House Hotel."

Neil touched the brim of his hat and gave the roan a kick. As he left, he heard the man holler again for him to slow it down. "This ain't a derned race course, ya know."

Neil pulled up in front of the hotel, and leaning over, he flipped the pack horse's lead rope around a hitching rail. Katie came alongside and did the same.

"You go in and get us a couple of rooms, Katie. I'll find the sheriff."

"What about the horses and the gear?"

"Just carry in whatever you need for now."

Katie nodded and dismounted. "I want to take a bath and put on fresh clothes."

"Fine. When I get back, I'll unload everything else and take the horses to the livery stable. Then I'll clean up, and we can find something to eat."

Neil headed over to Seventh Street and then around the corner to Crook. There, he located two small buildings. One was made of logs and bore a sign that read, "John T. Code, Sheriff, Custer County." The other was even smaller than the first — maybe eight feet by ten feet — and constructed of mortar and stone. It was clear that this little rectangle was the Custer County Jail.

Neil leaped from the saddle and hit the ground running. Without slowing down, he slung his reins around the rail and dashed inside.

The office was dark and austere. A man in his early forties sat in a swivel chair with his boots propped atop a pine desk. He was reading from a copy of *Leslie's Illustrated Newspaper.*

A boy of about twelve held a broom and was making an effort at sweeping, but about all he accomplished was relocating the dirt from the floor to the air.

When Neil came in, they both stopped what they were doing. "Whoa, slow down there, Mister." The man swung his feet down, folded the paper, and dropped it to the desk. He was a tall, lean man with large features and thick-fingered hands. He wore a shiny chromium badge with the word "Sheriff" printed across it in black letters. "What's the hurry?" he asked as he stood.

Neil could sense that the sheriff felt some trepidation and understood why he might.

It was no doubt rare that anyone ever rushed into his office like this bearing good news.

"There's been a robbery," Neil said, and then he told the sheriff about the driver and guards.

When he did, the man's faced blanched and his eyes went hazy. "You're sure they're all dead?" he asked in a low, soft voice.

Neil nodded.

The sheriff dropped onto the edge of his desk and looked away. "I knew them boys," he said. "I knew 'em."

Code took off his hat and ran a hand through his graying hair. "Damn," he added, "they was all good men."

"I never have seen a stage like this one," Neil said. "I don't think it was part of the usual line. It didn't have Stage and Express Company markings on it anyway."

"No, the bank and some of the well-to-do merchants up in Deadwood had it built in St. Louis and brought up here special about six months ago. We had two stage robberies last year where the bandits knew which runs was carrying the strongbox. It was clear that the information was finding its way to the wrong ears."

"Do you figure someone with the stage line might have been selling it?"

"Could be selling it, or maybe just sounding off to some Deadwood whore, and she was telling her boyfriend. Who knows? Me and the sheriff over in Deadwood sniffed around as much as we could, but we never came up with much. Anyhow, the big money boys figured it'd be safer if they had their own Monitor-style stage for transporting real high-dollar shipments. It seemed to solve the problem." He paused for a bit, then added, "At least for a while. I reckon they'll have to rethink that idea now."

He turned to the boy with the broom. "Benny, Luke's getting his hair cut. Get over to Stone's Barber Shop and tell him to meet me at the stables right away."

"Yes, sir, I sure will." The boy dropped his broom and was gone in a flash.

Sheriff Code crossed to the gun rack, brought down a couple of Winchesters, and tucked one under each arm. "How far out of town were you when you ran across the stage?"

"Maybe six or seven miles past the tall granite rocks that're just west of here aways. It's right on the road."

Code jerked his chin toward the door, and Neil headed out. The sheriff followed him into the street and watched as Neil mounted the roan. "Me or my deputy'll be needing to visit with you either tonight or maybe in the morning. What'd you say your name was?"

"Bancroft. For the next day or so, I'll be staying at the hotel around the corner here. Come by any time. I'm willing to help however I can."

The sheriff spit brown tobacco juice into the dusty street. "Every one of them boys had a wife," he said. "All but one had kids."

Neil didn't know what to say, so he didn't say anything. He couldn't tell for sure if the sheriff was even talking to him. It was just as likely that he was speaking only to himself.

Code stared west down Crook Street, past the scant buildings, in the direction of his murdered friends. "It's been quiet in the Hills here these last eight or nine months." He turned to Neil, his face still the color of milk. "I knew that was the sort of thing that was just too good to last."

Neil rode back around the corner, unloaded the horses, and asked the hotel desk clerk for permission to store the gear in the lobby while he took the animals to the livery.

The man didn't seem pleased with the idea, but he finally said it would be all right. "Would you be Neil Bancroft, by chance?"

he asked.

"That's right."

The clerk reached beneath the counter and produced a key. "Your room's on the second floor," he said. "Number twenty-one." With an oily smile, he added, "Right next to the young lady's." And with that, he gave Neil a sly wink.

It had been a long, eventful trip, and it had not ended well. Neil's patience was as thin as April ice. Taking the key from the clerk's hand, he leaned across the top of the counter and asked through clenched teeth, "You got something in that eye of yours, Mister?" Neil intended for it to come out harsh, and as it happened, it came out even harsher than he'd planned — which was fine.

Clearly the man caught the tone. "Er — uh, no, no, sir, not at all."

Neil slipped the key into his hip pocket. "I didn't think so." He turned for the door, and as he left, he jerked a thumb in the direction of the supplies that he'd stacked in the corner. "I'll be back in a while to take this stuff up."

"Oh, don't you worry about that, Mister Bancroft, sir," the desk clerk said, coming around his counter. "I'll be glad to carry it up for you myself right away."

Neil took the horses to the livery and paid boarding fees in advance for a day and two nights. He expected it would be at least that long before he and Katie headed north in search of the gold.

After collecting his money for the four horses and storing the tack, the liveryman led the animals to their stalls. As he did, Neil pointed toward the roan. "I'd be cautious with that one," he warned.

"Oh, why's that?" the man asked.

"He sometimes gets nasty with folks he doesn't know." Neil didn't mention that sometimes he even got nasty with folks he did know. "His behavior can get kind of rude." The word "rude" described the roan about as close as anything.

When he got back to the hotel, the clerk greeted him with a grin. "I took care of that gear for you, Mister Bancroft. I sure did."

Neil thanked him with a nod and proceeded up the stairs. He neither trusted nor liked that mousy little clerk, but he was glad the man had brought the supplies up. His arm, which had felt much better earlier in the day, now ached in earnest, and so did his back.

At the top of the stairs was a door labeled "Men – Bath." Neil peered inside and was hit with a wave of hot, muggy air. The room contained a large cast-iron stove. The stove's firebox was blazing, and a vat of steaming water sat atop the range. In the corner was a huge claw-footed bathtub. It was not in use and looked inviting.

When he got to his room, he unlocked the door and pushed it open. Just as the clerk had said, his and Katie's supplies were stacked against the wall opposite the bed.

The first thing Neil planned to do was to dig out what was left of the brandy and then take off his boots, kick back in the over-stuffed chair that faced the window, and have a couple of stiff drinks. Once the brandy was circulating, he'd have a leisurely bath. He would then doctor his arm, and he and Katie could find a good restaurant.

After their meal . . .

With a little chuckle, he stopped his woolgathering and stepped into the room. He didn't need to keep ruminating about what the evening might offer. Already, he felt that pleasant hum that Katie, or even thoughts of her, brought on. God knew that the woman could be as irritating as a thorn, but she could also be a joy. A real joy.

Those pleasant musings caused him to change his plans. Sitting in the room sipping brandy would be a waste of valuable time that could be better spent with Katie.

Instead, he'd kill two birds at once — take the bottle with him into the tub and have his drinks while he bathed. That would speed things along.

Part of him felt foolish counting any time away from Katie Burke as wasted time, but then again, it had been years since he'd had these kinds of feelings, so a little foolish behavior was allowed.

He took off his hat and sailed it over the bed and onto the big chair.

It was also a terrible waste of time to think about wasting time. That thought brought another chuckle.

He turned and kicked the door closed. When he did, the draft caused a folded piece of paper at his feet to lift and turn a graceful arc. He watched it float back to the floor, and then he bent and picked it up. He hadn't noticed the paper when he first came in, but apparently it had been slipped beneath the door while he was at the livery.

A coal-oil lamp sat on the table next to the bed, and he walked toward it, striking a match against the butt of his short-barreled as he did. He touched the flame to the wick and adjusted the knob. He brought the light up, which sent an amber glow chasing into the room's gray corners. Dropping to the bed, he tilted the paper toward the lamp.

He felt himself smile when he saw that written across the page in Katie's swirly cursive were the words, "Hurry up, slow poke. Time is wasting."

FIFTEEN

After more than a week of sleeping either on the ground or on the dirt floor of Raf and Lottie's cabin, no cloud in heaven could have felt as fine to Neil as the feather bed at the Kleemann House Hotel. Even finer was the feel of Katie snuggling herself into him and spooning her soft thighs against the backs of his legs. Though hovering in and out of sleep, he was aware enough to register his flesh prickling up into goose bumps as her breath tickled his spine.

It was all very nice.

With his eyes still closed, he pulled the covers tighter and drifted off again with the notion swirling about his head that if he had to choose a place to spend eternity, this feather bed might be just the spot.

That was his last thought before the banging on the door caused him to jerk back to consciousness. He made a grab for the short-barreled that was on the table next to the bed, but he caught himself before he did anything rash. Instincts suitable for the prairie needed to be tempered here in town.

Katie woke, too, and with a start, came up on one elbow. Shoving hair from her face, she whispered, "Who could that be?"

Without responding, Neil swung his legs out of bed and reached for his pants.

"What are you doing?"

"Well," he answered with a little laugh, "I'm going to see who's doing all that pounding, of course. What do you think?"

"Don't." Katie seemed anxious. She threw back the covers. "Just stay in bed," she said, "and be quiet. Maybe they'll go away."

He gave her a quizzical look and patted her arm. "There's no need for that." He pushed himself up from the bed, and as he came to his feet, he pulled on his pants. Crossing the room, he slipped one suspender over a bare shoulder, and as he did, he realized that the banging wasn't at their door at all — it was at the room next to theirs.

"Mister Bancroft, I'd like to talk to you, sir, if I could." Whoever it was who'd interrupted his peaceful musings in the feather bed knew his name.

Still holding the Colt, Neil opened the door. The man turned as he did, and Neil spotted the deputy's star pinned to his vest.

"I'm Neil Bancro —" Neil began, but he stopped when he realized that this man looked familiar. In fact, he looked damned familiar. It was Luke Sylar — Lieutenant Luke Sylar, from the Seventh US Cavalry. "Lieutenant Sylar," he asked, "is that you standing there?" Neil dug the sleep from his eyes and squinted for a better look. "By God, it *is* you, isn't it?" He shoved the revolver into the front of his pants and stepped into the hallway, extending his hand.

The man blinked a couple of times himself, and then, like the sun coming from behind a cloud, his face burst into a broad smile. "Neil Bancroft," he said. "Well, I'll be." He took Neil's hand in both of his and began to pump. "I had no idea that the Bancroft Sheriff Code sent me over here to talk to was you."

Sylar was a big man. At least six feet four inches and two hundred and fifty pounds. Back in their army days, he'd been as strong and tough as any man Neil had ever met. But it wasn't only his size that made Luke Sylar memorable. On his right cheek, just beneath his eye, was a purplish, two-inch-long birthmark that was the exact shape of the state of Kentucky. He had been a good man and a fine officer, but even so, behind his back, the troops had always referred to him as "Lieutenant Bluegrass."

"I can't believe it," Sylar went on. "How've you been? You're looking good." Then with a smile, he added, "Well, maybe a little bit older, but hell, aren't we all?" He took off his hat and tilted his head forward, exposing a pink scalp that shone through what Neil remembered had once been a thick shock of dark brown curls.

"I fear that affliction is in my future as well," Neil allowed with a smile, although he didn't lower his head so that Sylar could see for himself. "When did you get out?"

"It'll be two years ago this December." Sylar said. "I met me a school-teacher and got hitched."

"No, not you, Lieutenant. That can't be."

The man grinned. "Yep, it's the truth."

Neil smacked his forehead with the palm of his hand in an exaggerated gesture of disbelief. "You were the most popular bachelor I've ever known," he said. "You got more letters from more women than any three men in the Seventh."

That was the truth. Despite the prominent and not-too-attractive birthmark, Luke Sylar had been a ladies' man through and through. He had received well more than

275

his share of perfumed correspondence from every part of the country where he'd ever been posted, and he had half the daughters in western Dakota chasing him as well.

"My wife convinced me that the carefree, vagabond life of a soldier was no longer the life for me," Sylar said. "I resigned my commission and took this job as deputy. We got us a little one coming in November."

"You don't say."

"I surely do. Dora figures the way she's carrying it, it ought to be a girl."

"Well, that's fine," Neil said. "That's just fine. Congratulations." He'd always liked Sylar.

"Where've you been these past few years?"

"Most of the time over in Wyoming."

Sylar snapped his fingers. "That's right. Now that you mention it, I remember hearing that. You were range detecting, weren't you?"

"I did some of that for a while," Neil said. "Mostly, though, I've been punchin' cows and bustin' horses."

"Did you get rich?"

"A fella doesn't get rich tending other men's critters — not that I've noticed anyhow."

Sylar laughed, then said ruefully, "There's no money in the deputy business, neither.

Things can get very tight sometimes." Then with a shrug, he added, "It provides, though, I guess, more or less anyhow. And Sheriff Code's an easy man to work for."

Neil recalled Code's reaction to the sad news Neil had delivered at the sheriff's office the day before. "He seems like a fine fella, all right."

"Say," asked Sylar, "have you had your breakfast yet?"

Neil shook his head. "No, I was still sleeping when I heard you knock."

"Well, finish getting dressed, and I'll buy you some eggs. What d'ya think?"

"I think I'll take you up on that, Lieutenant." He turned to go back into the room. "Just give me a couple of minutes."

"You know," said the deputy, glancing at the number on the door, "I could've sworn the desk clerk told me you were in room twenty-one, not twenty-three."

Neil lifted his shoulders and held his hands out, palms up, in a gesture he hoped communicated there must have been some mistake.

"Right," Sylar said with a nod, but when he said it, Neil thought he caught a twinkle in the ex-bachelor's eye. "You go on. I'll head to the restaurant across the street and get us a table. Come on over when you're ready."

"All right," said Neil. "I sure will. See you in a bit."

When he got back in the room, Katie was sitting in bed with her legs folded in front of her. She held the corner of the sheet across her breasts. "Who was it?" she asked. The anxiety she'd shown earlier had eased some, but not much.

"Just the deputy. I figure he came by to ask about the robbery, but as it happens, I know the man."

"You do?"

"Can you believe it? He was my lieutenant in the Army."

"Small world. Was he at the big battle with Custer?"

Neil picked up the shirt he'd put on clean after his bath the night before and slipped it on. "No, he came in later that summer. He was one of the replacements for the men we lost. Fine officer. One of the best. We're headed across the street for some breakfast. Care to come along?"

"What time is it?"

Neil dug his watch from his pants pocket and popped it open. "A little past seven."

Katie shook her head and dropped to her pillow, allowing the sheet to fall away as she did. She draped a forearm over her eyes. "No," she said. "It's much too early for breakfast."

Seeing her lie there like that — her breasts exposed, her tiny waist and flat stomach bare and as smooth as butter — Neil was tempted to let Luke Sylar eat his eggs alone, but instead, he cleared his throat, turned away, and sat on the edge of the bed.

"That's right," he said. "I forgot. You like to sleep until at least ten o'clock." He put on his socks and shoved his right foot into its boot. As he pulled it on, he watched Katie from the corner of his eye.

"Ten at the very least." She stretched her legs, flexing shapely calves and pointing her toes at the bed's footrail. She then arched her back and stretched her arms toward the ceiling. When she let her hands drop, she allowed her fingertips to graze Neil's shoulder.

There was that hum again.

He put on his left boot and then turned to face her. Sliding his arms under her, he brought her to him, and without saying a word, he gave her a kiss. Their kisses seemed to get better and better, and he put everything he had into this one.

When he pulled away, Katie's eyes were just a bit out of focus. "Goodness gracious," she said, her voice a raspy whisper, "kiss me like that again." He did as he was told, and when they came apart that time, she lifted his hand to her lips and kissed his palm.

He smiled. "I'd like to stay," he said — and that was the God's honest truth. "But the deputy'll have some questions about what we came across yesterday." With a sardonic grin, he added, "It's my civic duty."

"You are such a good citizen."

He smiled. "Aren't I, though?" She now held his hand in both of hers, and he gently pulled it away. "Not that there's much I can tell him that he and the sheriff didn't see for themselves."

"Well," she said with a wistful tone, "if you have to go, then go."

"I'll be back before you know it."

Their plan had been to stay secluded until midafternoon and then bathe and eat an early supper. It turned out there was no play or recital in Custer City that night, but the Hill City baseball team was coming over to play the Custer team at five o'clock. Katie didn't have much familiarity with baseball, but Neil had played a little back in New York, and they planned to go to the game. Tomorrow, they'd rise early, and using Katie's crude map, they would head north to find the hidden gold.

What they would do once they found it had not been discussed. Neil noticed how they both had avoided that topic, and he wondered if Katie had noticed it as well.

He gave her another kiss — a quicker one this time — then let out a sigh. "You go back to sleep. I'll wake you when I get back."

Before he stood to leave, she took his chin between her thumb and index finger, tilted his head so she could see into his eyes, and said, "You're a good man, Neil."

"What?"

"You're a good man," she repeated.

He raised an eyebrow, and gave her a look he hoped communicated that he thought she was crazy. "Hell, girl, the first day I met you, I told you I was a prize."

"Yes," she said, "you did. And I believed you. I just didn't know how much of a prize you were."

He smiled and kissed her again, on the forehead this time, then he headed for the door. As he stepped into the hallway, he told himself — not for the first time — that Kathleen Burke was a strange one.

The café across the street was crowded and smoky, but Neil spotted Luke sitting at a table toward the rear. When the deputy saw Neil coming, he called to the waitress to bring over another cup of coffee.

"Have a seat, Neil," Luke said, nodding toward one of the three vacant chairs at the table.

Neil took off his hat, hung it on a chair back, and sat down. "Thanks, Lieutenant," he said.

"Enough of that," said the deputy. "Just call me Luke. We're civilians now."

"That's right, we are," agreed Neil, "and thank goodness for it."

"You never had much fondness for the military as I recall."

"Well, let's just say I'm glad to be out."

Luke nodded toward the young woman scurrying about, waiting on customers. "I asked Maggie there to bring us some eggs and a couple of ham steaks. Is that all right?"

"Sounds good."

Luke dug into a vest pocket for his makings and shook tobacco into a sheath of paper. Once he had the tobacco deposited in a neat line, he held out the pouch. "Care for a shuck?"

"No, thanks. I'll pick me up some cigars after we finish breakfast." He'd meant to get some the day before, but with all the excitement, it had slipped his mind. He hadn't had a smoke since sharing a bottle with Bill Cody on the far side of the Cheyenne River.

Luke used his teeth to pull the drawstring, closing the pouch. He tucked the small bag into his pocket. "It sure is nice to see someone from the old troop." He licked the paper, rolled it over onto itself, tapped the seam, and slipped the cigarette into his mouth. "I don't mind telling you, by the time I mustered out, I'd gotten a little fed up with army life myself." He looked a bit thoughtful as he said it. "But then again," he added, "there were some good times, too. Life was easier in those younger days." He struck a match and lit his cigarette, blowing a stream of smoke to put out the flame.

"There were a few good times," Neil allowed, but without saying it, he reminded himself that there had been damned few.

"I'm like you, though," Luke said. "I don't miss it much. It all got pretty boring after '77 when things calmed down with the Sioux."

"Maybe," said Neil, "but compared to the other choices, I didn't mind the boring times at all."

"I reckon not. Course, you had it lots rougher during your hitch than I ever did."

The waitress brought Neil's coffee and their food at the same time. "Here you go, boys," she said. "Eggs cooked easy and ham steaks." She set the plates down. Looking at Luke, she added, "We had us some mashed potatoes left over from supper last night, so I fried you fellas up some potato cakes to go along with it."

Neil glanced around and noticed that none of the other patrons were eating potato cakes.

"Looks as good as always, Maggie," Luke said. "Thanks a bunch."

"You're very welcome." Before she turned to leave, the waitress gave Luke a wide and very pretty smile.

It was clear to Neil that the girl was flirting, but Luke didn't seem to notice at all. That natural talent he possessed that made him so popular with the ladies was something elusive to Neil, but whatever it was, Neil wished he could pour it in a bottle. He'd become as rich as Carnegie if he could.

Neil started in on his food as soon as the waitress was gone, but Luke sat back in his chair and finished his smoke.

"You got out in September of '78, didn't you?"

"That's right. How can you remember that? Hell, I can hardly remember it myself."

"Because it was just a couple of weeks before the big ceremony."

"Ceremony?"

"The awards ceremony where you fellas who made a run for water got your Medals of Honor."

"Oh, that."

"We expected you'd be coming back to get yours. As I recall, you said you would, but then you never showed up. How come?"

"Who knows," Neil said. With a smile he added, "I was probably getting drunk with Raf Cossiga and missed it. You know how it goes."

Luke gave him a skeptical look but didn't press the matter. "Raf Cossiga. Damn, I haven't thought of him in years. The two of you got out at the same time, didn't you?"

"Joined on the same day, got out on the same day, and were together every day in between."

"He's quite a fella. What's that crazy little Basque doing these days anyhow? Do you ever see him?"

Neil had a fork loaded with egg halfway to his mouth when Luke asked the question. "He's dead," Neil answered after a pause.

"No."

Neil took the bite, then gave Luke an abbreviated version of the story.

When he finished, Luke snuffed what was

left of the cigarette into his saucer. "Ranchers," he said with disdain. "Some are all right, I reckon, but there's more than a few who figure they own every square inch of the West." He sipped some coffee, then took his fork and broke the yolks of his eggs. "I expect that's truer in Wyoming than it is over here because this is mining country and ranching is just now getting a foothold. But we have our share of cattlemen who think they're kings, and it's getting worse all the time."

Neil used his tongue to probe a piece of ham from between a couple of teeth. "That's for sure," he said. "Now that a man can travel from one place to the other without too much fear of getting scalped, I guess that bandits and obstinate landowners're about the only real disagreeable features to this country."

Luke snickered. "Sometimes it's hard to tell the two apart."

"I've worked for lots of ranchers," Neil said, "and there are lots more good ones than bad ones, but it does seem to me that the bad ones these days are especially bad. I think that's true of bandits as well. There may not be quite so many as there were a few years back when things were a little rougher, but the ones still around seem to be meaner than ever."

"Are you talking about what you found on the trail yesterday afternoon?"

"There's that, sure. That's an example, all right. But it seems to me that there's a wildness all over. You can't hardly spend an evening in a saloon anywhere in the territories without witnessing some kind of a ruckus, whether it's a fistfight, a knifing, or some poor bastard getting shot." He shoved his fork in the direction of the badge on Luke's chest. "Doesn't seem like the best of times to be going into the law enforcement profession, if you ask me."

"Oh, it's pretty peaceful around Custer. Most of the rowdies stay up in Deadwood. There was a time when this town's population was better than ten thousand souls, but since the big gold strikes over in the northern gulches, it's dropped down to only about four hundred, maybe fewer. That keeps things quiet and goes a long ways toward making this a real nice place to live. Plus," he added, "there's all the handsome country."

"It is scenic in these Black Hills, no doubt about it. I wouldn't mind finding me a spot up here and settling in, at least in the summer. It gets too cold, though, in the wintertime for me. I got rheumatism or some damned thing wrong with my back, and chilly weather doesn't help it." He washed down some egg with a slug of coffee. "Part of the problem, I expect, is I've gone sailing off the backs of too many surly broncs."

"Maybe," Luke suggested, "you're getting too old for that line of endeavor."

Neil lifted an eyebrow toward the deputy. "You're not the first of my acquaintances to point out that sad fact."

Luke smiled. "Well, Mister Bancroft, you're still younger than me, and the way I see it, we get two choices on this earth. We either suffer the years, or we're supper for worms, one or the other. Suffer or supper. And before I become supper, I've found me a peaceful little spot to settle down and enjoy a family. Maybe you should consider doing the same."

Neil gave him a skeptical look. "It's been a while since I've visited Custer City, but from what I saw yesterday, it seems you might be overstating how peaceful it is."

"That was pretty terrible, all right. Sheriff Code loaded the bodies into a buckboard this morning and left for Deadwood to tell the dead men's wives what happened. I was afraid he was going to send me on that errand, but he figured that was a chore he needed to do himself, thank goodness." He gave Neil a slap on the arm — his wounded arm — which got Neil's attention. "I drew the pleasant assignment of talking to you instead."

"I doubt that there's much I can tell you that you don't already know."

"There's damned little to go on, that's for sure, but mostly what we were wondering was did you notice any tracks around the stage when you first rode up?"

Neil gave that some thought. "Yes, I did. Of course, it was on a public road, so it's kind of hard to be sure, but I did see some fresh tracks right around the stage."

"Could you tell anything about them?"

Neil shook his head. "Not really, no. I guessed it to be three horses. It looked like two men had dismounted over by the stage and dealt with the strongbox. Other than that, there wasn't much to see."

"Were all the horses shod?" Luke asked.

"Sure."

"Did any of the horseshoes leave an unusual track of any kind?"

Neil thought back. "Nope, nothing special about any of 'em. Just averaged-sized mounts with standard shoeing."

"And you figure there were three of 'em?"

"That's what it looked like to me. Do you have any ideas who it could've been?"

Luke mixed his last bite of egg with his last bite of potato cake and finished it off. "Sheriff Code has a feeling that we might know who it was, but the bunch he's thinking of is a gang of four, not three."

"Is that so? What do you know about them?"

"Not much. That's the problem. And they may not even be the same ones. It's just that there was this wild group we figured was holed up somewhere around Deadwood that was raising a whole lot of hell all through the Hills for a couple of years there. They've been laying low now for nine months or so, and, like I said, they may not have anything to do with this holdup anyhow. It does fit their style, though, I guess. The reason we know so little about them is they try not to leave any witnesses around. One of the bunch we don't know anything about at all, but we've got a good idea who the other three are. About two years ago, they robbed a bank over in Spearfish. They put a couple of bullets in the teller, but he lived just long enough to tell the city marshal a little bit about them. The leader's a real vile son of a bitch by the name of Randall Frost. He's pretty new to the area, so we don't know much more about him than his name and that he's one cold-blooded bastard. The two others have been causing trouble around here to one degree or the other since the spring of '76. They came in through Buffalo Gap with some of the first pilgrims. From what I hear, they tried placer prospecting for a while, but that didn't last long — too much hard work, I reckon." He leaned forward, resting his thick arms on the table. "They're a couple of bad ones, too. They'd just as soon kill a man as spit." He pushed himself away from the table. "Hold on a second."

He stood and crossed the smoke-filled room, heading toward the far wall by the front windows. Attached to the wall was a bulletin board that contained various postings — the day's menu, notices of town council meetings, church get-togethers, items for sale by individuals, and a half dozen wanted posters. Neil had noticed it when he first came in. Luke pulled three of the posters off the board and brought them back to the table. Handing one to Neil, he said, "This here's Frost, the one we figure for the leader."

Neil took the poster. At the top, in bold type, it read, "$1000 Reward." Beneath that, in the same type, was Frost's name, and beneath the name was the man's likeness. It was only a drawing, not a photograph, but it had been rendered by an accomplished sketch artist. It showed a man who appeared to be in his late twenties or early thirties. There was nothing distinguishing about him apart from an unfriendly-looking sneer.

Luke held out the second poster. "This is Calvin Hoskins. He's one of the two I was telling you about who hit the Hills back in '76. He's none too bright, but plenty eager to use his six-gun and mean as holy hell."

It looked as if this fella was considered half as valuable as Frost — there was only a five-hundred-dollar reward offered for him. Neil glanced at the picture, stared at it for a moment, and then said in a surprised whisper, "Good Lord."

"What is it?"

"I know this fella. Or at least I've seen him. I shot him in the foot in a gunfight at Fort Fetterman just over a week ago."

"Shot him in the foot?" Luke sounded as if he was having a hard time believing it. "You did that on purpose?"

"That's right."

"Why?"

"It's a long story," Neil said. "But I'm sure he didn't have anything to do with robbing the stage."

"Why do you say that?"

"Because he's dead."

"Dead from getting foot-shot?"

"No, when I was leaving, this bastard Hoskins was going to put a bullet in my back, and another fella — a drunk by the name of Waldo Brickman — had to kill him." Neil finished off his coffee. "As it happens, this Brickman fella saved my life."

A couple of lines formed across Luke Sylar's forehead. "Did you say it was Waldo Brickman who killed Cal Hoskins?"

Neil nodded. "Hoskins went for his shooter as I was walking away, and Brickman stuck a knife in his heart right up to the hilt."

"Well, that surprises me some," said Luke. "I wouldn't've thought Waldo Brickman would care one whit whether Cal Hoskins killed you or not."

"Why do you say that?"

Luke slid the third poster across the table, and Neil picked it up. Staring back at him was the old silhouette cutter himself.

Sixteen

Luke Sylar went with Neil to the general store to pick up a half dozen long nines, and on the way Neil told him he was traveling with Katie, and how her husband, Edward, had been murdered the previous October while transporting his diggings out of the Hills.

Neil paid the clerk for the cigars, tucked five into his shirt pocket, and lit one as he and Luke stepped outside. Leaning his back against a hitching rail, Neil blew smoke into the sunny mountain air.

"It was clear to us back at Fetterman that this fella Hoskins was after Katie. He busted his way into her room, and she had to fight him off and escape through a window." As he spoke, the cigar went out, and he struck another match to relight it. "But it sure does come as a shocker," he said between puffs, "that Waldo Brickman was involved in it, too."

"How come?" Luke asked.

"Because he gave no sign of even knowing this man Hoskins."

"Oh, he knew him all right," said Luke. "They've been together for years, and they've been trouble the whole time. I expect they were just as much trouble down in Wichita, Kansas, too, before they slinked their way up here. It may be quiet in Custer most of the time, but the Hills gets more than its share of lawbreakers, and that was especially true back in '76 when those two scoundrels first rode in."

"That may be," Neil said, "but I have to admit that Brickman had me fooled. Course, it could be I'm just unskilled at telling when someone's lying, but I took him for nothing more than some loud-mouthed old coot who was forced by circumstances to kill a man he'd never even met. In fact, I thought he was going to keel right over from the sheer horrification of it all." He shook his head in disbelief. "Even if I am a poor judge of liars," Neil conceded once again, "he was damned convincing, I don't mind telling you. I expect Waldo Brickman could make himself a fine living on the theatrical stage."

Luke cleared his throat, spat, and wiped his mouth with the heel of his hand. "Believe me, Neil. Brickman wasn't horrified. That fella's probably killed more men than you've tipped your hat to. He's a clever one, though, smarter than he seems, and meaner than the dickens."

Neil dug in the dirt with the toe of his boot and thought aloud as he pondered the situation. "Katie and I figured Hoskins to be one of the bunch who murdered her husband, so Brickman must've been among them as well."

And, Neil added to himself, Brickman's being among them threw a lot of doubt on everything he'd said to Neil about Katie that first morning when Neil was trying to shave.

"And you're right, Luke, about what you said back at the café. It is surprising that Brickman would kill his own partner just to keep Hoskins from shooting me. It doesn't make any sense."

"It's hard to apply logic to anything that Waldo Brickman might do. He's smart but crazy."

"Maybe," Neil said. He turned to face the street, and as he did, he expelled a breath that carried not only a stream of blue cigar smoke but also the sound of frustration. "It's sure a puzzler." He rolled the tip of the stogie along the hitching rail's crossbar, causing the long ash that had formed to drop away. "I do think it's pretty certain that Hoskins and Brickman were among the ones who killed Edward Burke for his gold. Why else would they be after Katie? But she says there were three men in that bunch, and you said the gang Brickman and Hoskins rode with was made up of four."

"Yep, four, that's what Sheriff Code heard from Seth Bullock. Bullock's the law up in Deadwood."

"Doesn't exactly add up, then, does it?"

"No, it doesn't seem to, not in any way, but especially not as far as the robbery of the stage yesterday's concerned."

"How do you mean?"

"Let's say for whatever reason, Randall Frost's gang was down to three men when they murdered your friend's husband."

"Uh-huh."

"So with Hoskins getting himself killed last week over in Wyoming that would knock 'em down to two. You say you saw tracks from three horses at the scene of the robbery. It could be that Frost's bunch *didn't* have anything to do with the robbery yesterday."

"Maybe not," said Neil. "That figures, I guess."

Luke poked the brim of his hat with his

thumb, shoving it up a notch. Then he leaned against the rail, the corded muscles of his forearms standing out even through the cloth of his shirt. "And that's a likely assumption," he said, "but then that leaves us nothing at all to go on." He let out a sigh that hinted at his level of frustration.

Neil reached over and thumped Luke's badge. "I'm glad you're the fella who has to cipher it all out. I just want Katie and me to take care of our business and then get the hell out of Dakota. The truth is, I settled in Wyoming because I'd had enough of this place when I was in the Army. Montana and Dakota always meant trouble for me."

Neil and Luke bid each other farewell, and Neil headed back to the Kleemann House. As he crossed the street, he pondered these men being after Katie. He wished he knew more of what that was all about. He hadn't asked her any questions about her past since that first evening when they were camped at the confluence of Box and Lightning Creeks, and he hadn't pressed it even then. At the time, he figured she was leaving something out of her story anyway, and besides, at least until a few days ago, it hadn't mattered. As long as he received the thousand dollars he'd been promised if they found the gold, Neil hadn't cared what or who she was. She could be a miner's widow, a faro dealer, or the Queen of the Nile — it was all the same to him.

He took a hard draw on the cigar and felt the smoke swirl out behind him as he walked.

Since their first kiss, though, things had changed. Now he had to admit that his curiosity had taken a turn, but the first lesson he had learned after crossing the Mississippi was that on the frontier, a person's past was a private matter, and prying was the rudest kind of behavior.

Suddenly the long nine clenched between his teeth didn't taste so good, and he flicked the butt into the street.

On the other hand, he told himself, rude behavior or not, the time had come to ask Katie Burke some questions.

As he stepped through the hotel's door, he noticed a sign on the front desk that read, "Back in Five Minutes." That was good. Neil resented the leering grin that greasy little clerk always gave him.

He made his way down the hall to room twenty-three. It felt odd just letting himself into Katie's room without knocking, but he'd promised to wake her when he got back, and he had in mind a gentler way of doing that than pounding on her door.

He stepped into the room, turned, and closed the door as quietly as possible.

It was still his intention to pose some prying questions pertinent to their present situation, but with a smile, he decided it wouldn't be the first thing he would do.

Taking off his hat, he started for the bed but stopped short when he realized that the covers were tossed back and the bed was empty.

That was strange. He checked the time. It wasn't even nine thirty.

Thinking she might be digging something out of what few supplies they had left, he went next door to his own room, but she wasn't there either.

Where the hell could she be?

He walked to the far end of the hall and rapped a couple of times on the door marked "Women – Bath."

"Katie," he called out, "you in there?" There was no response. He tried again. "Is anyone there?" Still no one answered, so he decided to risk whatever criminal offense peeking into the women's bathing room might be, and he pushed open the door. The room was hot and steamy. Water simmered on the stove, but the place was empty.

He returned to number twenty-three and

sat on the bed to think. Where was she? His thoughts whirled, searching for possibilities. Finally, those whirling thoughts landed on the memory of Calvin Hoskins's breaking into Katie's room at that fleabag hotel back in Fetterman. That recollection shot a quick pang of foreboding into him, and he came straight up off the bed. His mouth went dry, and the bottom seemed to drop from his stomach.

Could that have happened again?

His eyes raced about the room. There was no sign of a struggle. He crossed to the wardrobe where Katie had hung the dress she'd worn to supper the night before. He jerked open the two mirrored doors, but the wardrobe was empty. Her satchel, which she had placed on the wardrobe's floor, was also gone.

Neil caught a movement out of the corner of his eye and spun toward the window. In the yard below, stepping out of a large privy, was the desk clerk. The clerk started for the hotel's back door, whistling some tune and carrying a newspaper tucked under his arm.

Neil sprinted into the hallway and was downstairs in the lobby waiting before the man had made it to the front desk.

"I'm looking for Kathleen Burke," Neil said as the clerk approached.

"Yes, yes, I thought you might be." He exhibited a smile even more unctuous than usual.

"Have you seen her?"

"Why, yes, as a matter of fact I have. She came down not five minutes after you departed."

"Where is she?" Neil asked. "Is she all right?"

The clerk stepped behind the desk and put down his paper. "Well, I certainly think so, Mister Bancroft. Why ever in the world wouldn't she be? She seemed right as rain to me."

Neil had no patience for this fella, but he fought the urge to drag the little man across the top of the counter. "Did she say where she was going?"

The man tapped his chin with the tip of his index finger as though he were trying to recall. "Nooo," he finally said, drawing the word out for the sake of drama. "No, I don't believe she did."

Neil was seconds away from giving in to his urge when the man must have realized that he had savored as much of Neil's discomfort as he dared.

"She did leave this for you, however." The clerk reached into a drawer and produced an envelope that had Neil's name written across the front in Katie's hand. "She told me to make certain to give this to you the very second I saw you."

He expected Katie had given the man a handsome tip to do it, too, and he certainly hadn't handed it over the very second he saw him.

Neil provided the clerk his dirtiest look, but at the same time, he felt a surge of relief as he took the envelope. "Did she say anything else?" he asked.

"Not a thing."

He locked onto the clerk's watery eyes, but the weasel was too furtive for Neil to read. Neil held his gaze until the man looked away, and when he did, Neil turned his attention to the envelope.

It was good to know she was all right. For some reason, his conversation with Luke Sylar and the memory of what had occurred at Fort Fetterman had him spooked. But apparently everything was okay. At least, unlike before, she'd not had to jump out of a window with some killer at her heels.

It was peculiar behavior, though. Of course, peculiar behavior for Katie Burke was not peculiar.

Feeling himself smile, Neil tried to imagine just what the hell she could be up to. After all, it was Katie who had wanted to lounge about the room all day.

He slipped a finger under the envelope's wax seal and popped up the flap. He was eager to see just what she had to say for herself.

But when he peered into the envelope, it took a moment for what he saw to wend its way into his brain. There was not a letter of explanation inside at all, and what was inside made no sense — not at first. Tucked into the envelope were ten green one-hundred-dollar National Currency notes. Abe Lincoln stared out from the corner of every one.

"Oh," said the clerk in his soft, smug voice, "now that I think about it there was one more thing the lady mentioned before she left."

Neil turned on legs that felt as though they were made of sand.

The little man seemed to be suppressing a smile, but he was doing a poor job of it. "She said for me to tell you to get on home to Wyoming, that she would not be coming back."

Neil returned to his room and checked their supplies. All Katie had taken were her personal belongings, a canteen, and one of the Marlin rifles. She was traveling light.

He ran the two blocks to the livery stable, but even as he did it, he knew he'd be too late.

"Yes, sir, she was here, all right," said the liveryman. "I was a little leery at first when she said that sorrel belonged to her. After all, you was the fella who paid the boardin' fee, but she showed me a bill of sale."

"How long ago was she here?" Neil asked.

"Better than an hour." He smiled, showing a half dozen blank spaces where there should have been teeth. "Ain't no way you could catch her, if that's what you're thinkin'. She lit out of here like she was afire."

"Which direction?"

"Toward Hill City. That's to the north. If you stick to it, it's the trail that'll take you all the way over to Deadwood."

Neil thanked the man and left the stable. Once he was outside, he stood at the edge of the street, watching the traffic pass on Custer Avenue.

The trail to the north, he thought. That trail might lead to Hill City and Deadwood, but first it led to the gold. He wished he had paid more attention to the map she'd shown him that first night at Archie's Café, but he hadn't.

Not that he gave a damn about the gold. No, what Neil cared about was Katie. He cared about her because she had made him care about her, and, like a fool, he'd thought she felt the same.

He reached down and touched the wad of hundred-dollar bills in his front pocket. His urge to find her had nothing to do with gold. She had paid him their agreed-upon price. They were even.

But he did have a few questions he wished he could ask. They were none of the questions he had planned to ask after his visit with Luke Sylar. That batch of questions had become meaningless. What he wanted to ask her now was why. It wasn't just why she'd left the way she had. What Neil wanted to know was why she had gone to so much trouble to make him feel this way, and why she had pretended to feel the same. What had she gained? Mostly what he wanted to know was what kind of woman would make a man love her and then run off? That was the first question Neil wanted answered. What kind of a woman lies like that to a man?

But he knew that asking those questions would not make any difference. For whatever reason, he had been lied to and used, and his chasing her down to ask the why of it wouldn't change a thing.

He wandered around for what must have

306

been four or five hours. He had no destination. He just walked. It was midafternoon when he found himself at the spot on French Creek, just south of town, where H. N. Ross and William McKay had first discovered gold when they were a part of the Custer expedition. That was right at seven years ago, but to Neil it seemed like a hundred.

He checked his watch. It was nearly three. As a rule, he didn't drink this early, but what the hell. He had a pocket full of hard-earned money — very hard-earned — and a day with nothing better to do. He could think of no reason in the world to postpone getting drunk.

He walked back to Custer Avenue, looked up the street, and located a large black-and-gold sign that read, "Geo. Palmer's Saloon."

That would do.

In less than five minutes, Neil was standing at the bar, staring into the golden swirls of a glass of Jameson's Irish. He took a sip and cringed. As smooth as the whiskey was, it didn't go down as easily as it might. His guts were roiling.

Neil sipped the drink and was still less than halfway into it when a giant of a man wearing a derby hat and walking on crutches hobbled through the door.

The bartender looked glad to see the fella. "Hey, Giovanni," he called out. "How're you doing?"

"How'm I doing?" the man repeated through gritted teeth. "You ever see anybody on crutches, Pete, that looked like he was doin' worth a damn?" The man spoke with the clipped, flat syllables of New York City. Neil had heard it some when he was growing up in Oswego, but he'd heard it even more after he'd joined the Army. It was the sound of second- and third-generation immigrants — Italian, German, Irish — Europeans of every ilk — who had learned to speak in the rough neighborhoods of south Manhattan Island.

"No," said the bartender with a laugh, "I reckon if a fella's on crutches, that's gotta be a sure sign that he ain't doing so good. What happened to you anyhow?" He turned the spigot on a beer keg and filled a glass. "The first one's on me," he said.

"Thanks," said Giovanni. He leaned his weight against the edge of the bar and placed his crutches on top. "I dropped a piano on my foot. Can you believe that, Petey? A goddamned piano."

The bartender's head snapped. "You did what?"

"A piano. The church is getting a new

piano. It's supposed to be coming up from Rapid City tomorrow, so the preacher's giving the old one to the school. He hired me and a couple of the fellas to haul it over."

"The preacher's giving the old one to the school?" repeated the bartender.

Giovanni, who didn't appear to be long on patience that afternoon, gave him a look like the man was stupid and then turned to Neil and asked, "Ain't that what I just said?" Without waiting for a reply, he repeated it, louder, like maybe the bartender was hard of hearing. "The preacher's giving the old one to the school, Petey. Jeez."

"That's what I thought you said, Giovanni. The preacher's —"

"— giving the old one to the school, fer Christ's sake," Giovanni said.

"Could it be your mood ain't so cheery today?" asked Petey with a smile.

Giovanni did not return the smile. "So's anyhow, the preacher, he's giving the old piano to the school, and me and a couple of the boys was hauling it over. These fellas're on one end of this piano, and me, I'm on the other, see? We're muscling this thing down the steps of the church, and the two guys, they lose their end, you know? It slips, and bam!" He slammed his huge palm down flat on the bar, and it hit with the sound of a ham dropped from a silo. "This damned piano, it lands right on my foot. Hurt like one holy son of a bitch, I wanna tell you."

"So what did you do?"

"What did I do?" He looked at Neil again and jerked his thumb toward the bartender. "What did I do, he asks. I screamed, that's what I done. I screamed, and I come out with a string-a words that ain't never been uttered on them church steps before. I guaran-damn-tee ya. Them words, they came out," he held up a hand like a copper stopping traffic or a witness taking an oath, "through no fault of my own, Petey. I mean, what's a fella gonna do when there's a god-damn piano on his foot, huh? I asks you, what's a fella s'posed to do? Anyhow, I'm screamin' out these words, the sort what you mighta heard if you was ever on the Bowery, you know? And I looks 'round, and there's the preacher. He's standing right there watching us the whole time. His eyeballs was the size of turkey eggs. Swear to God, Pete, for a second there, I thought maybe his ears was gonna start to bleed." The big piano hauler polished off his beer, and Pete refilled his glass. "Let me tell you something, Petey," Giovanni added, wag-ging his finger at the ceiling. "This goes for you, too, Mister." Again, he looked at Neil. "My advice to yous fellas is don't never drop no pianos on your foot."

The bartender nodded and allowed as to how he would try his best to bear that in mind. "So what did you do after you screamed and made the parson's ears bleed?" he asked.

"The guys, they toss me into the wagon we was gonna use for the piano, and they hauls me over to the doc's. Doc figures my foot's busted in about eight places. I'll be stumbling around with these things . . ." he scowled at the crutches, "for at least a month, maybe even two."

Neil was only half listening to all this, but when Giovanni mentioned the doctor, that gave him a thought. "How many doctors do you folks have in this town?" he asked.

"Just the one," answered the bartender. "Doc Green. I ain't sure he's even a real doctor, but he seems to know what he's doing . . . with the basic stuff anyhow."

"That's what *you* says," contradicted Giovanni. "I says he don't know shit. Especially he don't know shit about fixing no busted feet." He put all his weight on his elbows and lifted his foot onto the bar so his audience could see it better. "All he does is wraps up busted feet in cotton gauze, gives you a couple of sticks to hobble on, and tells you to go get drunk."

"Hell, Giovanni," said the bartender, "getting drunk ain't such bad advice." To Neil he said, "We had us a fella here for a while by the name of Flick who was a real doc, but he decided there wasn't enough sickness around Custer City to make a go of it. It was the mountain air, he used to say. It was so wholesome it kept everyone too healthy for him to make a decent living. One day a few years back, he packed up and moved down to Rapid City. He said down in Rapid City they's sick people coming outta the woodwork. He said in Rapid City, sick folks is as common as ticks on a dog."

"How long has this Green been around?" Neil asked.

The bartender squeezed his face up while he gave the question some thought. "Oh, at least a couple of years, I reckon. Wouldn't you say, Giovanni?"

After the exertion of placing his foot on the bar, Giovanni, who was now well into his third beer, seemed to have slipped into a funk. He didn't bother to answer Pete's question.

"Where's his office?" Neil asked.

"Just down a couple of blocks. It's across the street from the new courthouse."

Neil dropped a coin on the bar to pay for the Irish and headed for the door.

"If you's got a busted foot," Giovanni called after him, "you might as well just stay here and drink your whiskey."

Like most of the structures in Custer, Doc Green's clinic was built of pine logs. It was small and set back from the street, and a neat row of pansies lined the front of the building.

Neil stepped inside, and when he did, a tiny bell above the front door jingled. After a bit, a man in his mid-forties came in from the back. He was tall, thin, with a hooked nose and a walnut-sized Adam's apple.

"Yes, sir," the man said, "can I help you?" His voice was deep and pleasant, and unlike Giovanni's, it did not provide any clue as to the man's origins. "Are you feeling poorly, sir?"

Neil was feeling damned poorly, but he answered, "No, sir, I'm fine." He told the doctor his name and said, "I just wanted to visit with you some, if I could."

"Of course, Mister Bancroft." Wooden benches lined three of the walls. Neil assumed these were for patients awaiting treatment, but it did not appear the benches received much use. "Have a seat," the doctor said. He motioned toward one of the benches, and he and Neil sat down. "What's on your mind?" He reached in the side pocket of his dark frock coat and pulled out a large, curved briar pipe.

"From what I understand," Neil began, "you were the only doctor around these parts back in the fall of last year, is that so?"

The doctor tamped a large pinch of short-cut tobacco into his pipe. He then struck a match but made no move to touch it to the bowl. Holding the match as he spoke, he said, "Yes, sir, that's true. Only one then. Only one now. I began my third year of practice here in Custer just this past May." By the time he got around to lighting the tobacco, the match's flame threatened his fingertips, but to Neil's surprise, the doc got the pipe lit and the match shaken out just in time. "Why do you ask, sir?"

"Do you recall, by chance, treating a man for a gunshot wound last October?"

The doctor smiled. "Well, Mister Bancroft, I do treat gunshot wounds from time to time. Could you be a little more specific?"

"This man's name was Edward Burke. He wasn't from around here. He was just traveling through."

The doc nodded. "I remember the man. It was a sad case."

"Yes, sir. He died."

"Uh-huh. He held on for a day or so, but you're right. He eventually died. He'd lost a lot of blood by the time I saw him, and there wasn't much I could do. I didn't even bother to remove the bullet because he would never have survived the surgery."

"What can you tell me about this man?" Neil asked.

"Oh, not much. Like you said, he was just traveling through. Heading south, as I recall."

"Yes, sir, back to Texas."

"Texas? I didn't remember that, but you could be right. He wasn't all that lucid, so I didn't get a lot of information from him. He'd been living over by Deadwood. He said he had himself a cabin in Splittail Gulch just at the bottom of the steep hill going into town, although," the doctor added with a smile, "young Mister Burke admitted spending more of his time at Paulina Cardinale's Ace High hurdy-gurdy than he ever spent at his cabin."

Neil and Raf had ridden up to Deadwood as often as possible during their army days, but Neil was not familiar with Paulina Cardinale's. She must have come in after they had moved on. Neil was, however, familiar with what the doc meant by a hurdy-gurdy.

315

It was a term used in the Hills for a combination saloon, dance hall, and gambling emporium, and during their enlistments, he and Raf had become very familiar with these fine establishments.

The doc cupped his hand over the bowl of his pipe and puffed a few times, sending halos of sweet-smelling smoke spiraling about his head. "Mister Burke said he was tired of life in Deadwood, though. He said he was headed home when he'd been attacked by a gang of road agents."

"That's what I understand," said Neil.

"That isn't surprising, either," the doctor said. "We had us a rash of that sort of thing going on for a while last year."

"Burke had a wife," said Neil, "a young woman living in Amarillo at the time. I was wondering what all he told you about her."

Doc Green squinted through the smoke as he thought back. After a bit, he shook his head. "You know, I guess I don't recall his ever mentioning a wife."

"Really?" That didn't seem right. "He must've talked about her some, Doc."

"No, I don't believe he did."

"Are you sure? He wrote her a letter from here just before he died. I was told that he had you mail it for him."

"No, you must be mistaken. I suppose he

could have written a letter without my knowing it, but considering his condition, I figure that's pretty unlikely." His eyebrows lifted and his upper lip curled in a smile around the stem of his pipe. "My memory's not so sharp as it once was, but I think I'd remember mailing a letter for him." He took his pipe from his mouth. "And I assure you, sir, I did not. I would've been glad to, of course, but Mister Burke never made that request."

They sat for a bit without saying anything. Finally, the doc sat up straighter on the bench and wiped the tip of his pipe stem on his pants leg. "I guess, though, that if he did write a letter to his wife, he might've had his sister mail it."

"His sister?"

"Yes, sir, a pretty little thing. She was a year or so older, but you could see the resemblance once you knew they were related. She was the one who brought him in, and it looked like the two of them had gone through quite an ordeal in making their escape from the robbers." He rapped the pipe on the heel of his shoe, knocking the ashes and charred tobacco onto the rough wood floor. A couple of red coals still smoldered, and he scuffed the sole of his shoe across them.

"As far as any letter is concerned," the doctor continued, "if his sister mailed it for him, it must've been after he died because she was with her brother every second they were here. She never left his side — sat next to his bed night and day, holding his hand, wiping his brow. I've never seen a more caring nurse in all my life." He shoved the pipe back into his pocket. "I assure you, Mister Bancroft, a man could do much worse when his trumpet is played than to have a woman like Katie Burke helping to ease his passing."

SEVENTEEN

Before talking to the doctor, Neil had been willing to let her go. Now, though, he was determined to find her. He intended to learn just what the hell was going on. How he'd get the truth from her once he found her, he didn't yet know, but that didn't matter. He would find her just the same.

Although it was clear that Katie was a liar, he still believed that there was hidden gold. Why else would she have wanted to return to Custer? She had told him that first night at Archie's that Edward Burke had been wounded five miles to the north of Custer City, so Neil would ride out five miles and comb every gulch and ravine on both sides of the trail. Even if it took a month — a year — he would find her. If he didn't find her here, then, by God, he'd find her wherever she landed next.

Neil rushed to the stable, where he collected the roan and one of the pack horses.

He sold the second pack horse to the livery-man for half what they'd paid for it in Fetterman. He then went back to the hotel and loaded the few supplies that remained.

Heading north, he left Custer the same way he had arrived — at a gallop.

He kept the horses at that pace for close to a mile, then reined in when he topped the divide between Spring and French Creeks.

When he jerked the reins, the roan gave a churlish snort and chomped the bit. The roan was a runner, and after being cooped up in a livery stall, he was eager to stretch his legs, but Neil knew he had to slow down, not just for the horses' sake but for his own as well. Starting this search at a mindless gallop was not the way to go.

Neil took a deep breath of the scented air and looked out across a meadow so green it damned near hurt his eyes. He'd forgotten just how beautiful these Hills were. The meadow stretched toward a deep canyon, and beyond the canyon, the slopes were cloaked in thick forests of spruce and pine.

Looking down on it all was Harney Peak, the Black Hills' tallest mountain. Harney had snagged a passing cloud, and it lay cocked at a jaunty angle across the mountain's crest, just like one of ol' Raf's white berets.

Sitting in the saddle, taking all this in, Neil told himself that maybe what the doctor who had moved to Rapid City said was true. The air up here was wholesome enough to be therapeutic. Already he felt better — not a lot better, maybe, but some.

Out ahead of him, he watched a hawk circle above the meadow. It rarely moved its wings, but instead soared on lazy currents of warm summer air. That hawk had the right idea. There was no cause to rush, and Neil knew that somewhere in the green meadow, there was a mouse or rabbit fated to meet its maker.

After a while, he patted the roan's neck and put him into a trot.

Just before he reached what he figured to be the five-mile mark, he met a couple of riders headed south. They all three pulled up, and Neil gave them a friendly nod. "Afternoon, gents," he said. "Nice day for travel."

"Yes, sir, it sure is that."

These boys were in their early twenties. They were strangers, but Neil already felt comfortable with them because they bore the unmistakable look of cowhands. In this miners' country, he figured they were thinking the same thing about him.

"You fellas been traveling long?" he asked.

"Yes, sir," said the bigger of the two. "We started out at Deadwood yesterday afternoon and camped last night 'bout halfway between there and Hill City. We got up at first light and put in a good three hours of stream fishin' before we headed out. We been makin' real good time on this here fine trail."

"Yep, it's a good one, all right," Neil agreed.

The smaller man said, "It gets a little stumpy in a few places where it's been cut through the trees. If a fella was drivin' a wagon, it might slow him down a little from time to time, but on horseback, hell, it's easy going all the way to Deadwood."

"It's not my intention to go that far," Neil said, "but thanks for the information. When I first came to these mountains seven years ago, there wasn't a trail to be found. It's pretty accommodating up here these days compared to how it was back then."

"I expect that's the truth," the big man said. "So if you ain't going to Deadwood, where you headed?"

"Just up the road a ways. I'm looking for someone who's traveling alone, and I figure she left the trail around here somewhere and went down into one of these gulches."

The little man cocked his head so he could see Neil better from under the broad brim of his hat. "Did you say 'she'?" he asked.

"That's right."

The little man looked at his partner and then back to Neil. "Was she dressed in pants and wearin' a billed canvas cap?"

"I expect she was."

"And ridin' a handsome sorrel gelding?"

Neil nodded. "You fellas must've seen her."

"Sure have," said the big one. "She mighta left the trail around here like you say, but if she did, she done it hours ago."

"Why's that?" Neil asked.

" 'Cause 'bout ten o'clock're so, we run across her on the other side of Hill City. Had to be her. I doubt there's more than one woman on this trail wearin' a billed cap and ridin' a sorrel."

Neil had to agree, although he didn't say anything.

The big one glanced at the heavy stand of trees on both sides of the road. "I'd say it's lucky for you we come along. You coulda been looking for that girl down in them gulches 'til Judgment."

"When you met her," Neil asked, "did you

stop and visit with her any?"

The big one nodded to his friend. "PJ here tried to. He reined in and called to her, but when he did, the only answer that female give 'im was to pull a lever action outta her saddle scabbard and jack in a round. It was the unfriendliest thing I ever seen. Scairt us both near to death."

"No offense, Mister, if she's your wife or somethin'," PJ said, "but if you ask me, I'd hafta say that woman is pretty damned strange."

The two cowboys headed off, but Neil just sat there thinking and staring at a spot between the roan's ears.

Since Katie had been seen on the trail past Hill City, then the only place she could be headed was Deadwood, but that didn't make any sense at all. Why was she going there? She knew she was being hunted, and that was the most likely place for her hunters to be located. Somewhere around Deadwood was where they were last known to be holed up.

And what about the gold? If by ten o'clock she was already that far down the road, then she must not have had any trouble finding the gold. Of course, Neil realized with a start, she never needed any help finding the gold anyway. She knew right where it was stashed all along. It was probably Katie who had hidden it in the first place.

He stood in his stirrups, stretched his aching back, and then settled into the saddle. So she was past Hill City by midmorning. If she was making that kind of time, she should make Deadwood by shortly after dark.

Glancing at the sky, he saw the sun was still above his left shoulder. Four hours of daylight left. If he pressed it, he could be well on the other side of Hill City himself before he was forced to make camp for the night. And an early start in the morning would put him in Deadwood by late afternoon or early evening.

Unlike Custer City, Deadwood was a crowded place, but even so, there was a good chance he might find her by tomorrow night.

That thought sent an icicle into his chest.

Was he even sure he wanted to find her? There would be pain attached to seeing her again.

For a moment, he considered wheeling the roan, catching up with the cowboys, and returning to Custer. The three of them could raise some hell tonight — his treat — and he'd start back to Wyoming in the morning a lot richer than before he met Katie Burke — and hopefully a little wiser.

He gave that idea some real consideration, but in the end he admitted there was not much chance of his getting any wiser.

He spurred the roan toward Hill City.

Neil made his camp that night on the north bank of Rapid Creek, which was a nice, clear stream and the largest one flowing eastward out of the Hills. At this point, the valley was lush and wider than a mile. Some judge had come through there in '77 and named it Pactola. How the man came up with that name, Neil couldn't say, but it was a fine spot to camp. During his army days, they used to call the place Camp Crook because General George Crook had once used it on one of his expeditions.

The evening was pleasant, but Neil wished he'd taken the time to purchase a tent in town before he headed out. He rarely used a tent on the prairies because the nights there were warm and rain was rare, but the weather in these mountains was fickle. It was nice right now, but it could turn nasty in short order. He took his slicker from the pack, rolled it up, and used it as a pillow. If need be, he could make that do. He'd have to since it was all he had.

Plenty of clouds scudded by during the night, but his luck held, and the weather stayed mild. Still, he slept very little, and what sleep he got was fitful and full of dreams. About an hour before dawn, he finally quit trying to sleep, got up, and had a quick breakfast of coffee, biscuits, and jerky. After he ate, he doctored his arm, saddled the roan, and loaded the pack horse. The sun was still out of sight, just below the eastern ridges, but there was a soft gray light that was bright enough for travel.

He stayed at a walk until the sun made it above the crests, and then he touched spur to the roan's right side and brought up the pace.

It was well past noon when he came to the three branches of Boxelder Creek, and there he took a break. He was less than fifteen miles from Deadwood, but he figured the horses could use a breather.

He picketed the roan and pack horse in a stand of tall, green grass and then dug out the last can of peaches. Sitting on the creek bank, he finished that off, eating the syrupy fruit fast and trying not to think too hard about the cans of peaches he'd shared with Katie. For some reason that he chose not to dwell on, it was unpleasant to recall certain specifics, and it made him angry that those little thoughts could cause him such pangs. He threw the empty can at a tree trunk and fell back into the tall grass. The clear skies of the day before were gone. Threatening clouds now rolled just above the treetops.

He closed his eyes and made an effort to push down the anger he felt. Most of that anger he directed toward himself rather than Katie, though there was plenty there for her as well.

But he deserved to be angry at himself. He was a man old enough to know better. People were seldom what they seemed, and that had been his first thought with Katie Burke. On the very first day they met, she had shown herself to be a trickster. She'd proven that she was a woman not to be trusted, but, like the fool that he'd always been, Neil had allowed her to convince him otherwise.

He shoved his hat down over his eyes and blocked out the darkening sky.

He was a poor judge of both people and situations, all right, and to his disappointment, there were lots of occasions over the course of his life that had proven that.

Joining the Army where young men were ordered to their deaths on the whims of old men — that was a sign of foolishness.

Neil realized there were often times when events demanded that a man lay down his life for a just cause, but those times were absent during the five years he'd worn blue. Nonetheless, he had seen plenty of young men die. No, there was no doubt that Neil was a fool, but if there had still been some question about it, then this past week should settle the matter. He'd been duped by Waldo Brickman. He'd almost been duped by Norman Greasby. And God and Neil both knew just how thoroughly he'd been duped by Kathleen Burke.

He muttered a curse, pushed himself up from the grass, and squared his hat. It was time to fetch the horses.

Five miles from Deadwood, the rain started. Neil had his slicker snugged across the front of his saddle, and he pulled it on without having to stop. At first, the drops were few and as fat as marbles, but soon enough they thinned and came in hard, merging together and driving down in wide gray sheets.

The trail, which until the rain began had remained good, turned soupy fast, and neither the roan nor the pack horse was pleased. It took some coaxing to keep them moving up the divide overlooking White-wood Creek, and once they made it to the top and started down the steep and treacherous far side, Neil was forced to tie a gunnysack around the eyes of the pack horse and use more spur than he liked on the roan.

This part of the road was a well-known hardship for pilgrims entering Splittail and Deadwood Gulches from the south. Neil was amazed that anyone had ever gotten a wagon down the thing, but of course, they had. The trunks of trees at the summit were scarred from the hundreds of ropes tied to them over the years and used to ease wagons down the precipitous trail. But not everyone had been successful. The remnants of crashed outfits littered the ravine below.

The going was slow in the slick mud, but finally the slope eased. The trail still wended its way downhill, but it was no longer quite so steep, and he reached over and pulled the sack from the pack horse's eyes. The horse had behaved himself pretty well coming down but got skittish once he could see again. Neil tightened his grip on the lead rope and wondered if a gunnysack over the eyes might not be useful for humans, too, in bad situations.

At the bottom, just before it turned toward the northeast, the trail was washed out, and though the water that rushed across the road was white and churning, it wasn't too deep and was easy enough to ford.

Beyond this washout, to the right of the trail, Neil spotted what was left of an old, burned-out cabin. As he rode past, he guessed this was where Edward Burke had once lived. Doc Green had mentioned that Burke's cabin was at the bottom of Splittail Gulch, and this was the only building around.

The fire had not been recent, but whenever it was, it had burned the place to the ground. What little was left looked sad with its blackened logs sticking up in the rain at grotesque angles.

Away from the cabin, and a good hundred feet from the trail, a table was set off in a little copse of spruce. The table was a crude, unpainted, hammered-together thing, but even as rough as it was, it looked strange out-of-doors, nestled there among those scorched but still standing evergreens.

Neil could picture Edward Burke on pleasant summer nights taking his meals at this table — sitting there after he had eaten, smoking, perhaps drinking a bottle of beer or a glass of lemonade. The area was beautiful with its steep cliffs and forests, and its rich, wide meadows would make excellent pasture ground for cattle or horses, either one. Neil doubted that a lovelier spot could ever be found.

As he followed the trail around a bend, he still stared back at the place, particularly that rough old table. He couldn't take his eyes off it. He watched until it finally slipped from sight, and as he rode into Deadwood Gulch, he wondered if perhaps Edward Burke's sister might also have spent the occasional summer evening sipping lemonade there among the silver spruce.

EIGHTEEN

The little cabin in Splittail Gulch was not the only structure to burn since the last time Neil had been on this side of the Black Hills. Back in 1879, the town of Deadwood had been ravaged by fire. He'd read in the Cheyenne paper that an oven in a bakery shop had malfunctioned, and most of Main Street was lost before the fire finally burned itself out. But it seemed the town had recovered. There were very few signs of the destruction, and many fine stone buildings now lined both sides of the street.

It was raining even harder now, and Main was a bog. There was a wet sucking noise every time the roan lifted a hoof. At the corner of Lee Street, a large, overloaded freight wagon was stuck up to its axles in the muck. A half dozen men were pushing in an effort to help the teamster get the rig moving again, but they were having a hard go of it. Any other time, Neil would have been among the first to stop and lend a hand, but that day, he kept on riding.

There was a livery on Sherman Street that Neil and Raf had often used, and he stopped there, boarded his animals, and stored the bulk of his gear. He tossed his saddlebags over his shoulder and slogged through the mud over to the Wentworth House Hotel, where he took a room. Once he'd washed and changed his clothes, he sought directions to the Ace High.

Paulina Cardinale's Ace High was on the opposite side of the street and a half a block up from Nuttall and Mann's Saloon, the place where Bill Hickok was shot in the back of the head while playing poker. It was later renamed Number 10, but it had burned in the fire, too. When it was rebuilt, the owners stayed with the name, Saloon Number 10. Wild Bill had been killed in the summer of 1876, not two months after the disaster on the Little Bighorn River. Those had been raucous times, but even now, five years later, things did not appear to have been tamed much. As Neil walked up Main, he heard the sounds of piano music, bawdy laughter, and brawls. Rough-looking men leaned against every post. The air was charged with the dual enticements of hard drink and soft women.

Neil reminded himself that he had a pocketful of money. In the rowdiness of Deadwood, he could buy a hundred different ways to force Katie Burke from his mind. This was just the sort of wide-open town he'd found appealing in his youth, but for some reason it no longer held the same fascination.

All he wanted now was to locate Katie and demand that she admit . . . what? After a pause, he asked himself the question again. What in the hell did he want her to admit? That she had lied? That she had toyed with him?

At this point, he didn't know for sure what he wanted from her, but not knowing made him no less determined to find her, and that was just what he planned to do.

The Ace High was loud and crowded, and Neil had to push his way through the door. A grizzled miner with one pale blue eye and an empty pink orifice where his other eye should have been shouted, "Hey, goddamn it, who ya shovin'?"

Ignoring the man, Neil moved past.

The room was huge, twice as wide as most of the buildings on Main, and because of the dim light and thick blanket of tobacco smoke, Neil couldn't guess how far back it went.

There were twenty-five or thirty gaming tables scattered in front. At some, there was poker being played, at others, faro or twenty-one. The faro and twenty-one tables had women dealers. They were all pretty and wore tight, bright-colored dresses. The dresses were sequined and cut so low across the bosom that they offered the perpetual promise of a quick flash of nipple. Whether that promise was ever fulfilled didn't matter. Neil was sure that this was someone's calculated distraction, and he guessed that over the course of a year, it put many extra dollars into the gambling house's coffers.

The polished mahogany bar stretched toward the back at least sixty feet and perhaps more — that was as far as Neil could see. He considered ordering a drink, but men were shoving against that bar three deep, and there was not a spare inch available to elbow his way in.

A large, well-rendered portrait of a middle-aged woman hung above the glasses stacked behind the bar. The plain black dress she wore was austere and at least twenty years out of date, but the woman herself was not unattractive. Her expression was severe and unsmiling, and her dark hair was pulled back and pinned in an old-fashioned style, but even with all that, it was easy to see that she was a beauty — or had been in younger days. Neil stopped and stared at the sober, forbidding face with the thin lips and hard eyes and guessed that this was the proprietress, Paulina Cardinale. Clearly, the stern Miss Cardinale was a person to be reckoned with, and he suspected that how a woman like this had become the owner of such a place would make for an interesting story.

Turning away from the bar, Neil walked on through the crowd. The noise was deafening. A bald-headed man banged away on a piano at the front of the room, and some fat lady did the same in back. It was apparent that neither of them knew nor cared what the other was playing. The same was true of the patrons.

Squeezing his way in deeper, Neil spotted a teetering drunk urinating against the south wall. The man was having a great time, and as he did his business, he sang some old mule-skinner song at the top of his lungs. The song was at mid-chorus, and he was still in the process of relieving himself, when a man dressed in a cheap suit that was a size too small for his huge frame grabbed him by the scruff of the neck. The big man lifted the drunk off his feet and threw him headfirst — wriggling and squirming — into the very wall the man was using for his privy. To the displeasure of three or four unfortunate bystanders, the thrashing drunk's water didn't shut off even after he lost consciousness.

Although a freshet of blood streamed from a long gash on the now knocked-out singer's head and his equipment still dangled from his trousers, no one bothered to offer him any help. The big man who had tossed him into the wall sneered and then turned and joined two of his friends.

There were several of these large men dressed in tacky suits standing about the place. It was clear to Neil that they were there to maintain order, and judging by their size and the obvious shoulder holsters that bulged beneath their garish coats, he doubted it would be wise to question their authority — or their taste in clothes, for that matter.

He was halfway into the place now and could see a little better. There was a dance floor that sported fifteen or twenty couples clinging to one another and maneuvering about to the music produced by the fat lady at the piano.

Beyond the dance floor was another bunch of tables, and from this area the aroma of food fought its way through the stench of smoke, stale beer, and a score of even more unpleasant odors. A few of these tables were empty, and Neil, who hadn't had a decent meal since his breakfast the day before with Luke Sylar, made his way to one and sat down. After a bit, a young woman wearing a cotton print dress came to take his order.

"Steak," he said, "and a beer."

"Sorry, Mister. Roast beef and pinto beans is what's on the menu today."

"Then roast and beans it'll be." She turned to leave. "And the beer," he repeated. "I'd like it now if you please."

"Yes, sir."

The girl was young, but Neil guessed she was waiting food tables instead of dealing cards not so much because of her age but because of her plain appearance. Her hair was stringy and her face was pocked. The looks of the girls at the Ace High's gaming tables were of a higher caliber than in most places of this sort.

In less than five minutes, the young girl brought his beer and, at the same time, his food. He thanked her, handed her a shiny Morgan dollar fresh from the Philadelphia Mint, and began to eat. He was hungry, and the food was fine, but after a few bites his appetite was gone, and he shoved the plate toward the center of the table and picked up the beer.

If Edward Burke used to haunt this place, as he told Doc Green, then there was someone in here who knew him, and if someone knew him, then that person might know Katie as well.

The waitress returned with Neil's change.

"Keep it," he said.

"Thank you, sir." She smiled and turned to leave.

Neil called her back. "Before you go, I'd like to talk to you for a second."

She looked apprehensive. "I wait tables, Mister. That's all I do."

At first he wasn't sure what she meant, and then it came to him. "No, no," he said with an embarrassed smile, "it's nothing like that."

"I'm a good girl."

"I'm sure you are, Miss. I just want to ask you a couple of questions."

She still seemed reluctant, but in a wary voice she said, "All right."

"Do you happen to know a fella by the name of Edward Burke? I heard he used to come in here."

She gave it some thought and then shook her head. "No, can't say as I do. Lots of men come in here."

Neil looked out across the lake of drunken

faces. "I can see that."

"Could be he comes in and I ain't never heard of him. I just started working here last month. Miss Jackson might know 'im, though."

"Who's Miss Jackson?" Neil asked.

"Ellie Jackson. She's the boss. She runs the place."

"Oh? I figured Paulina Cardinale ran the place."

"She does, I reckon. That's who Miss Jackson takes her orders from, I guess, but I hear that Miss Cardinale don't like to be troubled with the small stuff. In the whole time I've been here, I ain't seen her come out of her apartment even once." She pointed to a set of stairs in the corner that led to a landing on the second floor of the building. "Not ever," she added.

"So where can I find this Miss Jackson?"

"She has an office in back yonder. I'll ask her to come out and talk to you."

"Thanks," Neil said. "I'll wait right here."

The girl disappeared through a door in back.

While he waited, Neil sipped his beer and considered how Paulina Cardinale never left her apartment. He guessed the stern-faced old prune might well be ashamed to look too closely at the evil manner in which she made her money, although he expected that despite her harsh expression, those thin lips parted in a smile every time that evil money got counted.

After a bit, his reverie was interrupted.

"You wanted to talk to me, Mister?"

Neil turned to see a petite Negro woman standing on the opposite side of his table. "Are you Miss Jackson?" He stood and took off his hat.

She motioned for him to sit. "That's right," she said. She pulled out a chair and sat down as well. "I see you're as shocked as everybody else when they first see who I am — or should I say *what* I am."

"Uh, no, ma'am, not at all." Neil placed his hat on the seat of the chair to his right.

She looked doubtful. "It's not common, even out here in the West, for a colored, especially a woman, to be in charge of anything, much less an operation like this." She waved her hand, taking in the place, then turned back to Neil and smiled. "Yet here I am." She did not appear to say this as a boast but merely as a fact, which, of course, it was.

"Well," he began, "I guess I . . . I . . ." His sentence ended in a series of stammers, which made Miss Jackson smile again. When she did, Neil had to smile, too. "I don't reckon there's any reason you shouldn't run a place like this if you can do the job."

"My thought exactly."

Despite the strands of gray that streaked her hair, Neil guessed her age to be just a shade on the other side of forty. She was barely taller than five feet, and though she was well proportioned, it was doubtful she weighed a hundred pounds.

"What's your name?" she asked, and Neil gave it to her.

Ellie Jackson's eyebrows were naturally arched, and her lashes were long and pretty. The eyes themselves were as dark as two pieces of midnight. The irises, being the same shade of black as the pupils, caused them to appear large, exotic, and a little unnerving. She had the sort of eyes that seemed capable of seeing more than nature had meant for eyes to see.

Lifting her chin toward the young waitress who was carrying a load of beef and beans to a couple of miners three tables away, she said, "Chrissy there told me who you're asking for. What's Edward Burke to you?"

"He's nothing to me, really."

"Then why do you want to find him?"

"I don't."

The woman started to push herself up

from her chair. "I don't have time for games, Mister."

"I'm not looking for him, ma'am. The man's dead."

She stopped, and, easing herself back into her seat, she asked, "How would you know that?"

Neil shrugged. "The way I know it for sure is the doctor in Custer City told me. He was with Mister Burke when he died. Mister Burke made it into Custer City, but he'd been mortally wounded out on the trail by robbers trying to steal his gold. Did you know the man, Miss Jackson?"

She nodded. "I knew him. He was a little wild, Eddie Burke was."

"Wild? How so?"

"Just always looking for trouble. Not in a mean sort of way, mind you. He wasn't mean, that boy, just wild and rascally, and easy to lead astray. Why're you interested in him anyhow, Mister Bancroft?"

"It's not him I'm interested in so much as his older sister, Katie."

The arch of the woman's eyebrows went up another half notch. "What makes you think he has a sister by the name of Katie?" she asked.

"That's more of what I learned from the doctor down in Custer. Katie was also with

344

him when he died. Do you know her, too, by chance?"

She held Neil pinned with those eyes for what seemed like a full minute. "What would be your concern with a dead man's sister?"

Neil wasn't sure how to reply to that, and there was another lull in their conversation while he tried to come up with an answer. The lull was long enough that before he finally got out a response, the silence became prickly. "I need to talk to her, that's all," he finally said. "Do you know where I could find her?"

The little woman pushed herself to her feet. "There's no Katie Burke around here, Mister. If you're looking for her, you'd best do it somewhere else." She squinted down at him. "You with the law?"

"No, ma'am."

"Pinkertons?"

Neil thought that was an odd question. "No," he said, "not them, either. I'm just here for myself, Miss Jackson. I want to visit with Katie Burke, and I plan to do it before I leave Deadwood, however long that might take."

"Well, like I said, there's no one named Katie Burke here, and there never has been. You best be on your way."

345

"I'll stay here and finish my beer, and then I'd like to visit with some of your employees and customers to see if any of them might know her. I'm sure her brother lived here in Deadwood, Miss Jackson, and I know she was traveling with him when he was killed. That makes me think she might've been living here as well." He found the woman's dark eyes in the dim light. "And I know for certain she came back to the Deadwood area last night. I expect someone in this crowd might be familiar with the Burkes, and I'd like to visit with them if you don't mind."

She placed both of her small hands on the table and leaned toward him. "That's just it, Mister Bancroft. I do mind. You see, Deadwood isn't like other places you might've been. Around here, if folks don't want to be found, then that's their right. That goes for men, and that goes for women, too. So unless you're the law with writs and warrants, I say get out. We don't like snoopers."

Neil also leaned across the table and held her gaze. She was standing, but even so, she wasn't much higher than he was. "It is my intention to find Kathleen Burke." He started to say more but stopped himself. As far as he was concerned, there was no more he needed to say.

"Not in here, you're not. The only thing in here you're going to find, Mister, is the door, and if you can't do that on your own, I'd be happy to have a couple of the boys give you a hand."

It was a threat and a promise rolled into one. After a bit, Neil asked, "What is it you're trying to hide, ma'am?" He was certain there was something.

She straightened when he asked that. Her strong jaw tightened, and her nostrils flared. Neil could tell from both the position she held in this establishment and the look on her taut face that, against any odds, this was a woman who accomplished what she set out to do, and what she wanted right now was to be rid of Neil Bancroft.

Turning away from Neil, she called out to one of the thugs standing beside the bar. "Mister Porter, would you and Mister Long step over here, please?"

Neil came to his feet. "This isn't going to stop me," he said.

The woman made no response. She was finished with Neil. When Porter and Long arrived, she said, "Would you escort this gentleman outside?"

"Glad to, ma'am," said Porter. There was the sound of the deep South in Porter's voice, yet despite her race, the man did not seem to mind in the least taking his orders from Ellie Jackson. The woman's dominion in this saloon did not seem to be questioned.

She stared into Neil's eyes as she spoke to the two ruffians. "And take him out through the alley," she added. Neil could guess what that meant. If she just wanted him thrown out, she'd have him tossed into the street. By having him taken to the back alley, she was telling her boys to provide Neil with something to remember them by.

Without saying more, she turned and disappeared into her office.

"They's two ways to get to the alley, Mister," said Long, a wiry man, an inch or two taller than Neil. "They's the easy way, and then, a-course, they's the hard way." He looked toward Porter and laughed, showing teeth almost as black as Ellie Jackson's eyes. Apparently they were going to pretend, at least until they got him outside, that if he cooperated, they meant him no harm.

Neil smiled. "Well, fellas, not being a fool, I reckon I'll choose the easy way. How's that?"

"It's smart," said Porter. Porter was a barrel-chested lug with orange hair that he combed straight back from his low forehead.

He motioned toward the rear of the building, and Neil picked up his hat and headed in that direction.

As they walked, Neil said, "Now, boys, I have the feeling that when we get outside, you're going to want to make this situation nastier than it needs to be."

"Shut up and keep walking," said Porter.

"I just want to let you know," Neil went on, "that there's no reason why this has to be unpleasant. We can go into the alley back here, and instead of making a fuss, we can just bid one another a cordial fare-thee-well. That way no one has to get hurt. I can be on my way, and you two fellas can go back to picking the lice out of each other's hair, or whatever it is that a couple of gorillas like you do in your spare time."

There was a few seconds' pause while it sunk through Porter's and Long's skulls what it was Neil had just said. Finally, Porter spoke to his partner. "I'm gonna like bustin' this one up."

"Maybe we can give him some special treatment," said Long, who took something from his pocket, then reached out and held his fist in front of Neil's face so that Neil could see the shiny brass knuckles that ringed his fingers. He then whispered in Neil's ear, "Before I'm done, I'm gonna make you get down on your knees and beg me to stop hurting you."

Neil knew it had not been wise to provoke these two, but he figured he wouldn't be able to talk his way out of this mess anyway, so what was there to lose? Besides, he'd had enough. In the last nine days, he'd been beaten and shot, he'd had to watch his best friend die, he'd damn near gotten hanged, and he'd had his heart stomped on by the lying Katie Burke.

Neil was done.

When they got to the door leading into the alley, Neil pushed it open and stepped outside. Porter came out directly behind him, and Long brought up the rear. As they walked into the alley, Neil sensed Porter reaching toward him to lift the gun from Neil's holster, and as Porter did that, Neil heard Long shut the door. Before Porter's hand could close on the Colt's grip, Neil beat him to it. In one quick move, he drew the pistol, spun, and brought the barrel down with everything he had into the middle of Porter's low brow. Blood squirted from Porter's forehead, and the big man hit the ground like a sack of onions toppling off a cart. Neil leaped over Porter's prone body, caught Long by the throat, and shoved the short-barreled Colt into the man's left eye with enough force to cause him to cry out in pain. Neil plowed him backwards, smashing him against the wall. Then, as he held him in place with the Colt buried in his eye, he reached inside Long's jacket and pulled out a medium-caliber Smith and Wesson. He tossed it into the darkness and then drove his knee into the man's groin. Long screamed, grabbed his balls with both hands, and slid down the wall to the ground.

Neil squatted in front of him, leaving the end of the Colt jammed in Long's swelling eye.

"Give me a reason not to kill you, son of a bitch."

"What?" Long asked in a choked voice.

"You heard me." Neil peeled back the short-barreled's hammer.

"I — I don't know what you mean."

"You can't think of even one good reason why you shouldn't die?"

Long looked like he was about to burst into tears. His features came all unscrewed, and his face started to fall apart.

"Puh-puh-please, Mister, d-d-don't shoot. We wasn't gonna hurt you none. Really, we was only foolin' with ya."

Neil took a handful of Long's oily hair, pulled back the Colt, and smashed it into the side of Long's face. The man's jawline split open, and a sheet of red cascaded onto the narrow left lapel of his ugly suit.

"Don't lie to me, you bastard," Neil said through clenched teeth, "or somebody'll be scrubbing your brains off this wall." The white of Long's left eye had gone blood-red. Without being gentle, Neil reinserted the Colt's muzzle into that red eye, and as he did, Long let out a terrified whimper.

"Now, listen close and answer the question. Do you want to die?"

Long's one good eye was as wide as a cup saucer. "N-no, no, sir, I don't. I surely don't."

"Well, that's unfortunate," Neil said, "because things're looking *real* bad for you right now." Neil slipped an extra little taunt into the tone of his voice. He didn't like this fella. "I'd say your only chance to come out of this in one piece is to tell me everything I want to know."

"Tell you everything you want to know?" Long repeated. He then began to shiver as though the month had been magically transformed from July to December.

"What do you know about a fella by the name of Edward Burke?" Neil asked.

"Edward Burke?"

"Goddamn it, man, are you going to repeat everything I say?" Neil still held a fistful of Long's hair, and he slammed the man's head back, hitting the wall hard enough to cause the eyeball without the pistol sticking in it to do a slow roll upward. Long was losing consciousness, but Neil wouldn't have it. "No, you don't," he said, and he shook Long's head the way a terrier shakes a rat. After a bit, Long's eyelid fluttered, and the eye slid back into view.

Once Neil was sure the man was still with him, he bent close to Long's face. "I'm asking you about Edward Burke. Did you ever hear of him?"

"Y-yes, sure — sure I have. Edward Burke. Sure. He used to come in all the time."

"What do you know about him?"

"Nothin'."

Neil raised the Colt, and Long cringed. "No, please," he shouted. "I don't know nothin' about 'im, really, except he had a cabin out south of town. It burned down a while back, and Burke stopped comin' around at about the same time."

"Did he work?" Neil asked. "Did he have a job?"

"I ain't never heard of him havin' no job, except maybe doin' a little placer minin' when he first come to town. He always seemed to have money, though, at least enough to keep 'im in whores and whiskey.

Sheriff Bullock even come in once about a year ago and talked to Burke about it. He talked to Miss Cardinale and Miss Jackson about it, too."

"What was he asking?"

"I guess the sheriff was just wonderin' how a fella who ain't got no job and no skills at gamblin' could always have money in his jeans."

"How did Burke answer?"

"Just a smartass answer is all I remember. I think he said he made it writin' poetry for *Harper's Bazaar* magazine, or some such. Burke was a smartass from what I could tell."

"Why did the sheriff question Miss Cardinale and Miss Jackson?"

"I don't know. It was their place where Burke was always spendin' his money. I reckon the sheriff thought they might have some idea where it come from."

"Did they?"

"Nah, as far as I know, they jus' told 'im they didn't care where it come from as long as it ended up in their till. Inside that bar, them two women don't put up with much from nobody, even sheriffs."

"What about kin?" Neil asked.

"What about kin?" Long repeated.

Neil jerked the man's head away from the

wall again, but before he could slam it back, Long screamed. "No, no, please, I'm sorry. Don't. Please."

Neil didn't smash his head, but he bent Long's neck backwards, forcing his face up, and shoved the Colt once more into the man's left eye. "Burke had a sister," he said, "by the name of Katie. I want to find her."

"He never had no sister that I know of."

"I heard that a while back, Katie Burke bucked faro in a place down in Cheyenne. Did a woman by that name ever do that here?"

"No, sir. I ain't never heard of no Katie Burke, and I done tol' you ever'thin' I know about Edward Burke. I swear to God." Sweat sparkled across Long's brow as he looked up at Neil with his one working eye. It was clear that the man was scared, and Neil figured he was too scared to lie.

"All right," Neil said, and he let go of Long's hair and stood.

Long exhaled, put his hand to the eye that had been holstering Neil's Colt for the last five minutes, then slumped back against the wall with his legs extended in front of him. He was still shivering and fighting back tears.

The man was pathetic, and as Neil stared down at him, he said, "I guess I won't kill you after all." He started to leave, but after a couple of steps, he stopped, turned on his boot heel, and came back. Without saying a word, he kicked Long in his right thigh as hard as he could. Neil figured he was not above kicking a man when he was down, and in Long's case, it seemed to be the right thing to do.

When Neil's boot landed, Long let out a yelp and grabbed his leg. "Jesus Christ," he whined, "why'd you do that?"

"Because I didn't like your remark about making me beg. That kind of trashy behavior is just uncalled-for."

NINETEEN

The next morning, after eating a quick breakfast of oatmeal and coffee at a restaurant next to the Wentworth House, Neil had a couple of ideas he wanted to try out.

First, he walked the two blocks to the post office and asked the postmaster if he had any memory of delivering mail to a woman by the name of Katie Burke.

The man gave the question some thought as he scratched his head. "No, sir," he said. "I don't. I'm sure she don't have a box, and if I ever had anything for someone by that name through General Delivery, I sure don't recall it."

Disappointed, Neil thanked him and made his way down the street to the office of Sheriff Seth Bullock.

The office itself was made up of one small room with a door leading to the back where Neil assumed the cells were located. When he came in, there was a young man of

357

maybe nineteen or twenty sitting with his boots on the desk and his chair tipped back. His chin rested on his chest, and Neil could hear the deep, even breathing of sleep.

It took Neil's clearing his throat three times to wake the man. When he did jerk awake, he almost toppled the chair over backwards and began pinwheeling his arms in an effort to stay upright.

"Whoa, watch it there, fella," Neil said as he shot a hand out and caught the man's foot just before he went tumbling ass-over-teakettle.

Once all four chair legs were firmly planted, the man said, "Whew, that was a close one." He looked up and smiled.

It was clear to Neil right away that this young fella had something less than the regular amount of intellect.

"Thanks, Mister. If you hadn't-a caught me, why, I'd-a gone over for sure."

"I didn't mean to scare you," Neil said. "Sorry for waking you up like that."

"Ah, that's all right. I gotta be sweeping out the cells anyhow." He stood and extended his hand. "My name's Skeeter Combs. What's yours?"

"Neil Bancroft. Nice to meet you, Mister Combs." He shook the man's hand.

"Just call me Skeeter. That's what everybody calls me. I'm the jailer here. Wanna cuppa coffee? I got some on the stove. It's already cooked up."

"Sure, I believe I will."

Skeeter poured two cups and brought them over. "It's nice and hot," he said.

"Thanks." Neil took a sip and then said, "The reason I came in, Skeeter, is I'd like to speak to Sheriff Bullock. Do you know where I can find him?"

"He ain't here," said Skeeter.

Neil nodded. "Yes, sir, I can see that he's not. Do you know where he is?"

"Sheriff Code from over to Custer come by t'other day, and him and Sheriff Bullock went to Lead."

Neil remembered that Luke Sylar mentioned that Sheriff Code was coming to Deadwood to tell the wives of the murdered men what had happened. Once he got here, Code must have asked Bullock for help with the unpleasant job.

"Why Lead?" Neil asked. "I thought the men killed in the stage holdup were from here. Did some of them live up there?"

"Yes, sir, one did. Webster Thurmond. He was the driver." Skeeter's brow wrinkled up. "Say, wait a minute. How did you know about that holdup? Sheriff Code and Sheriff Bullock said they didn't want the word on that to get out yet, and you are the second person what's come in here since yesterday who already knew about it."

"I am? Who else came in?"

"Why Miss Cardinale did."

"Paulina Cardinale? The woman who owns the gambling house?"

"That's the one, all right. Sure don't see her much, but there she was, big as life, standin' right where you are, wantin' to see the sheriff. I told her he went to Lead, the same as I just told you."

"Did she say how she knew about the holdup, Skeeter?"

"Nah, sir, but she knew about it, all right. Sheriff Bullock ain't gonna like that, neither. He said he didn't want no one to know until him and Sheriff Code had the wives done told."

"Did the sheriff say when he'd be back?"

Skeeter looked excited. "Yes, sir, he sure did. He always tells me stuff like that. He says I'm his right-hand man. He says to me, 'Skeeter Combs, you are my right-hand man.' That's just what he says." Skeeter offered a wide, proud grin.

"Well," probed Neil, "when did he say?"

"When? Why, heck, he's always sayin' it. 'Skeeter, you're my right-hand man.' That's what he always says."

"No, no, what I mean is when did the sheriff say he'd be coming back to Dead-wood?"

"Not until the end of the week or the first of next week. After him and Sheriff Code's finished up in Lead, they's going over to Custer City to investigate the crime. They doubt the robbers are still around there, but they figure that's the place to start the search."

So the sheriff wouldn't be back until the end of the week at the earliest, Neil thought. That was no good. He wanted to find out why Sheriff Bullock had been asking questions about Edward Burke. Clearly, he knew the man, and he had an opinion of him, too, judging by the sort of questions he'd been asking.

"Well, thanks, Skeeter, for your help." Neil held up the cup. "And for the coffee, too." He took a big slug, finishing off what he had left. "You make a fine cup of coffee."

Skeeter beamed. "Sheriff Bullock says my coffee is the best."

"Sheriff Bullock sounds like a real nice fella."

Neil stepped out of the sheriff's office onto the wooden sidewalk and pulled a long nine from his pocket. As he went through the

361

process of licking it, biting off the end, and firing it up, he considered what to do next. He was low on choices.

It seemed as if the more he poked around, the less he knew. He was getting no answers but a lot more questions. Like: what was Ellie Jackson trying to hide? And how in the hell could Paulina Cardinale know about the holdup so soon after it happened?

He huffed out a blue smoke ring that drifted away on the warm morning air.

Unless, perhaps, she knew about it *before* it happened. He couldn't picture a situation where an old biddy like that would have inside knowledge on a stage holdup. But who knew? Sheriff Code had said it was the feeling among the lawmen that someone was tipping the bandits off as to when and where gold was being shipped. The sheriff even speculated that it was some dance-hall whore who might be doing it.

Neil found it hard to believe that any man would be lonely enough to whisper anything into the ear of Paulina Cardinale, but he was still curious.

He expected that he'd worn out his welcome at the Ace High the night before, but he decided to walk over and see if he couldn't get an audience with the elusive Miss Cardinale, or at least ask a few more questions of her manager, Ellie Jackson.

The place was not as crowded at eight o'clock in the morning as it had been at eight o'clock last night. Only a half dozen tables were running any games, and Neil could count on one hand the number of men leaning against the bar.

He scanned the room. There were a few head-busters standing around, although not so many as the night before, and Ellie Jackson, Porter, and Long were nowhere in sight. Which was good. After his encounter with Porter and Long, these muscle boys had no doubt heard his name, but he didn't expect any of them knew his face.

Neil stepped to the bar and was greeted by a bartender sporting a waxed mustache with a seven-inch wingspan.

"Mornin', Mister. What can I get ya?"

It seemed a little early to Neil, and he looked down the line to see what other folks were drinking. It appeared that these boys didn't relate their drinking habits to the time of day. Every man among them was throwing back either beer or whiskey just the same as always.

Neil inspected the shelves behind the bartender. "Do you have any ginger beer back there?" he asked.

"One ginger beer coming up." The bartender pulled the cork on a green bottle that was an inch or so shorter than his mustache was wide, and said, "That'll be a nickel."

Neil paid the man, lifted the bottle, and took a sip. As the sweet, carbonated liquid washed down his throat, he looked up into the stony eyes of Paulina Cardinale. He stared into that rigid face and wondered if any man had ever received affection from this woman.

Earlier, he'd been unable to get so close, and he could see things in the portrait now that he'd missed the night before. Her hair was raven black, and her cheekbones high. He'd noticed that last night even from halfway across the smoke-filled room. From here, though, he could see that those stony eyes were blue, and that, all in all, she was attractive in a mean and heartless sort of way. Still, even as hard as she appeared, she looked as though there was a time in her distant past when those edges might have been just a little softer.

He guessed that it wasn't as much her physical appearance that was unappealing as the stiff way she held herself and the stark way she dressed. The neck of her dark frock rose to the line of her jaw, and its buttons were . . .

Neil felt his mouth drop open as he

lowered the bottle of ginger beer to the bar.

Clipped to the woman's dress just above her left breast was Henri Chenal's Flying Swan.

Neil pushed himself away from the bar and headed for the staircase leading to the second floor. Before he made it all the way, two of the big men in suits saw what he was doing and stepped in his path.

Neil lifted his left hand, pointed it at the men, and said in a cold, even voice, "I'd advise you two to step aside."

Before either of the men could respond, Neil heard someone behind him call out, "She doesn't want to see you. What she wants, Mister Bancroft, is for you to leave town."

Neil stopped and turned. It was Ellie Jackson standing at the doorway to her office.

She nodded toward a table. "Sit down. You and I need to talk."

The two big men still stood at the foot of the stairs, but they seemed less confident than they had before Miss Jackson had called out Neil's name. He looked past them toward the banister on the second floor and the apartment beyond that.

Ellie Jackson walked to a chair that was shoved up to a table and pulled it out for

Neil to sit down. "Please," she said.

With some reluctance, he did as she asked. Once he was seated, she sat across from him.

"I'll have you know that you cost me twelve dollars and seventy-five cents last night. That's what the doc charged for sewing up the hired help. Eighteen stitches in Mister Porter's forehead, and nearly twice that many in various places on poor Mister Long, including four stitches in his eyelid. I don't reckon I ever heard of anyone getting cut in the eyelid."

Neil sat silent.

"You play rough, Mister Bancroft. Porter's still having dizzy spells, and Long — well, sir, I don't know quite what to think about Mister Long. You must've put a real scare into that man. He doesn't hardly seem to be the same fella as he was only yesterday."

"If he's a different fella, then that's got to be an improvement."

Miss Jackson smiled. "What is it you want, Mister Bancroft?"

"I want to find Katie Burke. I don't mean her, or you, or Miss Cardinale any harm. All I want is to find Katie."

"You seemed to be taking a real interest in that portrait over yonder." She moved her head in the direction of the bar.

"She's wearing a pin. It's called the Flying Swan. From what I've been told, it's one of a kind."

"What you've been told is true. It was a gift to Annabelle Burke by her lover. That was in St. Louis, Missouri, back in 1866. Annabelle Burke is the woman in that painting you were staring at so hard a minute ago. She received that pin from a no-good Frenchie who later broke her heart."

"Henri Chenal."

"That's the man. Henri Chenal. Like Mister Long, she became a different person after that, only with Missus Burke it wasn't an improvement. She got religion. Too much religion, some might say. Her manner became stern." Ellie Jackson looked down at her dark hands folded together on the table. "Her young daughter never stopped loving her, though, and Missus Burke knew that, and the night she passed on, she pinned that swan to her daughter's dress. In all the years since, I have never once seen that girl without it." She looked up and met Neil's eyes.

"If that woman in the picture's not Paulina Cardinale, then are you telling me that Katie . . ."

The tiny woman nodded. "Her middle name is Paulina, and she thought that

'Cardinale' had a nice, exotic ring to it, suitable to the proprietress of an establishment offering various entertainments. That's not uncommon around here, Mister Bancroft. There are quite a few female owners of gaming establishments here in Deadwood, and, as far as I know, there's not one woman among them who's using the name she was born with." She glanced across the room at the picture. "An artist came through a couple of years back, and Katie had him paint that portrait of her mother from an old daguerreotype. I doubt that Miss Annabelle, having become a righteous Southern Baptist, would appreciate her current location hanging above whiskey bottles in a den of iniquity like the Ace High Saloon. But Katie loved her mother very much, and she thinks of it as a place of honor, even if her mother wouldn't."

Neil looked toward the apartment. "I'm going up," he said, and he pushed himself away from the table and started for the stairs. The two head-busters stiffened.

Miss Jackson came to her feet, too. "Please, Mister Bancroft, I was telling you the truth when I said she doesn't want to see you."

"I'll let her tell me that herself." He continued toward the stairs.

"She can't. She's not there."

Neil ignored her, made eye contact with the two goons, and lowered his hand to his holster. "I'm going up those stairs, boys. I hope I don't have to put any holes in either one of you to do it."

The one on the right blinked. The one on the left swallowed hard.

Again breaking the rule of gunfighting, he said, "I'll do my best to miss your vitals, but there are no guarantees. Do you fellas feel lucky?"

"Let him by," Miss Jackson said, and the two men looked relieved as they stepped aside and allowed Neil to pass.

He took the steps two at a time, crossed the landing, and knocked on the door. "Katie," he called out. "It's Neil." There was no response. "We need to talk. Let me in, Katie, please." He heard a kind of desperation in his voice that made him cringe.

Miss Jackson came up behind him, and with a wistful expression in those black eyes, she said, "Goodness gracious, but you do have it bad, don't you, Mister Bancroft?"

"I just want to talk to her, ma'am, that's all. Just talk."

"I told you she's not here."

Neil gave her a doubtful look.

"Go on in. See for yourself."

He turned the knob and stepped into the apartment's front parlor. The place consisted of a half dozen well-furnished rooms, and Neil walked through them all.

Ellie Jackson hadn't lied.

When he came back into the parlor, Ellie was waiting for him. "Until last night, she hasn't wanted to visit much since she got back. In fact, I didn't hear about the two of you until after I told her some wild-eyed cowboy named Bancroft had just beat the holy hell out of our two toughest men. Then it was like a dam busted. We were up most all of last night with her filling me in."

Neil's mouth felt dry, and the oatmeal he'd had for breakfast churned in his stomach. "Who are you to her?" he asked, dropping onto a divan upholstered with a luxurious flowered pattern. He felt suddenly drained.

"Annabelle Burke was her mother," Ellie said, "but it's me who raised her up."

Neil lifted his eyes. "You?"

"That's right." She folded her arms. "I reckon you've got enough invested in all this, Mister Bancroft, to learn about a few things. Would you agree with that?"

"Yes, ma'am, I surely would." He took off his hat and ran his hand through his hair.

Leaning against the doorframe, Ellie said, "You asked who I am to her. Well, sir, I was born a slave on her father's plantation in Itawamba County, Mississippi. When I was fifteen, Albert and Annabelle Burke had their first baby, a girl, which they named Kathleen. It was my place to tend to her. The same with little Edward a couple of years later when he came along."

"So you've known her all her life."

"I have. In those days, the mistress of the house didn't have time for such things as tending to babies. That wasn't unusual, of course. That's just the way it was. Then there was the war and Reconstruction, and after that, everything changed. Mister Burke fell with Barksdale at Gettysburg, the plantation was lost, and Missus Burke took me and the children up to St. Louis. We were there for eight hard years, during which time she met *Monsieur*," she pronounced it *Mon Sewer,* "Chenal."

"The man who gave her the Flying Swan."

"The man who gave her the Flying Swan, and, like I said before, the man who also gave her a broken heart. A couple of years later, Missus Burke finally died of that broken heart. When that happened, Edward headed out west, and Katie married the doctor who had treated her mother — yet another despicable fella, I might say."

"Katie married a doctor?" God, Neil thought, things were moving much too fast for him to keep up. "So she is married after all?"

"She was. It was a short marriage, thank the Lord. He moved us all to Amarillo where he contracted diphtheria in '77 and died. She stopped using the man's name as soon as we put him in the ground. He was a cocaine addict, a drunkard, and a wife-beater."

"It doesn't sound like life's been too kind to her."

"No, sir, it hasn't. The only good luck that girl's ever had has been whatever luck she made for herself. She tried to find work in Amarillo for a while, but she only had the nursing skills the doctor had taught her, which wasn't much, and, when you get right down to it, the only real talent she had as a nurse, anyway, was her compassion. When she had no success at nursing, she learned to deal faro. And she got good at it, too. In '79 we moved up here to take advantage of the rush for gold."

Neil ran his hand across his face and down over the back of his tight neck. He'd wanted some answers, and now they were coming in a flood. "I wish I'd ordered something stronger than ginger beer downstairs," he said. He felt as jittery as a cat.

Miss Jackson smiled and crossed the room to a cabinet. "What would you like?" she asked. "Whiskey? Brandy?"

Neil shrugged. "Ten minutes ago, I thought it was too early, but I'm thinking I was wrong. Some of that brandy will do just fine."

She poured him one and one for herself. "I don't usually do this so early myself, but this morning it seems fitting." She handed Neil a snifter of the amber liquid and sat in a wing chair across from the divan. "When Katie came back the other night, I thought all of this bad business was behind us. But it's not, is it? Not by a mile."

"What's going on?" Neil asked.

"What did she tell you was going on when you two first met?"

"That she was living in Amarillo, and her husband, Edward Burke, had come up here to mine. She said he had struck it rich, but that he'd been killed by robbers as he left to return to Texas. Why would she tell me all those lies? Why would she say she was married when she wasn't?"

Miss Jackson smiled. "Well, the lie was that she was married to Edward. What she was really telling you is that she was a widow, and she told you that because she knows men so well."

"What's that supposed to mean?"

"In spite of working in rowdy gambling emporiums down in Amarillo, and even owning one here in Deadwood for a while now, Katie Burke is not a loose woman." She added with a smile, "Don't misunderstand me. There are loose women around. We have plenty of 'em ourselves, but Katie Burke never was one. Over the years, though, she's learned a lot about how men think." Ellie tapped her temple with an index finger. "Now, if she'd told you she was a single girl, once you two got out on that lonesome Dakota Trail, she might've had to deal with you in a way that she didn't want to. But if you thought she was a recent widow, you would be less likely to try anything. And she *is* a widow. What she said was the truth."

"Sort of."

"No, sir, she's a widow, all right. It's just that her husband died years ago — long enough ago that a big ol' healthy fella like yourself might've looked on her the same way as you would if she was single. But since, as far as you knew, her husband had been in the ground only a few months, that slowed you down some, now, didn't it?"

Neil didn't answer, but he had to agree there was some truth in what she said.

"I can see it didn't stop you," Ellie allowed, "but it did slow you down. Also, those men were after her, and who knows, any lie she might drop about herself along the way might throw them off the trail. She told me that when she first left Deadwood, she dyed her hair blond. She hated it, and it wasn't long before she changed it back, but for a while there, Katie Burke was a blondie." The tiny woman raised her snifter, and just before she took a sip, she added with a smile, "My little Katie-bug with yella hair. Lordy, I'd've loved to've seen that."

"There's a lot I don't understand about all this," Neil said, "but I guess the first thing I'd like to know is why would she lie and say her dead husband had been a miner?"

"Because she figured you were an honest man, and if you knew the truth, you wouldn't've helped her out."

"That doesn't make any sense."

"We talked about you a lot last night, Mister Bancroft. Or I should say that Katie talked, and I listened. She found out as much as she could about you over at Fetterman before she approached you. She didn't know when or where for sure, but she'd heard you had participated in the Indian wars. She also heard that you were more than competent with a gun. And from what she says, I guess she even gave you a little test to find out just how fast you could think on your feet."

"Why was she afraid an honest man wouldn't help her if he knew the truth?"

"Because that gold she was after wasn't dug out of the ground — at least, it wasn't dug out of the ground by Edward Burke. It was gold stolen from the Deadwood-to-Rapid City stage. Eddie ran with Randall Frost's gang, Mister Bancroft. Sheriff Bullock suspected it, but he couldn't prove it. What's more, Bullock was convinced that Katie — or Paulina, as he knows her — was learning when the gold shipments were going out and then giving that information to Frost. The bankers and businessmen around here suspected it, too, and they were putting pressure on Bullock to do something about it or they were going to hire the Pinkertons." She leaned forward in the chair. "But she wasn't doing that, Mister Bancroft. They couldn't prove it because she wasn't doing it, and she never would."

Neil had to agree, although he couldn't imagine why he should give Katie the benefit of the doubt.

"Someone was doing it, though, that's for sure. Frost knew which stage was carrying the major shipments, but it wasn't Katie who was telling him, nor any of her dealers. She made sure of that." Ellie sat back in the chair. "Katie would never help Randall Frost."

"This Frost sounds like a bad one."

"He is a soulless creature, Mister Bancroft. The lowest I've ever run across. That trash who rides with him isn't much better. Our Eddie was a scoundrel, I have to admit, but he was some different than Frost and the others."

"I know from talking to the doc in Custer City that Katie cared a lot for her brother."

"She loved him with all her heart. When the gang robbed the Rapid City stage, there was a bunch of gunplay, and in the confusion, Eddie got hold of the loot, and when he did, he lit out."

"You mean he took off from Frost and the others?"

"That's right. There was a place up in the Hills that he and Katie both knew about, and he holed up there. A couple of days later, he got word down to Katie where he was and that he was leaving. He was going to use all of what they had stolen to get as far away from Randall Frost as he could."

"Did Katie go to him?" Neil asked.

"She did. She rode out and tried to convince him to turn himself in. She said if he didn't, that he'd never be free of either Frost or the law. She figured if he gave the money back and testified against the other gang members, the law would go easier on him, and he could still get out of this without getting killed."

"Sounds like advice he should've taken."

"He never had the chance. Waldo Brickman figured out what Katie was up to, and he gathered up Frost and Hoskins, and they followed her out to where Eddie was hiding. The rest, I guess you already know. Frost shot Eddie. Katie hid the gold, was able to lose them, and got her brother into Custer."

"And after he died, Katie just kept going."

"Yes, sir. She figured she couldn't come back to Deadwood, at least not until the law caught Frost, and even then, she was sure Frost would convince them that she had been the one providing him information on the gold shipments. She ended up running as far away as the Texas Panhandle and then back again with them tracking her down the whole way. She would lose them for a while here and there, but they always turned up. Randall Frost was intent on

378

catching her. He wants more from Katie than gold. He used to tell folks she was his woman, even though everybody within earshot knew it was a lie."

"I think when he was looking for her in Cheyenne, he was telling people she was his wife."

"That sounds like something he'd do, all right. They almost caught her in Cheyenne. By then, they must've figured out she was headed back to the Hills, but they couldn't be sure which way she was going. Katie figures they had to split up, with Frost following the regular stage line up through Rawhide Buttes and the Red Canyon, and Hoskins and Brickman coming the long way by Fort Fetterman."

"That's another thing I don't understand. It was Waldo Brickman who killed Hoskins, his own friend and partner. Why would he do that?"

"Katie couldn't understand that at first, neither. What she finally decided is since Brickman and Hoskins found her, Brickman, being a lot smarter, probably wanted to hold off doing anything until you were out on the prairie or even wait until you got all the way into the Hills and went to get the gold. But Hoskins was a hothead. He made a play in town, but thanks to you, it didn't turn out so good. Brickman must've figured if he let Hoskins shoot you in the back, then the law was going to get involved. If the law got involved, then somebody would soon figure out that Hoskins and Brickman were both wanted men."

Neil let out a long, exhausted breath. It all made sense, but it was a little dumbfounding.

"Katie was determined to get back up here to get the gold. There was no stage to the Hills from Fort Fetterman, so she figured to hire some honest and competent man to get her across the prairie back to Dakota where she would dig up the gold and disappear forever. She knew she was going to have to start all over somewhere, and the idea of starting from scratch didn't appeal to her."

"Even if it meant using ill-gotten gains? After all, she followed her brother out of Deadwood to try to talk him into returning the gold."

"These last months have been hard on her. When she was on the run, she wrote me two letters. One telling me what happened to Eddie and saying she'd decided to use the gold the same way he was planning, to get a new start far away. She wanted to give the Ace High to me. I wrote her back and said I didn't want it — said I'd sell the place and meet her wherever she wanted to go."

"If you did that, you might lead them to her like she led 'em to her brother."

"She thought that, too. She wrote me back saying we had to make a clean break. It was a plan that might've worked, too, except for one thing."

"What's that?"

"She had the bad fortune to fall in love."

TWENTY

At first, Neil wasn't sure he'd heard right. Then what the woman said wormed its way past his confusion. "Love?"

"That's right, Mister Bancroft. She has the sickness just as bad as you."

Neil didn't believe it. "I don't think she's in love. If she was in love, she wouldn't've run off like that back in Custer. She wouldn't have you telling me that she doesn't want to see me and that she wants me the hell out of town — out of Dakota." He put his glass down with enough force to slosh brandy onto the table. "A woman in love doesn't behave like that, Miss Jackson."

"Are you some kind of authority on how women in love behave, Mister Bancroft?" When he didn't answer, she said, "No, I didn't think so." Ellie reached toward the cocktail table between them, opened a pasteboard box, and took out a bonbon. "Care for one?" she asked.

Neil shook his head and picked up his drink.

She lifted the hand that held the candy. "I have to admit to a weakness for chocolate." She lifted her other hand, which held the snifter. "And brandy, too, for that matter." With a smile, she added, "I tell you, Mister Bancroft, to my recollection, we never got this stuff down in the slave quarters." She popped the sweet into her mouth.

Neil smiled, too, which surprised him some. He didn't feel much like smiling, but this little woman had a way about her. He tossed back what was left of his drink and then rolled the empty glass between his palms.

"Katie knew," Ellie continued, "just as soon as you saw those dead men on that stage outside of Custer City that Frost and Brickman were the ones responsible, and she figured they were still close by. That was why she wanted the two of you to get into town as fast as you could. With the price on their heads, she doubted that they'd try anything in town. That was when she decided she didn't want to hold you to your agreement. She'd been considering it for a while, but that's when she decided for sure."

"Before we even got to Custer?"

"That's right. Despite what she told you

back at Fetterman, she knew she could find the gold without your help. She just thought it'd be a good idea to have your able gun for protection along the way." Ellie helped herself to another of Katie's bonbons. "My, oh my," she said, "but these are tasty little devils. You oughta have one."

"What made her change her mind?"

Ellie gave him a bewildered look. "You mean change her mind about the agreement you two struck?"

"Yes, ma'am."

The high arches of her eyebrows moved closer together. "You know something? Katie told me that you weren't the sharpest hoe in the cotton patch, and I see she was right about that."

Neil frowned at that comment, but he was too confused by all this to defend himself.

"She didn't want to see you get hurt, Mister Bancroft. She knows you're capable in a fight, but Waldo Brickman and Randall Frost are something different. Even though he looks a fool, like I said before, Brickman is smart." She paused and ran the tip of her finger around the rim of her glass. "Randall Frost isn't all that smart, but he was the leader of that bunch for one reason and one reason only. He is as mean and deadly as any man who ever walked. He can work a six-gun like other folks bat their eyes. He prides himself on his skill." She lifted her gaze. "It had seemed like a good idea at first, but when it came down to it, Katie didn't want to pit you against those two. She wanted you out of the Hills, and she still does. She says she'll handle this situation on her own. It's her problem."

"If she wanted to take the gold and start over, why did she bring it back to Deadwood?"

"She's not going to use it to start over. She's changed her mind about that, too."

"How do you mean?"

"She's going to make a bargain with the sheriff. She's going to do what she tried to get Eddie to do. She'll return the stolen gold and agree to testify."

Neil nodded. "That's fine," he said. "She should do that."

"She should've done it a year ago," said Ellie, "but it's not so easy. Frost is crazy. He not only threatened her with that business regarding the gold shipments, but he said if she ever turned on him, he'd kill Eddie and me both. He promised that if she ever did something like that, that he would watch us die a slow death and see her rot in prison."

Neil felt his breath get shallow and his heart start to race.

"Now, though," she continued, "I expect we're far beyond worrying about what Frost might say to the law if he's caught. I'm sure that after what's happened these last few months, if Frost gets to Katie, he'll kill her, and he'll do it in the vilest way possible. Katie knows that, too, but she's decided to hell with him. She says that you've given her courage."

"Me?"

"You told her once that as far as you could tell, courage didn't really exist. You said in a bad situation people tend to stop thinking about what *might* happen if they do something and start thinking about what *will* happen if they don't." She sucked a dollop of melted chocolate from her index finger. "You claimed this wasn't anything special — that it was a common trait, and most folks do it naturally without even giving it a second's thought." She paused and smiled before going on. "Neither Katie nor I figure that you've got it exactly right. We doubt that it comes all that natural to most folks, but still, even though your way of looking at things is a little cockeyed, you're a good man, Mister Bancroft, and I think you're good for Katie. That's why I'm talking to you this morning, even though I know my Katie wouldn't want it."

She seemed to be waiting for Neil to say something, but he couldn't say what he was thinking, because what he was thinking was that he wished to God he'd never made those comments about courage. If anything he said ever caused her harm, he would never forgive himself.

"Anyhow, the deal Katie wants to strike with Bullock is she'll return the gold and testify, and in exchange, the law will give her and me protection, and no matter what lies Frost tells, the sheriff won't try to prosecute her."

"I don't know too much about the lawmen around here, but what little I do know, I like. I met Sheriff Code up in Custer, and he seems to be a good, competent fella, and I've known his deputy for years. I haven't met Bullock, but I have met his jailer."

"Skeeter Combs?"

"That's right, and just by how Bullock treats Skeeter, I figure him to be a man of pretty good character."

Ellie nodded. "He can be tough, but he's fair and honest. Katie believes that, too. That's why she sneaked back into Deadwood. The problem is, can she get to Bullock before Frost gets to her? There's been a lot of talk downstairs. The word is that Frost and Brickman are back in the gulch here, too, and they know Katie's here as well."

Neil sat up straighter. "Have they been in the saloon?" he asked.

"No, they'd never come in here. Katie has too much protection."

"Then why in the hell did she leave?"

"In case you haven't noticed, Katie can be a little stubborn."

Neil didn't respond.

"She's determined to see Sheriff Bullock. She tried to yesterday, but he wasn't in, so she went back this morning."

"Wait a minute," Neil said. "Are you sure about that?"

"Of course. She figures now that you're in town, there's no telling what stupid thing you might do, so there's no time to lose. She wants to take care of this right away. About thirty minutes before you came in, she left and headed back over to Bullock's office."

"That doesn't make sense. I spoke to Skeeter Combs this morning. He said Paulina Cardinale was in there yesterday, and he told her that Sheriff Bullock had left for Lead and would be gone until at least the end of the week. She knew that Bullock wouldn't be in his office this morning, and when I was there just a bit ago, Skeeter didn't mention that she'd come back."

Neil could see Ellie Jackson's black eyes fill with worry. She stood and ran from the parlor out onto the balcony that overlooked the Ace High. Neil followed.

"Walter," she called down to the bartender, "did you see Miss Cardinale when she left this morning?"

"Yes, ma'am, I sure did."

"How was she dressed?"

Walter laughed and twisted the end of his long mustache. "Well, not like I've ever seen her dressed before, that's for sure. She looked like she was ready to hit the trail. She had on riding clothes, and she was toting what looked like a brand-new Marlin that was 'bout as big as she is."

Ellie turned to Neil. Anxiety was etched into her strong features, and her fists were clenched at her sides.

Neil was starting to feel some anxiety himself. "Do you think she could be headed up to Lead to find Bullock and Code?" he asked.

"That," Ellie said, "would be just like her."

Neil rushed down the street toward the Wentworth House. When he got there, he spotted a couple of boys shooting marbles in the alley. "Say you two, do you know where the livery stable is over on Sherman?"

The smaller and cockier of the two boys spoke up. "Audie's? Why, sure we do, Mister."

Neil dug into his pocket and came out with four dimes and a couple of nickels. "I want you kids to get over there fast and tell Audie to saddle up Neil Bancroft's roan. You got that?"

"Yes, sir. Neil Bancroft's roan," said the little one. He answered as he stared at Neil's hand — the hand holding the money.

"Here." Neil divided the coins. "There's two bits in it for both of you. Now get along."

The boys shoved the money into their pockets and darted off down the street. Neil ran into the hotel and up to his room. He threw some things into his saddlebags and grabbed his rifle. As he passed the front desk on the way out, he called over his shoulder, "I'm leaving for a while, and I'm not sure when I'll be back. Hold my room."

When Neil arrived at the livery, the roan was hitched to a rail in front. He tied his bags to the saddle, and as he was checking his cinch, Audie came outside.

"That's one mean horse you got there, Mister. I think he's a goddamned meat eater." He rubbed his left forearm. "The

390

son of a bitch bit me so hard he drew blood."

Neil could cuss the roan, but he resented when other folks did it. "Damn, I can't believe that," he said. "I've always found this animal to be as gentle as a pup."

Audie responded to that with a dumbfounded stare.

Neil mounted and turned the roan toward the street. "I'll leave the pack horse and my gear stored with you, if that's all right. I won't be gone long, I hope."

The liveryman nodded. "That's fine. I'll take care of 'em."

Neil touched the brim of his hat and started off. As he rode away, Audie called out, "You best be watchful of that devil you're ridin'. I'm tellin' ya, he ain't no pup."

As Neil came up Main, he spotted a crowd in front of the sheriff's office. There didn't seem to be any order or purpose to the gathering — just a dozen or so people milling about. On the sidewalk in front of the office, a large man wearing a town marshal's badge was talking to a slender gentleman in a dark suit. As they visited, the gentleman held up a small tablet and made notes with the stub of a pencil.

Neil reined in and asked a teenager holding a fishing pole what was going on.

The kid pointed to the slender man and said, "Mister Richard Hughes there is a newspaperman. He went into the sheriff's office a little while ago looking around for any news for his paper." The kid shook his head. "And he sure found some, all right."

"What do you mean?"

"He come across Skeeter Combs shoved back in one of the cells beat near to death."

"Good God," Neil said. "Do they have any idea who did it?"

"Well, that's just it. You know Skeeter ain't the smartest fella to begin with, and from what I hear, he was kinda goin' in and out when Mister Hughes was trying to talk to him. I guess, though, that Skeeter said the ones who done it was Randall Frost and that Brickman fella. But that don't make any sense. Them two's got a price on their head. They don't never even come into Deadwood no more, much less the sheriff's office. Nobody's seen nor heard of 'em for goin' on a year. Ever'body figures ol' Skeeter must have it wrong."

"How bad is he hurt?"

The kid's eyes got big. "Oh, real bad. I seen 'em carry 'im outta there, and he was a mess." The boy swallowed and began to fidget with the line on his rod. "They figure he'll live, but he's bad."

Neil nodded toward the slender man talking to the marshal. "Did that Mister Hughes get out of Skeeter what it was the men wanted?"

"Well, sir, that don't make no sense, neither."

"Why's that?"

"Skeeter said them two fellas'd heard that Miss Cardinale had gone into the sheriff's office last night, and they wanted to know what she was up to. But heck, Miss Cardinale, she ain't been around for months neither. Nobody's seen hide nor hair of her since I can't remember when." He shook his head and added, "So folks figure poor ol' simpleminded Skeeter must've got that part all ass-backwards, too."

"Did Skeeter ever say what he told them about Miss Cardinale?"

The boy glanced around at the crowd, all of whom seemed to be discussing the situation in a kind of shocked stupor. "From what I hear, there wasn't much to tell. I guess Skeeter did let 'em know that she'd been looking for the sheriff, and he told her that the sheriff was up in Lead." Again, the boy shifted his eyes from Neil's and looked down at his fishing rod. "But I guess they worked 'im over anyhow."

Neil thanked the kid for the information

and headed out of town on the southwest trail.

In less than an hour, he was riding up the steep streets of Lead, Dakota Territory, a bustling community built around the gaping maw of the Homestake Mining Company.

The Homestake was the largest, most productive mine in the Black Hills, and the many fine homes snuggled into the steep slopes surrounding the town bore witness to that fact.

Looking around, Neil tried to imagine where Katie might go once she got here. Bullock and Code would have delivered their message and sad cargo to Missus Thurmond, the stage driver's widow, the previous evening, and they might well have headed off for Custer as soon as they had done so. On the other hand, it was possible they had stayed in Lead overnight and had started out early this morning. There was no way to know for sure.

If she could, Katie would want to make certain they were gone from town, though, before she lit out down the trail to Custer trying to catch them. That meant she'd need to talk to someone who had seen them, and the only person Katie could know for sure had seen them would be Missus Thurmond. It only made sense that Katie would go there first with the hope that Bullock might have given the woman some idea of their plans for today. At least that seemed the logical thing to do, and to Neil's way of thinking, Katie Burke was logical to a fault.

As he trotted up Lead's Main Street, he spotted a young man who appeared to be in his late teens or early twenties carrying a large bag of groceries. The man wore the white apron of a store clerk, and it looked as though he was making a delivery. If anyone would know the townspeople and where they lived, it would be a grocer.

"Excuse me, sir," Neil called out as he rode up to the man. "Do you happen to know where I might find the Thurmond residence?"

"Would that be Webster Thurmond?" the young man asked.

Neil couldn't remember what Skeeter had said the man's first name was, but that sounded right. "I believe that's it," he said. "He's a stage driver by trade." He almost said, "He *was* a stage driver," but he caught himself just in time. Not that it would make much difference. Missus Thurmond was the last wife that Code and Bullock had to visit, and the town would know soon enough what had happened.

"Yes, sir, Web Thurmond's house is over on Bleeker Street. Just 'bout half a block off Main here."

Neil touched the brim of his hat, kicked the roan, and found the Thurmond residence in short order.

There were a couple of buggies and a number of horses tied out front. It looked as though the mourners and well-wishers had already begun to arrive. He was glad. The more people there were around, the less awkward it would be.

He tied the roan to a bush away from the other horses. If it was one of his moody days — as judging by what Audie had to say, it must be — the roan could be a bad neighbor. Neil crossed the yard and knocked on the screen door. The morning was already turning warm, and the wooden front door stood open.

There were ten or so people inside. An attractive woman in her early thirties fluttered about, tending to everyone's needs. She answered Neil's knock.

"Yes, sir, could I help you?" she asked, pushing the screen door open a foot or so.

Neil took off his hat. "Yes, ma'am, I sure hope so. I hate to bother you now, but I'm looking for a young woman, and I was thinking she might've stopped by here this morning."

"A young woman?"

"Yes, ma'am. In her twenties, dark hair. She would've been dressed for riding."

She pushed the screen open wider and said, "Come in, please. We're letting in flies."

Neil did as she asked. The front room of the house was small and didn't accommodate this number of people very well. Against the far wall from where Neil stood, atop a long table, lay the body of Webster Thurmond. The last time Neil had seen the man, he had been pulling him out from under the driver's seat of the stage and loading him inside the coach in order to avoid the crows, magpies, and buzzards. That was a detail he would spare the man's friends and family.

The woman extended her hand in a businesslike fashion. As Neil shook it, she said, "I'm Margaret Cosgrove, Edith Thurmond's sister." She nodded toward the crowd. "It's been like this most of last night and all this morning. Web and Edith have a lot of friends."

"Yes, ma'am, I'm sorry to intrude. I know this is a difficult time."

"Yes, it is. My brother-in-law was tended to by the mortician in Custer, but Mister

Farquhar, our local man, is bringing over a casket." She glanced at a small watch pinned to the front of her dress. "He'll be here any time now. I just know he will." It was clear that the woman wished Mister Farquhar would hurry. "Now, what is it you were asking? You're looking for a young woman, did you say?"

"That's right."

"There was a woman here a couple of hours ago asking about Sheriff Bullock. Might that be the one you're after?"

"Yes, ma'am. That's the one, all right. It's my expectation that the sheriff planned to head out for Custer either last night or this morning, and I believe this young woman would've been inquiring as to when he might've left. It's very important to her that she not miss him."

"I didn't speak to the sheriff myself. I wasn't here last night when they arrived with the . . ." she cast a nervous glance at the body across the room, "with the horrible news. But when the young woman was here, my sister told her that the two sheriffs said they would be leaving town last night as soon as they had some supper. They hoped to make Rochford, but they doubted they would get that far. They were traveling by buckboard, you know, so they didn't expect to be making very good time."

"So they left Lead last night, did they?"

"That is what I'm given to believe, yes, sir."

With that kind of head start, Neil knew that Katie would never catch them. The question was, would she go ahead and follow them, or would she return to Deadwood and wait for Bullock to do the same?

"When your sister provided that information, did the young lady indicate whether she would follow after them?"

"That was the impression I got, yes, sir. She said she had hoped to catch them on the trail, but it looked as though she'd have to ride all the way into Custer."

"Well, thank you, ma'am. I better get going. I appreciate the information. You've been a big help. If she's got a two-hour head start, then it'll take me at least five or six hours of hard riding to catch her." He shrugged and offered a smile. "It looks to be a long day."

As he turned toward the screen door, the woman said, "That young lady is very beautiful. I can see why she's so popular."

Neil stopped. "I beg your pardon, ma'am?"

"About an hour after she left, another gentleman stopped by here asking for her, too, and he was just the nicest man that you'd ever want to meet." A thought seemed to cross her mind. "Well, here, I know you're in a hurry, but if you have just a second, I'd love to show you what he gave us. It was just the most wonderful thing. Can you spare the time?"

"Sure," Neil said. "I guess."

The woman went to a chest of drawers in the corner and pulled out a twelve-by-nine-inch folder constructed of stiff white paper. As she returned, she said, "He told us that he'd heard of our terrible loss, and that when he was a child, his father always performed this service free of charge for the family of every departed soul in their small town back in Indiana. It was just a little token, he said, to help them better remember their loved one. His father was sort of an artist, you see, and he'd passed his skill on to this kind gentleman who was here." She handed Neil the folder. "I couldn't believe how quickly he did it. I swear it didn't take him three minutes once he got started."

Neil opened the folder. Pasted inside was a perfect profile in black silhouette of the dead man on the table.

TWENTY-ONE

Neil pushed the roan harder than he should've for more than an hour before he finally admitted to himself that he would never catch up to Frost and Brickman before they caught up to Katie. It wasn't possible. His only hope was that he could get to them before they killed her. And, he reassured himself, there was a chance of that since he doubted they would kill her right away.

That thought did not make him feel much better.

If he was going to be of any help to her, though, he had to consider his horse. He reined in and slowed the pace, but he still pushed the animal, stopping only twice for water — once on Whitewood Creek and once a couple of hours later at some little damp spot of a stream. If the stream had a name, Neil didn't know it.

At the second stop, Neil gave the roan a

nose bag of oats but didn't have the patience to allow the animal to finish. After ten minutes, Neil pulled off the bag and mounted up.

"Sorry, roan," he said as they returned to the trail, "but once we've taken care of business, I'll let you eat your fill. That's a promise."

It was going onto four o'clock in the afternoon when Neil spotted the smoke of a campfire swirling above the trees. He knew it could be anyone, but the population in this part of the Hills was sparse, and travelers along here were rare. He felt sure it was Frost and Brickman.

Castle Creek ran close by, and when the roan smelled the water, he got antsy and even harder to control than usual.

"It's all right, boy. Settle down. Your part's almost done." Neil left the trail, and when he did, he lost sight of the smoke. It made sense that they would camp close to the creek, though, and if he stayed near the water, he'd come to them eventually.

Just less than a quarter of a mile upstream from where he figured they were, he allowed the roan to drink. He then dismounted and had a drink himself.

The water was cool and clean and eased the sour feeling that had settled into the pit of his stomach. This was a feeling he'd had before. He knew what it was — pre-battle jitters, and the jitters came to everybody in one way or another. With Neil, it was a sour stomach. With Rafael, it had been a twitch. The twitch in Raf's face was the damnedest thing Neil had ever seen. It was like a tiny toad had climbed down inside Raf's skin just below his right eye.

Sometimes, Neil thought, Rafael seemed very far away, and other times, like now, he was close.

The day was warm, and Neil pulled a bandana from his back pocket, dipped it in the creek, and tied it around his neck. He then filled his canteens and led the roan away from the water into the trees. There, he took off the saddle and replaced the bridle with a halter. He dug the hobbles out of his bag, draped them over his shoulder, and led the roan back for another drink. This time, he let him have a little more than he had before and then took him back into a grassy area where he bent and buckled on the hobbles.

"You could use a good brushing," Neil said, "but there's no time for it now."

He pulled the last of the oats from the gear and poured them onto the grass. "You get to take a breather," he said, and the horse snorted.

Neil liked this surly bastard, though he couldn't for the life of him figure out why. He'd had other horses over the years that rode as well and were just as strong and easy to look at, but this mean son of a bitch had won his heart.

Neil rubbed the animal's neck and whispered in his ear. "I'll be back for you soon," he said. Then, as an afterthought, he added, "If I don't get shot."

He felt bad about leaving the horse hobbled like this in case the worst did happen, but he decided there was nothing else he could do. Besides, he'd be back. That was what he told himself, anyway. A fella needed to keep his outlook bright.

Neil took the empty oat sack back to his saddle and tucked it into one of the bags. He then dug out some extra rifle shells, shoved them into his pocket, and pulled the Marlin from its scabbard.

He saw the roan was making short work of his oats, and Neil wished he had more to give him, but the grass here was high and green, and the water close by. He'd be fine.

"See ya in a bit, roan," Neil said, and when he did, he wondered if Katie was right. Maybe he should give this ill-tempered horse a name. He tried to imagine what a fitting name would be, and finally decided "Roan" was good enough.

What was it the poet had said? Neil tried to recall but couldn't. He was sure that he'd once read something about how, in the end, a name didn't mean all that much. The true nature of the thing being named didn't change, no matter what it was called.

That was sure true of the roan. He could name this beast "Fluffy" if he wanted to, but a man would still be wise to make his turns wide when he walked behind him.

"I'll be back," Neil said again. "You rest for a while." The horse lifted his head, offered Neil what looked to be an annoyed expression, and returned to his supper.

Neil made his way through the timber. The trees provided perfect cover, but it was quiet enough out here that he had to move easy to keep from making too much noise. He had figured Frost and Brickman to be about a quarter of a mile away, but as it happened, he'd misjudged. He came upon them less than three hundred yards downstream from where he'd hobbled the roan.

He could smell the fire before he could see anything. They had made their camp in a small clearing, and as Neil edged his way up to where the trees stopped, he could see the back of a man sitting at the fire. The man was drinking a cup of coffee and smoking a cigarette.

Standing in the tall grass at the far side of the clearing was another man. This man was buttoning his pants, and as he did, he stared down at something lying at his feet.

Neil didn't recognize the man, but he figured him to be Randall Frost because, even with his back to him, Neil could tell that the one sitting at the fire was the silhouette cutter, Waldo Brickman.

Neil had found them.

"Do you want some of this, Waldo?" the man asked. He had his gun belt thrown over his shoulder, and once his pants were buttoned, he strapped it on.

"I don't know," Brickman answered. "I reckon I might have a taste."

"Well, make up your mind. If you do, you best do it while I'm down at the creek, 'cause when I get back, I'm gonna give her one more chance to tell us where she stashed it."

"And if she don't?" asked Brickman.

"If she don't, then I'm gonna slice open her guts an inch at a time 'til she does decide to tell." Frost looked down and spoke more to whomever was in the grass than he did to Waldo Brickman. "It'll be her choice," he said. "She can watch her intestines spill into the dirt, or she can give up the gold. It's just that simple."

"Either way," Brickman said with a laugh, "it sounds like an afternoon's entertainment, that's for sure."

Frost gave a smirk. "I got her warmed up. Get over here and do 'er if you want, but be quick about it. I'll be back in a bit." He turned and disappeared into the trees.

Neil watched as Brickman finished his smoke and tossed the butt into the fire. After a couple of minutes, he pushed himself up, unbuckled his own gun belt, and let it drop. When he was halfway across the clearing, Neil stepped out.

"Hold it, Brickman," he said.

With a start, the man spun around.

Leveling the Marlin and not moving his eyes, Neil bent and pulled Brickman's six-gun from the holster on the ground. It was an older Remington in need of a good cleaning. Neil flipped it around, caught it by the barrel, and threw it end over end as far as he could into the trees.

Brickman watched all this with wide eyes. It was clear that he expected he was about to die, but Neil resisted the urge to shoot the son of a bitch. He'd gladly have done it, but he didn't want to give himself away until he had a better idea of where Frost had gone.

After a bit, Brickman must have sensed that Neil was hesitant to shoot because he drew in a breath and was about to call out. But before he could do it, Neil sprinted the ten feet between them and swung the rifle butt into the man's jaw. Blood, spit, and at least one tooth went flying. With a grunt, Waldo Brickman hit the ground.

Neil made sure he was knocked out, and then he crossed the clearing.

What he found made him wince. Katie lay semiconscious and nude in the tall grass, her legs splayed, the perfect features of her face beaten almost beyond recognition. Her left eye was swollen closed, her lip was split open, and her nose was broken. Blood covered her face and breasts.

He dropped the Marlin and fell beside her. He had to do something, but he didn't know what to do. "Katie," he said, "I'm here now. You're going to be all right. I promise. You're going to be just fine." His hands began to shake, and he couldn't control them. "I promise you're going to be fine."

Katie's one good eye rolled and finally found him. It took a moment, but he was sure she knew who he was. While he was in the trees, he had spotted a canteen by the fire, and he went back for it now. When he returned, he said, "Here, Katie. Take some water," and when he lifted her head, she flinched with pain. She drank two or three small swallows, which seemed to bring her around a little more.

She raised her hand to her swollen jaw, and with a moan, she tried to speak. "Th . . . th . . ." Whatever she was attempting to say seemed very important to her, but she couldn't get it out.

"No, Katie. Don't talk."

He looked for her clothes and spotted them a few feet away. He brought them to her and helped her put on the shirt. Once her arms were through the sleeves, she lay back onto the grass, and Neil buttoned it for her. As his shaking hands fumbled with the buttons, he watched the sun wink off the Flying Swan, which, as always, was pinned to the front of her shirt.

"It's going to be okay," he said. "I'll take care of you, Katie. They won't hurt you anymore. I promise."

Her one eye had locked on him, and again she tried to tell him something. "Thr . . . thr . . ." But she couldn't make her voice work. She shook with the frustration of it.

He bent forward and kissed her forehead. "Just be still," he said.

He could see fear in her eyes. Swallowing, she tried again to speak, but it was no use, and she seemed on the verge of hysteria.

Neil thought if he held her it might calm her down, but just as he put his arms beneath her to lift her up, he heard a noise. Turning, he saw Waldo Brickman five feet away and coming fast. In his right hand, he held the knife he carried in the sheath sewn into the leg of his pants. Neil had first seen Brickman use this knife to slice river mud from his boots and had next seen it protruding from the chest of Calvin Hoskins.

Brickman hit Neil at a dead run, knocking him to his back and landing astride his chest. From high above his head, Brickman brought the knife down. Neil threw up his hands and caught the man's wrist just before the blade plunged into his neck. It was close, but Neil soon realized that he'd only slowed the knife's descent. He had not stopped it.

Brickman put all his weight and strength into shoving the knife downward. "I figured you'd be coming," he said between his teeth as he pushed, "but you didn't get here in time, did ya? Ol' Frost got to make that little girlie his wife after all, and just as soon as I whittle you up some, I'll be goin' on a honeymoon with 'er m'self." He leaned on the knife, and it came another inch closer. "She's a juicy little minx," he said with a smile, "but I reckon you already know that." The knife continued down.

Brickman had the leverage, and Neil knew he couldn't hold him much longer. While he still had the strength, Neil twisted under Brickman's weight, lifted his right leg, and wrapped it around the front of Brickman's neck. Now the advantage of leverage belonged to Neil, and he flipped Brickman over backwards. As the man went down, Neil stripped the knife from his hand. Brickman let out a curse and made a dive to get it back, but he was too slow. Neil buried the blade into Brickman's left thigh. The man cried out and snatched again for the knife, but before he could grab it, Neil jerked it from his leg and swung it like a scythe.

Brickman must have seen it coming, but there was nothing he could do. The blade sliced across his throat, sending a fan of scarlet onto the grass. He gasped and toppled over. The wide gash beneath the line of his jaw sputtered red foam as he lay on his back, staring at the sky and twitching.

After a bit, the foam and the twitching stopped.

Neil used his sleeve to blot sweat from his forehead, and then he returned to Katie, who still lay where he'd left her.

"Katie, listen to me," he said. "I'm going after Frost." He nodded toward her jeans and boots. "Try to get dressed."

She stared at him without moving. He picked up his Marlin. "If I don't come back and Frost does, you've got to kill the son of a bitch. Do you hear me?" He placed the rifle beside her. "Don't think about it twice. Just do it. You've got to do it."

He brushed the hair from her brow, and as he did, he could tell she still wanted to tell him something, but she couldn't make the words come out. There were beet-red marks appearing now on her throat, which showed Frost had choked her as well as beaten her.

Struggling with the pain, she braced herself and made another attempt. "Thr . . ." But she stopped in frustration.

"No," Neil said. "It doesn't matter. Just remember, if Frost comes into this clearing, you kill him. You shoot him as soon as he shows himself. Do you understand me?"

He wanted her to at least nod her head and indicate she knew what he was saying, but all she did was stare at him with that one haunted eye.

He got the canteen, gave her a little more water, and then put it beside the Marlin. "I'm going now," he said and squeezed her hand.

He stood and started for the trees, but before he left the clearing, he stopped, turned, and came back. Bending down, he placed his lips next to her ear and whispered, "I love you, Katie." She looked up at him when he said it, and a lone tear leaked from the slit of her swollen left eye. "I love you," he said again, and with that, he left to search for Randall Frost.

Neil found him sitting on the creek bank smoking a cigar. His dark hair was wet and combed straight back. His shirt was off. He must have washed it, because it was in the sun, stretched across a rock to dry.

As he smoked, Frost absently tossed pebbles into the stream. When he heard Neil walk up, without looking around, he asked, "You done already, Waldo?" With a laugh, he added, "Damn, but you're fast for an old man, ain't ya?"

He then swiveled around, and when he saw Neil, his broad, crooked smile froze. "Well," he said, "I don't believe you're Waldo."

"You're right about that," said Neil. He

jerked his thumb over his shoulder. "Wal-do's busy."

"Is that so? Is he still enjoying the charms of the woman who was fool enough to steal my gold?"

"No," Neil said. "No, sir, I'm pretty sure he's not doing that."

"Then what's he busy doin'?" Frost asked, clearly enjoying the game.

"Well, the last time I looked," Neil said, "he was busy bleeding in the grass."

Frost laughed, turned back to the creek, and tossed in another stone. "I had a feelin' you was gonna say somethin' like that. You must be that cowboy I've been hearin' so much about. What's your name? I think I was told, but it seems to've slipped my mind."

Neil gave it to him.

"Bancroft, that's right. Waldo said he watched you draw against Calvin Hoskins. Put a bullet in his foot before ol' Cal could even say boo. Did you do that on purpose? Shoot 'im in the foot, I mean?"

It seemed like everyone always asked him that question.

"As foolish as it seems looking back on it," Neil said, "yes, sir, I did."

"That ain't the way I do things," said Frost.

"No, I wouldn't think so. I'd expect you to be a chest and head man."

Frost smiled. "Waldo said you're quick and accurate. Maybe even quicker'n me."

Neil didn't respond.

"I guess you're also a little bit stupid." Frost lifted his cigar and blew the ash away. "You could've killed me just now."

"That's right."

"But you didn't."

"Not yet."

Frost took another puff on the stogie and then placed it on a rock, stood, and faced Neil head on. His shoulders were sloped, and he showed the beginnings of a gut, but Neil could tell what little extra weight the man carried covered a lot of muscle. "It would've been easy enough to shoot me from them trees back yonder," Frost said. "I'd-a never been the wiser. What with the water rushing by in the creek here, I never heard you until you was right up on me. Why didn't you do it?"

"Because," Neil said matter-of-factly, "I was hoping to look into your eyes when you die."

Frost smiled again. His two front teeth were large and stood out just a bit from the others — not enough to be considered bucked, but enough to give his smile a strange, unnatural appearance. "My eyes, huh?" He lifted his left hand and scratched behind his ear with his thumb. "Well, sir," he added, "I'd say that choosin' to not kill me when you had your chance might prove to be a mistake, Mister Bancroft. Maybe even a fatal mistake."

"We'll see."

They stood there for a bit, not talking, just staring at each other, Frost's smile never flagging. "Are you waiting for me to make a move?" he finally asked. "Are you one of them fellas who hates to go first for some reason?"

"You know," said Neil, "except for that part about wanting to see into your eyes when I kill you, I don't really have many rules or preferences on how this goes." He shrugged. "One way's about as good —"

As Neil spoke the words, Frost's right hand jerked toward his gun. At the very moment Neil's bullet slammed into his bare chest, Frost's shooter was almost out of its holster.

But not quite.

Frost dropped to both knees. A round, black hole between his nipples leaked a single line of red.

The short-barreled Colt left a trail of blue smoke as Neil crossed to the man. Stopping in front of him, Neil said, "When I'm not shooting people's feet, I'm basically a chest and head man myself."

Frost swallowed and stared up at him. The color had drained from the outlaw's face.

Neil thumbed back the hammer and placed the Colt's muzzle at a spot just below Frost's hairline. Staring into the man's cold eyes, Neil pulled the trigger.

When he returned to the clearing, he saw that Katie had gotten dressed. One boot was on, and as she pulled on the other, she kept looking back over her shoulder. She still had that lost, vacant expression about her, and it appeared that getting dressed had taken about all the strength she had, but she seemed at least a little better.

He came up beside her and dropped onto one knee. Again, she looked behind her and then back at Neil.

"Frost is dead," he said, and she released a sigh and closed her good eye. "It's over now, Katie. It's finished."

Shaking her head, she clenched her fists and forced the sounds to come out. "Thr . . . three . . . men."

"What? Katie, what did you say?"

"Three . . . men. Fr-r-r-rost . . . B-b-b-rickman . . ." She turned and looked behind her. "And man . . . with the . . . horses."

As soon as she said it, they heard the snort and whinny of horses in the trees on the far side of the clearing in the direction of the Custer City trail. And then the man came into sight. One rider holding a long lead rope. Attached to the rope were Katie's sorrel and what Neil assumed were the two horses belonging to Frost and Brickman.

He was a large man, but his hat was pulled low, and other than his size, Neil couldn't make out anything about him.

"Who is that?" he asked Katie, but she shook her head. Either she didn't know the man's name, or she was telling Neil that her voice was finished. At least for a while, she had used it up. It could have been that she was telling him both of those things.

Neil stood and watched as the man galloped off, leading the three horses. Whoever he was, why would he go to the trouble to take all those mounts? Neil could just make out the trail in the distance, but instead of going in that direction, the man cut back to the west, the way they had come.

Like a fist in the teeth, it hit Neil what this man was up to. He was taking the horses so that he could get away without Neil's following. And now he was headed in the direction Neil had come from. The man was headed for the roan.

"Stay here, Katie." And as soon as he said it, Neil was on his feet.

He ran with everything he had back to where he'd left the roan, but the thick brush made the going hard. Twice he fell, tumbling headlong over rocks and rotting timber. He plunged into a shallow but craggy ravine, banging his head and twisting his arm. The breath was knocked out of him, and he'd landed hard enough that for a second he was convinced his arm was broken, but then he discovered that the fingers still worked, and with some effort, he climbed out and started off again.

As he fought his way through the trees, he could hear the roan scream. The sounds the animal made were almost human. And mixed with the horse's screams were other screams that were definitely human.

Neil was still fifty feet from the clearing, but through the trees, he could see what was happening. The big man's back was to Neil, and he was down on one knee. He was making a frantic attempt to get the roan's hobbles unbuckled, but the roan would have none of it. The horse tried to sidle away from the man, but his fettered legs wouldn't allow it. He jerked his head, bared his teeth, and then bit into the man's shoulder. The man screamed as the roan ripped through the shirt and into the flesh.

"Goddamn it," he yelled, grabbing his shoulder. It was clear as the man wrenched himself away from the furious horse that he'd given up on trying to remove the hobbles.

Standing, and with his back still to Neil, he pulled his sidearm, cocked it, and leveled it at the roan's head.

"Nooo!" Neil shouted as he raced out of the trees. He lowered his shoulder and drove it into the small of the big man's back. The six-gun flew into the grass, and so did the two men.

Neil was certain that he'd hurt the man when he hit him, but the bastard made a quick recovery. He was on his feet in a flash. He lifted Neil up and plowed a rock-hard fist into Neil's stomach, sending him reeling. As Neil tried to stand, the man lashed out with his boot and kicked Neil square in the face. The blow knocked him onto his back, and Neil watched as the sky went from blue to gray to brown. Before it faded into total blackness, the man was on top of him with his huge hands around Neil's throat.

Neil clawed at the man's wrists, but there was no budging them. He gasped for breath, but try as he might, no breath would come. It was as though, in an instant, the world had been depleted of all oxygen, and Neil could feel himself start to fade away.

From somewhere far off, he heard a raspy, unintelligible sound, and though he couldn't make out the words, as if by magic, the pressure on his windpipe was gone, and the air rushed in.

Neil rolled onto all fours and coughed and gagged and gulped at the air. He gorged himself on it. He let it fill him up.

After a few seconds, his senses began to check back in, and he looked up to see Katie standing above him. She still looked like hell, but at the same time, she had never looked better. In her hands, she held the Marlin, and the old mustachioed bartender back at the Ace High had been right. The gun was damned near as big as she was.

She had not had to fire a shot, but by the way the rifle was cradled, it was clear Katie knew how to use it. The hammer on the long gun was back, and the barrel was slanted toward the man who sat in the grass next to Neil. Neil turned to take a look at the son of a bitch who had almost killed him and his horse. When he did, he felt his jaw go slack.

It was Luke Sylar, his friend and lieutenant from the Army.

TWENTY-TWO

When Katie awoke, Neil was sitting by her bed in Doc Green's clinic in Custer City.

"You're looking some better," he said. And she was. The swelling had gone down a little, which made her face appear less distorted. The doc had sewn up the cut in her lip and straightened, as much as possible, her broken nose. It would never be what it had been before, but that was okay. Her features had been too perfect, and now her face would have more character.

After Katie and the Marlin had convinced Luke Sylar that choking Neil to death was a bad idea, Neil had tied Sylar to a tree while he rounded up Brickman and Frost and tied them to their horses. He then lashed Sylar's hands behind his back, and he and Katie rode with him into Custer. When they got to town, Neil left Katie with the doc and took Sylar to the sheriff.

"Did you find Bullock and Code last

night?" Katie asked. Her voice was still hoarse and almost inaudible, but after a good night's sleep, it was working better than it had the day before.

"Sure did. They were over at the jail, drinking coffee and wondering just where the hell Sheriff Code's deputy had gotten off to. They were a little surprised when I brought him in all trussed up."

"I bet. You gave them my map?"

"I did. They were more surprised by that than they were the deputy. I expect they were out there north of town at first light to dig up the gold. I don't mind telling you, Katie, I was a little surprised by that myself. I assumed all along that you'd stopped to get it when you left here the other morning."

"I thought about it, but it seemed safer where it was than anywhere else."

"I guess that makes sense," Neil said.

Katie started to reach for a glass of water on the table beside the bed.

"Here," said Neil. "Let me get that for you."

She drank a couple of sips. He could tell it hurt her to swallow. He wasn't swallowing all that well himself. Yesterday had been hard on both of their throats, but, Neil guessed, if a prize was to be awarded for throat damage, it would have to go to Waldo Brickman.

"It's too bad about Luke Sylar." She pushed herself to a sitting position, and Neil fluffed her pillows for her. "I know he was your friend."

"It's hard to believe that he'd do something like that, but he did. He confessed to everything last night while I was still there. He was the one who told Frost of the two gold shipments last year that Bullock suspected you of doing. By the way, Bullock sends you his apologies for those misplaced suspicions."

"That's nice," said Katie, with just a hint of sarcasm.

"The bankers always informed both Bullock's office in Deadwood and Code's office over here in Custer whenever the gold was being moved. That's how Sylar knew. Same with the stage robbery the other day. Sylar also told Frost about that one. Since Cal Hoskins and your brother were no longer around to help Frost and Brickman with the holdup, Frost forced Sylar to go along. That explains the three sets of tracks I saw. Sylar denies having anything to do with killing the driver and guards, though. He claims that was all Frost and Brickman."

"Maybe he's telling the truth," Katie said.

"Maybe," agreed Neil. "I guess a jury will have to decide that."

"He didn't want to have any part of what they were doing to me yesterday. That's why he stayed with the horses."

"When I knew him," said Neil, "he was a good man. I guess he just got greedy and fell in with Randall Frost. Once Frost got his hooks into him, Luke was lost."

"Just like my brother," Katie said.

Neil helped her drink a little more water and then returned the glass to the table. He pulled the straight-backed chair he'd spent the night in a little closer to the bed and sat back down.

"I guess Brickman followed us out of Fetterman last week as far as Raf and Lottie's, and then he headed on up to Custer. It was the plan for Frost and Brickman to meet here and wait for us. They were going to jump us once we got to town and force you to turn over the gold they had stolen in the stage robbery last October."

"Then why didn't they?" Katie asked.

"Because Sylar told them about this current gold shipment, and they decided to pull that job instead. After they did it, Frost and Brickman figured they'd better lay low, so they went to some hideout they have over by Deadwood."

"They were just going to forget about me?" Katie asked.

"No, they weren't really the forgetting types, but since you were back in the Black Hills, Frost figured he could take care of you later. Sylar was supposed to keep an eye on you. Then when you left Custer unexpectedly," Neil looked down at his hands, "I trailed you and Sylar trailed me. He met up with Frost and Brickman somewhere around Deadwood, and Frost decided that even though things were pretty hot right now, it wasn't clear what you were going to do, so they needed to deal with you now."

She pulled her covers tighter and turned her head. "He did bad things to me, Neil."

Neil felt his heart fill up and his chest constrict. "I know, but he'll never hurt you or anyone else ever again."

"Did you mean what you said back there?" she asked.

"About loving you?"

She nodded.

"You don't have to ask that, do you?"

"I don't know. Do I?"

He leaned in closer to her bed. "Katie," he said, "I love you with every bit of me."

She smiled. It wasn't her big, beautiful smile, the one that always made his insides bang together. This smile was softer, more subdued, yet even so, it seemed to come from some deep place. "I'm sorry about leaving the way I did," she whispered. "I thought it was for the best."

"I know."

"If you'll give me another chance, I swear I'll never leave you again."

Neil bent forward and gave her a soft kiss on her battered lips. "That sounds like a fine idea," he said.

He knew Katie was not a crier, yet for the second time in less than twenty-four hours, he was seeing tears bud in her eyes.

"Would you mind living here in the Hills?" she asked. "I have land just south of Deadwood. Edward had a small cabin on it next to the trail, but Frost burned it down right after Edward left. It's good land," she said.

Neil knew it was good land. He remembered the beauty of it and the lush meadows that would be perfect for pasturing animals.

"And we could build another house," Katie said. "Our own house. I wouldn't want it where Edward's house was, though. I would want to build ours back in the trees as far away from the trail as we could get."

Neil tried to imagine what it would be like. He liked the idea of building their own place back away from the trail, and it would be pleasant to spend the summers there. He could picture sitting at the table in the copse of silver spruce, watching the breeze play with Katie's hair. On the other hand, Neil didn't much like the idea of wintering in this high country. He started to tell her that, but he decided, what the hell, the winters wouldn't be so bad if he had her to snuggle against. In fact, with Katie to keep him warm, the winters would be fine.

"We could raise horses." She smiled. "And kids."

"Horses and kids?"

"Sure. You want kids, don't you?"

"Kids sound okay. It's the horses I'm not too sure of." He rubbed his aching back. "I've been giving real consideration to getting out of the horse business."

"Well, I think you should leave the horse breaking to someone else. You're much too old."

It seemed they'd had this conversation before.

"But we could hire that done," she added.

Neil snapped his fingers. "By golly, I almost forgot. Bullock says I'll be getting a thousand-dollar reward for Frost, five hundred for Brickman, and as soon as he confirms Cal Hoskins's identity with the provost marshal at Fort Fetterman, I'll get another five hundred for him."

"That's wonderful. I always hoped to marry rich."

"I doubt you'll ever see the day when I'm rich, Katie Burke." *But,* he told himself, *who knows.* That place south of Deadwood looked like a fine spot for horses. "Do you think you could be happy being a horse rancher after your exciting life owning a hurdy-gurdy in the West's wildest town?"

"I never did much at the Ace High. The success of that place was all Ellie Jackson's doing, every single bit of it. She's a born businesswoman."

"I had a nice visit with her," Neil said. "She cares about you."

"I know. Ellie's been more of a mother to me than even my real mother was."

"She said she pretty much raised you."

"She did." She gave a little shrug. "I love her like a mother, but I loved my real mother, too. I worshipped her. After the war, if it hadn't been for my mother's determination, none of us would have survived. Not me, or Edward, or even Ellie. Despite being raised a pampered Southern belle, my mother was the strongest woman I've ever known."

"Ellie told me some about her."

"After her bad experience with Henri

Chenal, she became a different woman. Something seemed to have snapped inside her, but even then she never stopped loving us and taking care of us. And she never lost that strength that had seen us through those bad times."

"Ellie told me some of that, too," Neil said.

Katie smiled. "Ellie's one reason I want to stay in the Hills. I know she would be willing to go anywhere, but the Ace High is the only place where she can ever be treated the way she deserves to be treated. It's the only place where she can be given the chance to take advantage of her skills."

"She's smart," Neil said. "If it hadn't been for her talking to me yesterday, I would've never found you."

"It's a miracle that you did. I thought I was hallucinating when I looked up and saw you." She reached out to him, and he took her hand. "Once again, you risked your life for somebody else," she said. "It seems you do that a lot."

"I just did what had to be done."

"That's what you always say, isn't it?" She turned and nodded toward a chair in the corner. "Is that my shirt draped on the chair over there?" she asked.

Neil followed her eyes. "Yes, I believe so."

"Would you get it for me?"

Neil brought it over.

"Let me have your hat."

"My hat? What for?"

"Just do it," said Katie in a tone that would brook no quarrel. It was a tone Neil told himself he was apt to hear for the remainder of his days.

He handed it to her, and she took the Flying Swan from her shirt and pinned it onto the side of his hat just above the band. She held it at arm's length to see how it looked.

"What are you doing?" he asked.

"You have your reasons for not accepting your medal," Katie said. "I don't agree with it, but I respect it. I figure, though, that what you did for me deserves a medal, too, and this one you're going to take, whether you want to or not." She handed him his hat. "Besides," she added, "that ratty old hat could use a little decoration."

Neil looked down at the gleaming pin. It did improve the hat's appearance. But the gift was too much. "I can't take this, Katie," he said. "Ellie told me how much it means to you."

Again, Katie's eyes glistened, but this time she was also smiling her beautiful smile. "You're right," she said. "That pin means everything in the world to me. There's nothing that I have that means so much."

"Well, then," he began, "I can't —"

Katie cut him off by placing an index finger against his lips. "Hush," she said. "And give me a kiss."

AFTERWORD

Although *Dakota Trails* is a work of historical fiction, Neil Bancroft actually lived and was awarded the Medal of Honor for bravery at the Battle of the Little Bighorn. The major events in the novel regarding Bancroft's life prior to his discharge from the Army on September 20, 1878, are — as far as the historical records can tell — true and accurate, including the fact that he was never presented his medal.

It is known that he died in Highland Falls, New York, on May 14, 1901, but all that occurred in his life between his discharge and his death is unknown.

Some speculate that his failure to receive his medal was due to his leaving the Army before the awards presentation, and therefore he didn't know it existed.

That speculation never rang true with me. The honorees received their awards on October 5, 1878. Nearly two and a half years had passed between the events on the Little Bighorn and the presentation. It is logical to assume that Neil must have learned during that time that the water carriers' names had been nominated for the medal. It's my speculation that when it was finally determined by the powers that be in Washington to award the medals, the recipients would have been told at that time (or very shortly thereafter). Neil probably would also have known of the presentation on the fifth since his discharge was only two weeks earlier.

The Battle of the Little Bighorn was one of the biggest, most reported-upon, and historically dissected events in the last quarter of the nineteenth century. The nation was transfixed by the battle just as much then as it is today. In the unlikely event Bancroft did leave the Army without knowing, it is implausible that he would have never learned about it in the twenty-three years between the awards presentation and his death.

For me, the questions are less about whether he knew than why, assuming he did know, he chose not to stay for the presentation, or why at some point over the next two-plus decades he didn't contact the Adjutant General's Office to have the medal forwarded to him, which the AGO certainly would have done.

I have pondered all these questions ever since my first visit to the Little Bighorn Battlefield National Monument when I learned that Private Neil Bancroft was awarded, but never received, his Medal of Honor. Unfortunately, there are no definitive answers, and there never will be. They are, like the entirety of the courageous private's life subsequent to his discharge, lost to history.

Therefore, everything that appears in *Dakota Trails* regarding his life after September of 1878 — his adventures, relationships, and opinions with regard to all things, including his medal — are solely products of the author's imagination and are presented with the greatest respect for the man and the true hero that he was.

ABOUT THE AUTHOR

Award-winning author **Robert McKee** draws inspiration for his writing from his own diverse history, including four years in the military and employment as a radio announcer, disc jockey, copy writer, court reporter, and municipal court judge. After school in Texas, Bob settled in Wyoming, where he has lived for thirty years.

McKee's short fiction has appeared in more than twenty commercial and literary publications around the country. He is also a recipient of the Wyoming Art Council's Literary Fellowship Award, as well as a three-time first-place winner of Wyoming Writers, Inc.'s adult fiction contest, and a two-time first-place winner of the National Writers Association's short fiction contest. One of his stories was selected for inclusion in the prestigious annual publication Best American Mystery Stories.

"The western," says McKee, "is a uniquely

American literary genre. Both its history and its mythology appeal to me as a writer. Plus," he adds, "who can resist a good shoot-'em-up adventure?"

When not at his computer writing, Bob can be found rummaging through antique stores in search of vintage fountain pens or roaming the back roads of Wyoming and Colorado with his wife and two children.